MW01136201

WOLF OF STONE

Thank you!
God Bless

[signature]

WOLF OF STONE

Gypsy Healer Series

Book 2

Quinn Loftis

Published by Quinn Loftis

© 2014 Quinn Loftis Books LLC
All rights reserved. No part of this publication may be
reproduced, distributed, or transmitted in any form or by
any means, including photocopying, recording, or other
electronic or mechanical methods, without the prior written
permission of the publisher.

This book is licensed for your personal enjoyment only.
This book may not be re-sold or given away to other people.
If you would like to share this book with another person,
please purchase an additional copy for each recipient. If
you're reading this book and did not purchase it, or it was
not purchased for your use only, then please return it, and
purchase your own copy. Thank you for respecting the hard
work of this author.

Photography Keeton Designs
Cover Design Mirella Santana

ISBN: 1503386481
ISBN 13: 9781503386488

For my sons, Travis and Jonivan.

Also By Quinn Loftis

The Grey Wolves Series
Prince of Wolves
Blood Rites
Just One Drop
Out of the Dark
Beyond the Veil
Fate and Fury
Sacrifice of Love
Luna of Mine

Elfin Series
Elfin
Rapture
Book 3 Coming soon

The Gypsy Healer Series
Into the Fae
Wolf of Stone

Stand Alone Works
Call Me Crazy

ACKNOWLEDGMENTS

As many of you know while writing this book my husband and I adopted a new born little boy. He is truly a miracle and we praise God for him. Having a new born, and one with the problems that Jonivan came into the world with, made finishing this book the biggest challenge I've faced so far in my writing. I praise God for giving me the words, the energy and the stamina to get it done. Thank you to Bo for being so patient with me as you edit my books. Thank you for taking care of the boys, the house, the cooking, the laundry and everything when I fail to… which is most of the time. You are simply supernatural and I praise God for giving me you. Thank you to Candace, the best PA in the world. I couldn't do what I do without you. Thank you to Shelley Carman for being an amazing Beta reader who is honest and so very thorough. I truly appreciate your time and diligence. Thank you to Kelsey Keeton, your vision for my characters amazes me and I'm so thankful to get to work with you! Thank you to the Hell Cats for being such wonderful friends and for helping me keep my sanity. Thank you to all the readers who cheered me on as I wrote this novel. It has been a long road and filled with so many emotions in my personal life as well as while writing what the characters went through. Thank you to everyone who has stood by me and been patient. I truly am blessed beyond measure.

Prologue

"There is no sound loud enough to silence their screams. There is no vision serene enough to diminish the blood. No matter how many times I breathe in the fresh morning air, the scent of their terror and of my own torment linger still. I have resigned myself to a life forever filled with memories so dark and terrible that no light could ever penetrate them." ~Dalton Black

1780. Small village just outside of Salem, Massachusetts.

"If we torture his wife in front of him, it will force him to use his magic, then we will have definite proof that the Black family is practicing witchcraft."

The voice of the short, worm-like man echoed in Dalton's ears. He, along with ten other males, had captured him and his parents. The intruders had caught them unaware while Dalton and his parents slept, sneaking into their home in the dead of night. Dalton and his father and mother hadn't even know what had happened until they awoke chained like animals in an underground cell.

One of the men was a physician and had given Dalton and his father a potion that had disoriented and weakened them. Unimpaired, Dalton would have ripped the chains from the wall.

"She is a beautiful woman," another man spoke up and Dalton could smell the lust rolling off of him. His stomach turned violently as he realized what the man was insinuating.

"Lying with one such as these would be an abomination. We will not lower ourselves to such things, no matter how attractive she is. She is probably using her magic to lure us to her so she can cast some sort of spell over us."

Fools, Dalton thought. Even though the witch hunts were slowly losing power, some of the most zealous witch hunters still believed that magic practitioners were secretly among them. They were correct of course, but more than half of all the so–called witches they had murdered had been mere humans. Another twenty percent had been werewolves like him and his parents leaving only about fifteen percent of the condemned that had actually been guilty of such crimes.

He pulled at his chains again, straining against the bonds that refused to budge. He knew that if he did not get them out of the clutches of these evil men, then they would die and it would not be a quick, honorable death. It would be slow, torturous, and gruesome. He could not bear such a fate for his gentle, kind mother.

"Father," he whispered to the wolf across from him chained to the opposite wall. "Can you call on your wolf yet? Can you phase?" Dalton had been trying to phase but whatever the doctor had given him was affecting his ability to communicate with his wolf.

"No," his father answered grimly. "My wolf is silent."

The whispering of the humans continued and Dalton had to tune out their vile words. He had no idea how long they had been held before they finally came for them. His mother was first, just as they said she would be. And they indeed tortured her in front of him and his father, but not before giving them more of whatever concoction the good doctor used to keep them from phasing. Of course, the humans thought they were simply weakening their "magic" so that they couldn't use enough of it to escape. His father fought violently against his bonds trying to get to his mate. Blood poured from the wounds he inflicted as he threw himself against the pull of the chains and they dug into his neck, wrists, and ankles.

His mother's screams—calling out for his father—was the last thing he ever heard her say. They tortured her for hours, screaming at her to admit her so–called sins, to confess to practicing witchcraft. They mocked her for her pleas for mercy and taunted her to curse them and show her true nature. Once her body lay lifeless, bloody and mangled beyond recognition, they turned to start in on his father, only to find him already dead. His true mate was gone and so his life ended with hers. Dalton at least found comfort in knowing that they were both at peace, no longer enduring agony at the hands of those driven by fear and hate. They burned his parents' bodies, believing that it was the only way to keep them from somehow bringing themselves back from the dead. Dalton had thought that would be the worst of it. He had been wrong.

They left him for days with no food or water, chained underground. He didn't know how much time had passed until at last he heard voices. He recognized the sound of several of the males, but there was a new voice in the group, a feminine voice. His heart began to beat hard against his chest as her familiar but unwelcome scent filled the stale air. Then she was standing less than a dozen steps away from him.

"Tell me it is not true," Gwen's high voice bounced off of the walls around them. "Dalton Black, tell me you do not use magic."

As usual she was demanding her way, and as usual he was going to ignore her wishes.

"Why are you here, Gwen?" he all but growled at her.

Dalton had met Gwen on one of his trips into Salem to sell the furniture that he and his father built to earn their living. They were both master craftsmen at woodworking and they were often commissioned out for many months. He had been unloading his wagon of rocking chairs and tables when she had walked up to him, telling him how she admired the furniture. He could not understand how she could possibly say such a thing since she had not taken her eyes off of him since he had driven his wagon into town. His sharp senses had picked up on her stares as she followed him down the main street. It was not uncommon for humans to be attracted to their kind. They were unusually handsome and fit, but for a female to be so forward was uncommon. From that day on she made it very clear that she intended to have him as her own. She had cornered him several times demanding that he court her. His usual response was to simply walk away; it seemed to irritate her most when he did not engage her in any way. But on the rare occasions that he did speak to her, he would ask her why she thought her demands would be endearing to him. Why any female would think a man would want her taking the lead in the relationship was beyond him. And now here she stood once again attempting to lead him around like a lap dog with no mind of his own.

"I want to hear from the lips of the man I intended to marry that he is not practicing witch-craft," she snapped at him.

"Then I suppose you should go searching for your betrothed because I have told you repeatedly that I would never take you as my bride."

"Even if I could save your life?"

"My heart will only ever belong to one, and I would rather die than betray her that way." Dalton hadn't found his true mate yet, but that did not mean she wasn't out there. His species did not search for a mate by courting female after female.

They were preordained for only one, the one who held the other half of their soul. Each male had one perfect match and only for her could he ever yield. Any other female paled in comparison.

"If I cannot have you, then no one will." Gwen's words were laced with such venom he was sure she would turn into a snake at any moment.

Dalton could have never guessed at how deep Gwen's depravity ran. Her veins were filled with ice and her heart was made of stone, for only one such as that could do the things that she did. He was tortured all day—flesh peeled from his body, toe nails torn off, and lips sewn closed. The latter she had done herself when he was too weak from blood loss to protest. And then each night after the day of enduring such things, Gwen would come and clean his wounds, bathe him, and lie next to him as if she were his lover.

"Why do you make them do this to you?" she cooed to him after a particularly horrid day. Her hands didn't even shake as she removed the thread from his eyelids. His captors were convinced that if he could not see, then he would not know where to throw a curse.

"If you would just let me take you from this place, let me make you mine, then this would all end." Her voice was deceivingly sweet but he could hear the poison beneath it.

He did not open his eyes once she was finished removing the thread. He did not want to look at her because he did not want her face to be the last thing he saw before he fell into the exhausted sleep that he longed for. It was the only time that he was able to push away all the ugliness that had become his life. He thought that surely he would have nightmares after all he had suffered, but instead there was just nothing. His sleep was as empty as his soul felt—devoid of any emotions, thoughts, or fears. The touch of Gwen's fingers on his arm jerked him from his thoughts and he forced himself not to cringe.

"I love you, you know? I could make you happy." Her warm breath against his ear made his insides roll in nausea.

"You are the last female on earth who could ever make me happy, Gwen." He usually tried not to talk to her but her tongue against his ear was too much.

"I bet I can change your mind," she whispered as her hands wandered.

He swallowed down the bile that instantly rose and felt his wolf stir, fighting against him. If he thought he despised Gwen, it was nothing compared to the way his wolf felt about her. To be touched by one other than his mate in such a way, to have something that should have been beautiful turned into something dirty and abhorrent, was unforgivable to his wolf.

He grew to hate the night worse than the torture he endured during the day. Her touch was revolting to him. Like millions of ants crawling all over his skin, he cringed under her fingertips. Her lips on his flesh was like acid and the few times that she had tried to kiss him on the mouth, he would find himself retching trying to remove the taste.

Over time he began to pretend to be weaker than he truly was, and the doctor began to give him less of the drug. Dalton made it appear as if he was finally giving in. His captives began to drop their guard. Under the constant command of Gwen who wanted privacy with him, he was left unattended as his strength began to return.

He knew that she was growing tired of his resistance and that she would follow through with her threat to kill him. Over the past several weeks she had made it abundantly clear that if he did not choose her, then he was choosing death. Frankly, death was looking very appealing.

"Tomorrow is your last chance, Dalton," Gwen told him through narrowed eyes and stretched lips one evening after she had once again cleaned his wounds and attempted to seduce him. He could see that his lack of response to her physically and emotionally was beginning to upset her more and more. "You will give me what I want or I will see to it that all know you as the witch they claim you to be and you will be burned alive. I don't want that for you, but as I said before...if I cannot have you, then no one will."

Thunder rumbled across the sky and rain pelted the earth on the night Dalton finally found his chance to escape. His strength was back, his wolf was enraged, and he wanted blood. But the man just wanted to be free. Gwen had finally left him after hours of torture and then her so–called ministrations. By the time she finally removed her hands from his body, he was ready to skin himself just to be rid of the smell she left on him. He waited about an hour to make sure no one would return, and then without much effort at all he ripped his chains from the wall then broke off the links at the cuffs. All that remained was the circular metal around his ankles, wrist, and throat. Those he would be rid of as soon as he phased. He followed his nose, breathing in the fresh air that led him straight to the door that stood between him and his freedom. It was chained closed, but with his full strength returned it posed no true obstacle against his wolf's power. He ripped the chain from the door and tossed it aside as if it were no more than an old, shredded rope. The door did not even squeak as he pushed it open. He closed it back and then followed the stairs up to another door that was above his head. This would be the one that opened to the forest.

As he stepped out from the underground jail, he took in a deep breath filling his lungs with fresh air. It had been so long since he had felt the breeze on his face and smelled the glorious scents of the forest. He wasted no time as he phased into his wolf form, allowing his clothes to be shredded in the process and the shackles to fall away, and took off into the night at a dead run. He was not running away for good; he would be back to deal out his retribution. His wolf demanded that the evil ones responsible for torturing and killing those that belonged to him pay for their deeds. If they knew what he was, they would scream animal or beast or claim him to be a savage—a monster—when in reality they were the monsters.

Dalton paused after running for several miles and looked up at the full moon that lit his way. He let out a long, deep howl, part in memory of his parents and part in victory of his escape. As the sound died he felt peace wash over him and knew that the Great Luna had heard his pain, knew his grief, and mourned the loss of her children with him. He did not know if he would ever recover from his time in captivity. He did not know what his future held for him, but he knew that his Creator had not forgotten him. As he began running again, the wind ruffling his fur and replacing the scent of his torture with that of the beauty of nature, he pushed away the memories that would torment him. For that moment in time he simply let the wolf take over. He buried the man's emotions under the iron determination of the beast, knowing that it might be the only way he would be able to survive. For the first time in his life he realized that some things were just too much for the human. But the blessing of being Canis lupis was that the wolf could handle what the man could not. His wolf would shield him from the memories, allowing him to do the things necessary in order to move on with his life. And he would move on, after those who killed his family were crushed between his jaws. He would survive, but little did he know then, surviving did not equate to living.

1

"We can make plans for our life. We can schedule
appointments, pencil in vacations, fill our calen-
dars with important dates, and even set long-term
career goals. But the reality is all our planning
amounts to nothing. There is no guarantee,
no contract promising the outcome, no dotted
line where we can sign our names to guarantee
the outcome of these plans. Truly we are at the
mercy of the chaos around us. We can choose to
bend when our plans take a sudden turn, or we
can stand rigid and risk being broken." ~Sally

Present day

"When will the males begin arriving?" Dillon
Jacobs stood holding his cell phone to his
ear, waiting for the Romania pack Alpha's response.
He stared out into the forest that surrounded Peri's
home, wishing he could enjoy the beauty of the
place. But there had been too much ugliness, too
much death in their lives recently for him to be able
to notice the beauty in anything. All he could hope

for in that moment was a measure of peace, but he knew it would not last long.

"I am leaving that up to you and Peri. I imagine that regardless of what I say, she will do whatever she wants. So if she wants them to stagger their arrival, then fine; if she wants to flash them all in at the same time so that they land in a big heap on top of one another just so she can get a laugh, then so be it. Frankly, I don't care, as long as they all show, and they behave," Vasile answered. "Regardless of the unity between the packs that has been established, we are dealing with dominant wolves. They are coming into a situation that is dangerous and potential mates, not to mention gypsy healers, are caught in the middle. The protective nature of the men will be very high."

"Let me guess," Dillon nearly groaned. "All the males coming happen to be unmated Alphas and Betas."

"They are the ones that most need to come. Can you blame them?" Vasile asked. "Kale, Beta of the Ireland pack, and Banan, the pack's Third—both unmated—will be the ones Peri goes for first. She should be getting them this evening."

The Colorado pack Alpha pinched the bridge of his nose as he considered the consequences of what they were willingly walking into. There was no doubt that the help from the other packs would be beneficial. He just wondered if it was worth the possible blood that might be spilled within their ranks.

"I have spoken with each of the wolves coming, Dillon," Vasile interrupted his thoughts. "They know the repercussions of their actions if they do not conduct themselves with control. It has been explained that when they initially arrive, the healers will not be paraded in front of them like meat for the taking. As much as we rejoice in males finding their true mates, that is not the intention of this gathering. If they find their mate while there, so be it. They are still to assist in finding Volcan. I do not think you will need to worry about the males fighting."

"I hope you are right."

"Perizada will have no problem putting any misbehaving wolves in their place if need be," Vasile added. "Not to mention my brother is dominate enough to put most in their place, even Alpha's."

Dillon chuckled. "That is true. We might actually need to worry more about Peri's patience with the males. Knowing Peri, if she gets too irritated with them, she'll make good on any threats to turn them into rabbits."

"Do I even want to know why she threatened to turn them into rabbits?"

"Let's just say that the old adage, *going at it like rabbits*, had something to do with it and leave it there."

Vasile let out a tired breath and Dillon could tell that though the Alpha had not been present for the horror that had taken place, his worry for his wolves and the healers was taking a toll on him. "Keep me posted if you do not mind, Dillon, and please keep them safe."

Dillon knew that Vasile cared for everyone in Farie, but he was truly asking Dillon to look out for Crina, Sally, and Costin. Though Sally and Costin were technically members of the Serbian pack, Vasile would always consider them his own. "You have my word."

Dillon disconnected the call and continued to stare out into the forest. He knew his Beta, Dalton, was out there roaming in his wolf form. Two days had passed since he had informed Dalton that he would be allowing the incoming males to meet Jewel. He was hoping that it would provoke some action in Dalton and that it would drag him back from the dark place that he had lived in for so long. Dillon felt in his Alpha bones that Jewel Stone was indeed Dalton's true mate. But just as you could lead a horse to water and not make him drink, so you could also lead a male to his mate and not make him claim her.

He had to believe that Dalton would accept her, but he wondered how many lives might be in danger of being lost before that finally happened. If Dalton saw another male touch her, there was a very real possibility that his Beta would not be able to control his wolf's reaction. Dalton had already proven to be an incredibly strong wolf. If he went feral while other male wolves were around his unclaimed mate, he would become virtually indestructible. He knew that if that happened, he would have to do whatever was necessary in order to destroy his Beta. He could not have a feral wolf running lose while

4

they were in the middle of dealing with a diabolical villain as well.

"Isn't my life just a ray of sunshine," he muttered as he turned back towards Peri's home. He needed to inform the others of the visitation schedule Vasile had laid out. Hopefully it would give the other pack members time to prepare for being around eleven dominant males all hoping that one of the precious healers would be theirs. He released another tired sigh. "Yep, a freaking ray of sunshine."

———

Sally stared down at the battered–looking Jewel, frustrated that her patient was showing no signs of improvement. The wounds had closed, yes, but she could not get the scars to fade. The poor healer also remained unconscious, unable to communicate to Sally what she might need. Over and over Sally had used her healer abilities to push her essence into Jewel, searching for anything that would help wake her. But it was no use. The young healer had buried herself inside of her own mind. Sally couldn't say that she blamed her. Anyone, especially a seventeen–year–old girl who had endured what she had, would want nothing more than to escape not just the torture but the memories as well.

"How is she?" Peri asked from the doorway.

Sally had to bite back the retort that gathered on her tongue because she knew it would do no good to take her anger out on anyone else. One by one the pack would stop by to ask about Jewel, and Sally would tell them each the same thing.

"No change."

"Do not kick yourself, Sally," Peri said as she stepped further into the room. "At this point, and after all the things you have seen in the past year, surely you know there will be no change until her mate intervenes."

"He has not been to see her in two days. She has not had any more of his blood in nearly four days. Any male who could leave his true mate in this state does not deserve her," Sally growled.

"Perhaps," Peri said nonchalantly. "Or perhaps a male many centuries old has many demons with which to wrestle, and he does not want his young mate to have to face them. Remember also that she is a healer and not yet of mating age. The full emotions of the mate bond will not hit until she turns eighteen. Once that happens, he might not be able to fight it, no matter how badly he tries."

"Do you know something of his past?" Sally asked as she turned to look Peri in the eyes.

"You *know* who I am, healer. Of course I know; I was there. But, as much as I love a good wolf tale, it is not mine to tell. Let's just say that Dalton Black has a past as dark as his name implies."

"Is it too much to ask for a normal wolf, with no baggage attached, to come along and sweep our healers off of their feet?"

Peri smiled. "Did you just use the word normal and wolf in the same sentence?

"Poor choice of words," Sally admitted. "I have a feeling that once she turns eighteen and those mating signs appear, Dalton will be even more dangerous. When did you say her birthday was?"

"Since they seem to lose what little sense they have when they see the mating signs, you are probably correct. But since her birthday isn't for another month and a half, nothing can be done about it just now. Come," Peri said and motioned her to follow. "Dillon has information to share and, as moody as he has been lately, I can tell he only wants to say it once. Jewel doesn't look as though she will be sneaking off any time soon; you can step a way for a bit."

"Tacky, Peri," Sally grumbled.

Peri shrugged. "I call them like I see them. She's a healer trapped in a coma induced by torture at the hands and teeth of a possessed fae. She is in need of her mate's care who refuses to give it—ergo, no sneaking off."

Sally rolled her eyes at her couth-less friend. "Whatever, let's just get this little meeting over with. I'm sure it is bound to be filled with encouraging tidbits and not in any way overflowing with the possibility of more things that could and probably will go wrong."

Peri glanced at her from the corner of her eye as they made their way into the living room. "My, my, you are just a happy little Smirf, singing and dancing and raining on everyone's freaking parade."

Sally started humming the Smirf song quietly drawing an unladylike snort from the high fae.

"Just sit down and try to contain your jovial spirit; it's getting on my nerves."

"I make no promises, Peri Fairy. If Dalton shows his too handsome face, I may just dance the jig right up to him and spit in his eye."

"Just one eye?" Peri asked as her brow drew together.

"Oh, don't worry, I'll stab a spoon in his other eye."

"Good to know you are an equal opportunist when it comes to causing bodily harm."

"Who's causing bodily harm?" Costin asked as he wrapped an arm around Sally from behind and pulled her down with him to the couch so she was sitting on his lap.

Peri waved him off. "Never mind, just try to keep your blood thirsty little healer under control."

"Is everyone here?" Dillon asked as he stepped into the room.

"Everyone except your Beta," Peri answered.

"Then everyone that matters is here," Sally piped in.

Anna, Stella, Heather, and Kara had taken seats on the floor across from the couch where Sally sat and were staring at her with wide eyes.

Dillon glanced at the healer wrapped in Costin's arms, and pain rushed through him at the sorrow in her eyes. She was a gypsy healer; it was in her nature to take care of those around her, to nurture them, and it was obvious she felt totally helpless when it came to Jewel. She also knew that Dalton was partly to blame.

"I spoke with Vasile," he began, effectively drawing everyone's attention to him. "Four of the twelve packs will be sending males to assist us in capturing Volcan. Ireland will be sending the Beta, Kale, and third, Banan. Italy's Alpha, Ciro is coming and bringing his Beta, Aimo. Spain's Alpha, Gustavo, will be coming and bringing his Beta, Antonio, and the fourth pack is Canada. The Alpha Drayden will be coming and bringing his Beta, Nick. That's eight new dominant males added to our group."

"Why only three Alphas? Is Volcan not a threat that warrants the attention of all the Alphas?" Elle asked from where she stood by the stairs next to her mate, Sorin.

Dillon let out a long breath. This was the part that he had been dreading. Emotions were already high, and now he was asking them to accept a situation that might just push some of those emotions out of control.

"Well, I know that we are dealing with some pretty heavy stuff now that Volcan is again on the loose," he began. "But the fact remains that we have five newly discovered, unmated gypsy healers here, three of which are of mating age."

"They are sending only unmated males?" Sally snapped and tried to stand but Costin would not relinquish his hold on her.

Dillon met her eyes and waited until she dropped them to continue. "Having the strength and power of more dominant males is something we need, especially in order to protect such precious pack members. These females," he motioned to the four women sitting on the floor and then towards the room where Jewel lay, "are precious to us, as all our females are, but they are healers and that makes them more vulnerable than others."

"Mated males can protect them just as well as unmated," Crina pointed out as murmurs of agreement rippled through the room.

"And what mated female is going to want her mate around a group of unmated gypsy healers?" Dillon challenged. "You? I'm sure wouldn't have any problem if Sorin was assigned to their protection. How about you, Sally? Let's let Costin follow them around twenty-four-seven and see how you like it."

"Enough of this." Lucian stepped forward. The power in his words had the room silenced before his next breath. "There has to be a solution to this that will benefit everyone. If we stop arguing long enough to think like a pack, then I am sure that we can come up with something. So unless you have something useful to say, do not speak."

Dillon didn't take offense to Lucian's command because he felt none of the wolf's power ripple over him. But he did give the male a sideways glance as he was surprised that Lucian was able to control and direct who his orders would affect. But then he was the brother of Vasile and as such came from a line of strong Alphas.

"Think," Dillon encouraged. "We have to allow these males to help us and allow them the opportunity to interact with the healers. But we also have to keep from having them tear into one another?"

"Oh, is that all you are wanting a solution for?" Crina muttered. A low growl from both Dillon and Lucian had her dropping her eyes and clamping her mouth shut.

Heather sat with the other girls, quietly contemplating the dilemma before them. Not being able to see gave her the benefit of being able to really listen to the tone in a person's voice when they spoke. As she had been listening to Dillon, she heard the compassion that he felt towards the men that were coming to help, but she also heard the very real worry that something bad would happen. She still didn't fully understand the whole true mate thing. From the way everyone talked about it, it sounded more like a burden than a blessing. However, she could not deny longing to be loved in such a way as Sally and Peri had described the way the males loved their mates. As she considered all the things Dillon had said, she remembered that Peri had said something about the mate signs not appearing until the healers were eighteen. Would that mean that the males could safely be around the two girls that weren't yet eighteen?

"If I may," she spoke up into the quiet room. Everyone else was obviously taking Lucian's words seriously and trying to come up with a feasible solution.

"Go ahead, Heather," Dillon told her.

"If I remember correctly, Peri said that for gypsy healers the mate signs did not appear until the female was eighteen. That raises the question; can the males be around Jewel and Kara without knowing for certain if the girls were their true mates? Or at least not feeling it to the extent where they want to kill anyone who gets near her? Sally has told us about how she and Costin met and how he felt a pull towards her before she turned eighteen, but it wasn't that all-consuming need to claim her." No one responded immediately and Heather took that to mean that her question had merit.

"You may be onto something, Helen," Peri spoke up. The girls gave an exasperated sigh nearly in unison at the ridiculous nickname that Peri was hell bent on using for Heather. Heather wasn't bothered by it and she knew that just aggravated Peri more. Peri continued after a few moments of thought. "We could take the three females that are of age to another location, giving some of the males currently present the responsibility of protecting them. The unmated males could come here, without worry of mating signs with Jewel or Kara, and be briefed on our situation. From there we can decide how to proceed in our pursuit of Volcan without allowing Anna, Stella, and Heather to come into contact with the males."

"That could work," Dillon agreed.

It didn't go unnoticed by Heather that Dillon and Peri were both totally avoiding the whole Dalton–sized elephant in the room when it came to

Jewel. If they were going to ignore it, then it seemed like so could the rest of them.

"You do realize that when the males get here and find that there are no healers for them to meet that could possibly reveal the mate bond, they are going to be a tad upset, right?" Elle asked Peri.

Peri shrugged. "What is new about a male werewolf being a tad upset over females?"

"She has a point," Sally agreed as she nodded.

"Where will you take us?" Heather asked drawing the attention back to the girls on the floor. She waited as Peri clucked her tongue, obviously lost in thought, considering her question.

"I have a certain Pixie King that owes the wolves and I a debt," she began. A collective groan from the males had Heather wondering just how much trouble Peri was about to get them into.

"Pixie King?" Anna asked hesitantly.

Peri narrowed her eyes. "You have discovered that fae and werewolves exist, and yet you are surprised there are pixies as well?"

"I try to refrain from making assumptions," Anna admitted.

"Wise little healer." Peri nodded approvingly.

"You will entrust their safety to the pixies?" Lucian asked his mate.

"I'm finding it hard to have a whole lot of faith in my own race right now. Having two high fae turn to the dark side tends to have that effect." She turned back to Dillon. "I suppose Vasile told you that I would be gathering the hounds instead of them flying in?"

Dillon nodded. "Vasile left it up to you in regards to how and when, but he mentioned you would begin with the Irish wolves tonight. Are you sure you want to exert yourself?" His tone was slightly patronizing but Peri seemed inclined to ignore that fact as she answered.

"It will be easier than listening to them complain about long flights," Peri said "I'll flash them here starting with the Irish pack." She said is if Dillon hadn't already mentioned it. "Might as well start tonight and end tonight because honestly they aren't going to get along any better if we bring them in a day at a time. Better to just get it over with quickly."

"So soon?" Kara blurted out after having successfully kept quiet throughout the meeting.

Dillon's eyes softened as he looked at the young girl. "Unfortunately, evil does not wait for those willing to fight back to be ready. Every day that we aren't pursuing Volcan is a day that he can gain strength."

Kara nodded her understanding but the apprehension in her eyes did not abate.

Peri clapped her hands together and began speaking in her no nonsense tone. "Dillon, I think it would be best if you stayed here to welcome the newcomers along with Lucian. We will need dominant males to deal with any lack of control they might have." She turned then to look at Costin. "Sally will need to stay here to take care of Jewel. I imagine that it is your desire to stay with her?" Peri knew it was a stupid question, but she didn't miss an opportunity to goad the cocky bartender.

"Naturally," Costin replied dryly.

"Sorin and Adam, along with their mates, will also accompany the healers. I realize that isn't very many males to protect such precious cargo, but Crina is no lightweight, and Elle has no problem holding her own in a fight. I will do my best to keep tabs on both groups, but I also need to get in contact with some of the other supernaturals. Any questions?"

Stella raised her hand. "Yeah, is there any way we can get off this crazy train?"

A wicked grin spread across Peri's face. "You can try. However," her face suddenly serious, "you are a gypsy healer, unmated, and out there in this big wide world is a male who has the other half of your soul. Can you honestly tell me that there is something back in your old life that's worth walking away from that?"

Stella shook her head as she let out a long, deep breath. "No, honestly I cannot. I can, however, tell you that living with pixies in order to keep the peace among a bunch of possessive, controlling, allbeit no doubt incredibly good looking, werewolves doesn't seem like much of a step up from dancing on a bar."

"If it makes you feel any better, when this is all said and done, I'm sure Costin would be willing to let you dance on his bar."

The room erupted into chuckles at Peri's words. Costin stood helping Sally up to her feet as he shook his head at the fae. "That just sounded wrong on so many levels."

—

Dalton slipped quietly into the room where Jewel Stone lay. She was still as death and yet just as beautiful as the last time he had been in to see her. Regardless of all that had been done to her, all the marks she bore because of those things, to him she looked like an angel. He could hear Dillon's voice from the main living area as he discussed the new wolves that would be arriving soon. Dalton didn't want to care, didn't want to feel as though he needed to feel flesh between his teeth at the thought of one of those males near Jewel, but he did. In his long life he had never felt such possessiveness or jealousy toward another, and the lack of control it ignited in him left him rattled.

He took a seat in the chair next to her bed knowing he would at least have a few minutes while the others were distracted. He tried to stay away. He lasted all of one night before he was slipping unseen back into her room. He had to see her with his own eyes to know without a doubt that she was still holding on. His eyes roamed over her small form, noticing that she had lost even more weight, not that she had any to lose to begin with. Her strawberry locks seemed dull as they fanned out around her. The porcelain skin that was covered in scars that she would bear for the rest of her life appeared even paler than it had the day before. He wanted to do something. His wolf, caged inside of him, snarled, imploring the man to take their mate and protect her.

He dropped his head forward as the memories—the reason that he could not touch her again, could not be what she needed—rushed through his mind. His stomach rolled at the images that played out like a horror movie that would not end. He saw all the things that had happened to him beyond his control. Worse than that, however, were the things he had done in order to cope with those atrocities. Jewel deserved better than the likes of him. He would not condemn her to live with one who had truly become a monster, caged though he may be. He knew that if she was his, if he claimed her, if he took her and bound her to him, then the monster would be set free. For if she accepted him with all of his ugliness, if she pardoned him and bestowed grace and love upon him, he feared he would never let her leave his side. He would shackle her to him so that he could keep her safe. He would want her all to himself and the life of a gypsy healer was the complete opposite of that. She would be needed by others. Her life would be one of service and sacrifice. He would have to share her and even the sanest of their males did not share well.

Dalton lifted his head when he heard the voices get louder, indicating that his time was up. Sally would be back to check on Jewel, and he did not want to be caught by her. The animosity she felt towards him was palpable from more than fifty feet away, and he had no desire to listen to the healer berate him.

Dalton looked back at Jewel as he stood. His feet felt as though they had turned to concrete as he stepped back. "Keep fighting, little dove," he whispered as he backed toward the window, his usual point of retreat when unable to use the door. The desire to grab her was stronger now that he knew of the unmated males that would soon be there. Instead of acting on that desire, he opened the window and carefully managed to squeeze his large frame through the opening. He would be back. He could tell himself a thousand times that this was the last visit, but he knew the wolf would take over eventually. Over the centuries, Dalton had secluded himself more and more, living a solitary life. During that time, the beast had gained more and more control over him. And the control he lacked over the beast would keep him from leaving her. He might be able to force his wolf to watch from a distance, and to convince him that just being close to her was enough. Then again he might also kill all eight of the wolves that showed up to help find Volcan. Really it was a tossup.

—

Kara Jones watched as Anna, Stella, and Heather gathered the possessions that they had accumulated over their time in Peri's home. The high fae had managed to procure them each clothes, toiletries, shoes, and anything else they had told her they needed. When questioned about where and how she got it all, she simply shrugged and said, *I'm me, do you really have to ask?* They left it at that deciding that they really didn't want to know.

"Sucks that you have to stay here," Anna said, breaking the silence that had hung heavy over the room.

"What if they're wrong and the mating signs do show up, even though you are only sixteen?" Stella paused in her packing as she looked over at Kara. "Would they expect you to *bond*, or whatever, with the guy even though you are underage?"

Kara shrugged her shoulders. "If he treated me in a manner even close to the way those guys out there," she pointed towards the door, "treat their mates, then I can't say that I would be opposed to the idea." Kara at first had been very leery of the idea of being tied to one man, and of having no say in the matter. She was young, and that was a big decision. Besides that, what did she know about relationships? She wouldn't know what a healthy relationship looked like if it slapped her in the face. But after years in the system, jumping from home to home with no love or affection, she could not deny the appeal of having someone look at her the way Lucian looked at Peri.

"You do not have to do anything you don't want to, Kara," Heather spoke up. "And if whoever your mate is truly loves you, he will wait for as long as you need him to."

Once their bags were all packed, they headed back down to the living area. Peri wanted them to leave as quickly as they could so that she could remove their scents from the house.

As they stood waiting for the others to join them, Anna's eyes wandered toward the front door. Whatever magic that lived in her that longed to heal others was being drawn outside. She moved toward the door, not saying anything as she quietly slipped outside. As soon as the walls of the house no longer separated her from the pull, it hit her full force. She followed it, letting it guide her toward the forest. As she broke through the trees she saw a huge, steel grey, wolf. His pale blue eyes bore into her as she moved slowly toward him. She knew it was Dalton because she would never forget seeing him stand over Jewel in his wolf form as she lay broken and battered on the altar.

She could not see a wound on him, yet she could feel his pain radiating toward her. Anna remembered some of the things Sally had been teaching them about their magic—how to use it to evaluate a person. From what she understood, she knew she would need to touch him in order to look inside. But as she took another step forward and his eyes began to glow, she knew touching him was out of the question. She didn't know if his wolf had been calling out for help or if she had just been drawn to him because of his anguish.

"I am not the healer you need," she told him gently. "I don't know much about this whole true mate thing, but I do know that opening yourself up to a person is scary. It's humiliating, humbling, and excruciating. I'm not going to tell you that you need to claim her or whatever. I'm not going to say that what you're doing is selfish because honestly I don't even know you." Anna took a deep breath as she thought about her next words. She wasn't lying to him, but at the same time Jewel was a friend now, and she wanted what was best for her. If Dalton was what was best for Jewel and he could help her get better, then that is what she wanted. "Just," she paused. "Jewel loves to read. She told us that she practically lived at the library back in her hometown. She also loves to learn. She's probably the smartest person I've ever met. She is constantly spouting off random facts that most people would never care to know." A huff of laughter escaped her as she remembered the things Heather had told them about her time in the forest with Jewel and Kara. "She carries a heavy burden of self-doubt and hides behind her knowledge. Just know that you aren't the only one with hurt or shame in your past."

She turned and left him with a certain amount of peace filling her. She hadn't had to heal a physical wound, but perhaps that's not the only types of wounds gypsy healers helped with. Anna didn't know if her words would make a difference, but she hoped that somehow she had been able to plant a seed of doubt about his choice to walk away from his true mate.

—

Dalton watched the young healer called Anna walk back toward the house. As he sat staring out into the woods, he had been completely surprised when she emerged into the forest. He had not considered how his pain and longing might affect the healers now that it was no longer held under such a tight reign. He was a little shocked that she hadn't berated him for his behavior but instead had tried to understand his part in the matter. Dalton was even more shocked that Anna had revealed things about Jewel. Things that would make her seem more like a person and less like an unconscious stranger. For that he wanted to growl at Anna. He didn't want to know Jewel's likes and dislikes or habits and quirks. If he knew those things, then he would long to know more. Knowing more would lead to caring and he wasn't sure there was enough emotion left in him to care for anyone.

He sat silently in his wolf form, his body stiff and his senses alert. He had tried to go further, to put some distance between him and the fae's home, but his wolf had literally stopped him in his tracks. He would not let the man budge from that spot. Dalton's wolf had forced his phase and it had been over a century since he had done that. He decided not to fight it. He knew that his own wolf wanted to be close by when the new pack members began to arrive. Some he knew personally and others he just knew of; but he wanted to get a good look at all of them.

The daylight faded and darkness swallowed up the forest and still he sat, waiting. Finally he saw

Peri flash, appearing just in front of her home with two large men on either side of her. They were here. Single males. Here to help? Yes, but like any unmated Canis lupis, they were also searching for their true mates. The door closed, cutting off his view. His wolf trembled as though bolts of electricity were being shot into him as he battled his need to get to her. Suddenly Dalton threw his head back and let out a soul–baring howl. He poured his rage, fear, worries, anguish, and shame into it, and the power that he released shook the trees around him. As it died down and his eyes were once again focused on Peri's home, for the first time, he truly feared that he would not be able to keep his wolf from killing any male that touched Jewel. Slightly more disturbing was that the man was in agreement with the wolf. He didn't know if he wanted to stop his wolf from ripping their throats out.

Unable to stand it any longer, he paced over to the house and stood just outside the window to Jewel's room. Peering in he saw Sally close her eyes and lay her hand on Jewel's head. Several minutes later she opened them with a frustrated growl. He knew she had not been able to reach the injured girl. Costin wrapped an arm around her and kissed her temple.

"We have company. You can check on Jewel again in a bit," he told his mate as he led her from the room. The door closed and Jewel was alone. Now was his chance to see her before the other males did. He considered breathing on her to cover her in his scent as he phased and snagged the pants and shirt he had stowed in the bushes. If she was covered in his scent, then they would know not to pursue her. Dalton reached for the window and just as his fingers touched it, a violent shock ripped through him. He jumped back with a painful curse as he shook his hands. He looked down at them to see the damage but there was nothing, no burn marks or cuts. His eyes narrowed as he looked back at the window, and he growled as if it was the window's fault he had been electrocuted. He stepped towards the house ready to attempt to open it again but was brought up short by the sound of his Alpha's voice.

"You can't get in."

Dalton turned slowly and his wolf peered out of his eyes at Dillon. "Why?" he growled.

"There is a reason we keep high fae around. Peri has bound you from the house. I know you have been visiting Jewel; your scent has been all over her room. The draw to her is undeniable and yet you still refuse to claim her. This is your doing." Dillon pointed to the house behind Dalton. "I told you that I would give the other males a chance to see if Jewel was their true mate. After all, it was you who said there were no mating signs, only the need to protect her."

Dalton's head dropped forward as he felt the fight rush out of him. Those were his words. Dillon was right; he had been the one to claim that Jewel might not be his mate, and in doing so he had left her available for other males.

"You have to let your past go, Dalton," Dillon told him. "Everyone has a past that haunt them, but you are letting yours control you."

Dalton looked up and his eyes met Dillon's for a count of three before settling on his Alpha's right shoulder. "Some pasts are darker than others. Some pasts cannot be healed or excised."

"When you go feral, I will have no choice but to kill you. Consider what that will do to your mate before you decide *for her* that your past is too much."

Dillon left him standing there in the dark. He had not missed what the Alpha had said. He'd said *when you go feral* not *if.* And he was right. Dillon was also right that he would have to kill Dalton once it happened. Because once his wolf took over the dam would burst and all the rage caused by being separated from their mate would be let loose on anyone in his way. Man, woman, or child—mated or not—they would all bleed for his own sins.

2

"Change is inevitable in this life. Whether this change is good or bad ultimately depends upon our response to it. Most of the time we assume any change that is painful or difficult is bad, but the truth is probably quite the opposite. We shy away from the changes that will bring us suffering and test our will. When in fact we should be running into it with our arms open wide embracing that which will most likely make us stronger." ~ Heather

Heather's hand lay gently on Stella's shoulder as the group followed Adam through a thick forest. Elle had mentioned that the home of the pixies was deep in the Carpathian Mountains. Strange, she thought, that they were looking for pixies as they trekked through a range of mountains that were notorious in fiction for harboring vampires. Heather laughed to herself as she considered how different her life had become in such a short amount of time. Some of those changes were good, and some, well some flat out, sucked. Hearing the horrible sounds of the battle that had happened only days ago was something she thought she would only ever hear in a movie. Finding out that she, a blind dog trainer from Texas, was special for something other than her lack of sight was almost too much to hope for. She didn't want much out of life, but to be loved the way the men of the Canis lupis species loved their mates was something she could completely be okay with.

"Are you thinking little-blue-demon-looking things for the pixies?" Stella whispered to Heather.

Heather snorted. "You say *blue* like I know what that means." She felt Stella shrug.

"What should I say?" Stella asked.

"Good point," Heather conceded. "Whatever they are, I don't think Peri would put us in a situation that would be dangerous to us."

"Are we talking about the same fairy that had us running headlong into a battle between a band of werewolves and two psycho fae?" Anna spoke up.

"Exactly," Stella agreed.

Heather ignored them and instead directed her next question to Crina. "Have you met these pixies, Crina?"

"I have met some," she admitted. "They are a finicky race. Typically they aren't necessarily good or bad. They simply choose the side that is most likely to win. In other words they look out for number one above all others."

"And yet she trusts them with our safety?" Anna asked.

"Yeah, what exactly is this debt that is owed by the king?" Stella piped in.

"Maybe we should stop for a break and fill them in," Elle suggested. As she drew to a halt, the others followed suit. Sorin and Adam got out the water bottles they had packed and began passing them out as they each sat in a small circle. The three healers sat side by side staring back at the two couples who had been charged with their care and waited for the tale that no doubt would be full of unbelievable information.

"We've shared with you a little about the past year and all the trials the Romanian pack has faced. So many changes have been taking place and with changes come challenges," Elle began. "It seems that with the reappearance of the true mates, which is a good thing, also came great evil. It was as if the world was somehow trying to balance itself out. One of these evils was Desdemona, a witch of incredible power and a heart so full of evil that the grass she walked upon died beneath her feet. She, like Volcan, was also hell bent on obtaining her own gypsy healer. Now as you all may or may not know, in the supernatural world, like draws like. It works kind of like a magnet. Evil forces are able to draw other weaker evil forces to serve them or work with them. Mona was able to call all sorts of evil beings and powers to her to help her in her quest. Though the pixies are not necessarily evil, they are not necessarily good either. They had no resistance when she came calling—no light, no purity that would repel her. She managed to coerce them into assisting her.

"Ainsel, the pixie king, agreed to help send some of Vasile's males, including Vasile to the *In Between*."

"Which is what exactly?" Stella asked.

"A place of hopelessness and torture. Not somewhere you ever want to go," Sorin answered and the look in his eyes made it clear that he had firsthand experience.

"If Ainsel did something as terrible as that, then why on earth is Peri trusting him?" Stella asked, this time directing the question to Elle.

"Vasile, the most powerful Alpha of the Canis lupis chose to spare the king. Ainsel's decision to help Mona was not made out of a desire for power or greed, but by the need to protect his people. Though this did not excuse the king's mistake, neither did it make him evil. Vasile only destroys that which he feels has no hope of being changed for the good."

The group was quiet as the three healers seemed to consider the information given to them. After several moments Stella stood and brushed off her pants. "Well, I can't judge because I know that there are times in life when you have two choices, and it's the lesser of two evils that you must choose from. If Peri says we will be safe there, then that is good enough for me." She looked down at Anna and Heather. "What about you two?"

Heather stood and Stella held out an arm for the blind healer to hold onto to help gain her footing. "I figure I've got two choices myself." Her Texas drawl made the others grin. "I can keep going deeper into the rabbit hole, or I can head back towards the jaws of the big bad wolf. For some reason, at this moment the rabbit hole—no matter what pixie might inhabit it—seems a tad bit safer." This brought a chuckle from the two males.

"Smart healer," Adam praised.

"Well contrary to popular belief, fairy boy, blind does not equal dumb," Heather snorted.

Elle clapped her hands as she stood up and grinned at Adam. "How come it never gets old when these humans call you fairy boy?"

Adam shrugged, unoffended. "They don't know any better. They've probably never been in the presence of such beauty and masculinity all wrapped up into one and it's blowing their little healer circuits."

"Okay, on that note, I think we better get moving," Heather said and gave Stella a small nudge. "If he continues spouting off that much crap we'll be knee deep in it in a matter of minutes. I don't know about y'all, but of all the crap in the world, male fairy crap is the most repugnant."

Another round of laughter rippled through the group as they once again headed off. Elle assured them that it wasn't much further, though in truth she didn't know when they would find the entrance to the pixie realm. This wasn't because she didn't know how far away it was. On the contrary, she happened to know that they were basically on top of the veil to the pixie realm, but Ainsel was hiding it from her. He was watching them, letting them walk in circles, no doubt so that he could gain as much information on them as possible before allowing them entrance. Peri had told her that she had spoken to the pixie king, but that with everything that had taken place over the past months he was especially paranoid. She didn't want to worry the healers. It was bad enough that she had had to tell them about their history with the finicky pixies; she didn't need to add to any apprehension they might already have towards the creatures.

"Elle," Adam's voice broke through her thoughts. "Why are we going in circles?"

"So much for not worrying them." Sorin's voice reached through their bond. She smiled to herself at the exasperation in his voice. She should have known he would know what she was doing. As her mate, he was privy to any of her thoughts, though he usually tried to give her privacy.

"Adam is not known for his discretion," she responded.

"True enough. Might as well let them know, love," he told her gently.

She let out deep breath but didn't stop walking as she answered. "The pixie king doesn't quite trust us yet so he is keeping the veil hidden until he's ready to let us in."

"Wait." Heather came to an abrupt halt. "You mean to tell me that we are just walking around aimlessly until this king decides to invite us in for tea? I'm going to give you the benefit of the doubt and think that maybe I gave you the impression that as a blind woman I love stumbling through a forest completely unworried about tripping over roots and face planting into some pixie droppings." Heather ignored the cough covered chuckles. "I am not about to think that you let us walk around for no reason at all because you didn't want to worry us over the weird pixie king."

Elle had stopped and turned to look at the blind healer, trying not to cringe at the obvious irritation, though no doubt warranted, in the woman's voice. She had a feeling if Heather could see she would be staring a whole into Elle's skull.

"Elle, will this Ainsel let us in when he feels we aren't a threat?" Anna asked gently.

Elle nodded, still unable to speak after having been thoroughly berated by Heather.

"Then how about we just sit and rest," Anna suggested.

The group was quiet as they sat and the tension was thick until Heather finally spoke again. "Elle, I apologize for blowing my gasket. I think I'm just tired. But nonetheless, I shouldn't take it out on you."

Elle smiled at her and knew that Heather would hear that smile in her voice. "Or it could be that you were taken from your life, tossed into a world of wolves, fae, blood and magic, forced to endure a friend being tortured, subjected to the realization that one day a possessive, hairy male would claim you as his own, and then told that we were going to try and hide you from said male for as long as we could while seeking out the evil that tortured your friend."

"Naw, it's definitely just because I'm tired."

—

Sally stood next to Costin in the living area of Peri's home trying not to fidget. She was restless. Since the others had left in search of the pixie realm, the house had felt empty and the lack of distractions only made her mind dwell on all of the difficulties that they faced. Kara was upstairs in the room where the girls had all been staying per Peri's suggestion. She had wanted to sit with Jewel while she waited to be introduced, but Peri had said she wanted her as far away from the males as possible without her leaving the house. The sound of the door opening had Sally gripping Costin's hand tightly which made him chuckle, causing her to want to kick him in the shin.

"Why are you worried, Sally mine?" he asked her through their bond as they watched Peri walk in with two males on her heels.

"Oh, I don't know, could be because we have a sixteen-year-old gypsy healer upstairs, a seventeen-year-old gypsy healer unconscious in the room twenty feet away, neither of them are mated, and two unmated males are walking into this house hoping that they might find their true mate?"

"Lucian, Dillon, and I won't let anything happen to the females. Quit stressing about it and relax. You know Peri's about to bust these twos' balls and it's bound to be

hilarious. You wouldn't want to miss fully appreciating getting to see her rip into unsuspecting werewolves now would you?" The playfulness in his tone had her biting back a smile.

"OMG, I would never want to miss out on Peri busting balls," she said dryly. Costin looked at her from the corner of his eye; a mischievous grin spreading across his sexy lips.

"What?" she whispered with raised eyebrows.

"You said *balls,*" he muttered, attempting to cover his laughter with a cough.

Peri's head whipped around and her eyes bore into them both at the sound of Costin's laugh. The look was definitely one of warning.

"Welcome to Farie," Perizada said to the two males. "This is my mate, Lucian. And this is the Beta of the Serbia pack, Costin, and his mate and gypsy healer, Sally."

Sally watched as the first man that stepped forward gave a formal bow to Lucian. He was several inches shorter than Lucian putting him at about six foot one. He was big, Sally noted, like most of the wolves she knew and had dark chocolate eyes, black wavy hair that brushed his collar, and his face was chiseled and masculine. He was handsome, very handsome. His movements were confident and smooth.

"Lucian Lupei, it is so good to see you alive and well. You knew my father, Ramone. I am Gustavo Rivera, Alpha of the Spain pack. This is my Beta, Antonio." His thick Spanish accent was alluring and rich.

"Could you please refrain from ogling the Spanish wolf, beloved?" Costin growled in her mind.

Sally grinned. *"You have nothing to worry about, Costin. Any male that can't spin a bottle in one hand while pouring a shot with the other isn't worth a second glance."*

He let out a snort but coughed quickly when Lucian glanced at him from the corner of his eye.

"Thank you for coming, Gustavo," Lucian said and bowed his head in return. Sally noticed neither male bared their necks to the other. She wondered if that meant that they weren't sure who was more dominant.

The Spanish wolf then stepped in front of Costin and Sally. "Costin Miklos." Gustavo gave a curt nod of the head.

"Gustavo," Costin said and tilted his head to the side bearing his neck ever so slightly. "Thank you for coming. This is my mate, Sally."

Gustavo held out his hand to her, his head slightly bowed. She fought the urge to giggle like a school girl as she placed her hand in his. To her surprise he didn't kiss it, but simply leaned a little lower as he spoke. "An honor to meet you, healer."

"Thank you," Sally told him pulling her hand away quickly as she felt Costin tense next to her. If Gustavo noticed the tension between them, he didn't give any indication as he righted himself and turned back to Lucian.

"Where is Dillon?" he asked.

Lucian glanced towards Jewel's room as though listening for something. "He's dealing with a pack issue; he will join us shortly."

"Perizada, thank you for allowing us to stay in your home," Antonio spoke for the first time. His accent was just as thick as his Alpha's, though his voice wasn't quite as deep.

"As much as I would like to say that I would gladly open my home to all the wolves and that you are most welcome here, I try not to lie, unless it will benefit me somehow." She shot her mate a look when he growled at her. "No offence, Antonio, but werewolves are not my company of choice; they tend to tread on my nerves with their sharp little claws."

Antonio frowned. "But you are mated to one."

"Hmm," she nodded. "Yes, well, let it never be said that the Great Luna doesn't have a sense of humor."

"Don't let her fool you," Sally smiled. "She loves wolves, especially her big white one; she just likes to have something to complain about."

"Why don't we take a seat?" Lucian interrupted whatever it was Peri was about to reply. Sally was sure it would have been laced with colorful words.

Just as they all were seated, the front door opened and Dillon walked in. "Gustavo, Antonio, so glad you made it." He nodded to the two wolves. Dillon took the remaining seat across from the Spanish wolves leaning his forearms on his knees with his hands clasped in front of him. Sally knew this to be his no nonsense pose. Dillon wasn't about to exchange pleasantries or small talk. She could see in his narrowed eyes that he was all business.

"Peri, when do you have to go for the next pack?" he asked her.

Peri glanced at her bare wrist as though looking at a watch. "Whenever we are good and ready for the next ones."

"Very well." He looked at Gustavo. "I don't like to have to repeat myself a hundred times so how would you feel about letting Peri retrieve the remaining packs and then allowing me to fill you all in at the same time?"

Gustavo's lips twitched and Sally could tell he was trying not to smile. "What Alpha does like to repeat himself?"

Dillon chuckled. "Good point."

"We are fine to wait, Dillon. There is no sense in wasting time speaking with each of us separately."

Dillon looked over at Peri again. "Do you mind bringing all the wolves now?"

"Oh, sure, wolf delivery service, that's me." Peri plastered on her sickest fake smile before rolling her eyes and disappearing.

"She's a tad moody this evening," Sally muttered.

"Oh, like that's different from any other day?" Costin laughed.

"I thought she would be less moody now that she has Lucian," she said as she looked over at Peri's mate.

Lucian's face remained blank as he responded. "She is less moody, just not with the general public."

Costin grinned. "Sally mine, if I didn't know any better I'd think Lucian just made a joke."

"Guess it's not true that you can't teach an old dog new tricks."

Gustavo's brow rose. "Are they always like this?" he asked Lucian.

Lucian shook his head. "Worse."

An hour later Sally's foot bounced restlessly as she sat next to her mate and her eyes darted around the packed room. All of the huge male bodies reminded her of her time at the Gathering when Vasile and the other Alphas had attempted to find mated pairs by bringing all the unmated members of the twelve packs together. Yeah, that had been one big happy party. Deep voices rumbled as the males introduced themselves to one another in various accents and languages. Most of them seemed to know one another, which Sally realized shouldn't be surprising considering they were all probably older than dirt.

"Depends on which layer of dirt you are referring to, love," Costin's voice interrupted her thoughts.

"Do you know who the oldest in the room is?" she asked him as she glanced from male to male.

"Lucian is probably the oldest; although the one who probably runs a close second isn't here yet. That would be Kale, the Ireland pack Beta."

"Does their age have anything to do with how powerful they are?"

Costin nodded as he answered through their bond. *"Yes, generally the older the wolf the more powerful, but being mated makes a male stronger as well."*

Sally started to respond but stopped when Peri appeared once again in the living room with two more men. She wasn't surprised to find that they were both at least six feet tall.

"I'm just going to go out on a limb and say that there are no small male werewolves," she muttered to Costin through their bond.

Costin didn't turn his head away from the new males as he answered. *"Not that I have ever seen."*

"Good to know," she whispered as she smiled at the newcomers.

Peri left again without bothering to make introductions, and by Sally's count this would be her last trip. As they introduced themselves, Sally tried to take note of their names and faces, as well as their pack locations, because she knew the other healers would be asking her for details. There was Drayden, the Canada Pack Alpha, and his Beta, Nick. Drayden was blonde and blue eyed with classic good looks. He had an intriguing scar above his right eye that Sally was sure held an interesting story. Nick, his Beta, was the epitome of the biker bad boy, in looks at least. He was tall and broad in his chest and shoulders. His head was shaved, though not smooth like with a razor, but just down to the shortest he could get it with clippers. His eyes were black with a sheen to them that reminded her of obsidian. The black t-shirt and black boots only added to the overall effect. His eyes had a calculating look that slightly unsettled Sally.

The next ones brought by Peri were the Italian Alpha, Ciro, and his Beta, Aimo. Both of them had olive toned skin and dark chocolate hair. Ciro had light brown eyes, whereas Aimo had hazel eyes that were similar to her own mate, Costin. Again they were tall, but instead of being bulky, they were leaner and reminded her more of Adam in build. Both were very handsome and Sally had decided that the Great Luna had made the males of their race nearly irresistible in looks because it certainly wasn't going to be their personalities, with all their demanding grunts, that won their true mates over.

"I heard that," Costin told her as he listened to the Ireland wolves introduce themselves.

Sally ignored him as she looked at Kale, the Ireland Beta, and Banan, his third. Kale had dark hair but the goatee and mustache on his handsome face were a deep red color. His eyes were bright green framed in long eyelashes. She frowned as she thought how unfair it was that a man should have such beautiful eyelashes. As his eyes met hers, he smiled and two deep dimples appeared causing her to smile back. He was a charmer and the accent only added to his appeal. Banan was more what she would consider a classic Irish look. He had red hair and freckles, which in no way subtracted from his manliness. He had a boyish face with round cheeks, and his green eyes seemed to dance in delight as though he knew something no one else did. Sally liked him immediately.

"Maybe you should go check on Jewel," Costin suggested coolly.

"Maybe you should get over the fact that you aren't the only hottie in the room. Regardless of that fact you are the only hottie that I want."

"You try my patience, Sally mine."

"You'll live."

Dillon took a deep breath as he prepared to explain to the males that had joined them just what they were up against. Introductions had been made. They were short, but then they weren't here to find out each other's favorite hobbies. They were here because the unsuspecting world needed them. Vasile had put it best when he said, *if not us, then who?* Dillon completely agreed. If they did not step up and fight the evil, who would?

"Thank you all for coming on such short notice," he began as he met each of their eyes. "I know that Vasile gave you the abridged version of what has taken place over the past weeks. I will try to give you a little more information, and then I'll open it up for questions." He waited until he had received nods from each of them and then began.

"Some of you may remember a high fae named Volcan. A very long time ago he began practicing dark magic, and the witches that once occupied this world were all created by him. The fae and some of the wolves that agreed to help attempted to destroy him, and they thought they had succeeded. But now, centuries later, another high fae, Lorelle, has defected and stumbled upon Volcan's castle along with his essence that he had somehow managed to preserve. Lorelle has been dealt with, but Volcan remains at large," Dillon continued while they silently listened. He told them all of the things Peri had shared with him regarding the healers, her sister, and Volcan's past. The males all listened intently and when he was finished the room was silent as they all absorbed the information he had just given them.

"Do you have a place to start looking?" Drayden, of the Canadian pack, finally broke the silence.

It was Peri who answered. "Of course we do. We wouldn't have dragged you across the world into this mess without having a starting place."

Drayden looked at her expectantly. "And?" he drug out the word.

She let out a deep breath. "And, we will start with looking on each continent, in each realm."

"Glad to hear you have it narrowed down," Nick chuckled but bit it back as Peri's sharp eyes met his. "I mean, uh, where do we start?"

Peri's lips curved up into a wicked smile as Lucian laid a hand on her thigh. "Good to know there is at least one smart one in this bunch."

"What of the lasses? Are they alright? Are they well?" Kale of the Ireland pack asked, his voice a deep timbre filling the room and drawing everyone's attention.

"You mean the healers?" Dillon asked. Kale nodded.

Peri's nose scrunched up as she glanced at Sally. She let out a small laugh that was about as real as the tooth fairy. "Yeah, about them...."

—

Darkness was all she knew. Jewel couldn't remember a time when she hadn't been surrounded by the bleak, black hole that she seemed to be falling further and further into. The only time that she felt like a sliver of light was penetrating the dark was when she heard his voice—the deep timbre that soothed her and made her want to crawl back to reality. She hadn't known his name until she had heard Sally say it after one of his many visits. From what she could gather, Sally didn't know that Jewel could hear everything that was going on around her, but the more experienced healer spoke to her continuously as if the constant conversation would somehow bring Jewel back from the brink. Jewel had felt Sally attempting to heal her, but the girl could only do so much. When Sally had realized that there was nothing else she could do, she had gone off on a bit of a tirade about this male named Dalton who kept coming to visit Jewel but refused to, as Sally put it, grow a pair and be the mate that Jewel needed. Jewel had been a little shocked to hear Sally say something so blunt. In the short time that she had known the gypsy healer, she had only seen gentleness and kindness and loads of patience.

From that moment on Jewel found herself drifting further and further away from life, only to be drawn back when Dalton was near. She could literally feel him when he came close to her without him ever speaking. A sense of security and peace would rush over her, and she felt as though, in that moment, nothing could touch her, nothing could hurt her, not ever again. But though it felt safe and secure to have him near, it felt equally panic inducing when he left her. It was during these times that she tried to draw on the facts that she knew. She had deduced that her state was induced by the horror and pain that she had endured at the hands and mouth of Lorelle, the twisted fae woman who had been under the control of an evil spirit. It made perfect sense. Okay, so, a team of psychiatric professionals might not agree that it made perfect sense. But in the alternate reality that had become her life when she had been ripped from her home by Lorelle, it totally made perfect sense. Knowing what was wrong with her helped her keep from panicking, but then that was the story of her life.

For as long as she could remember she had been the butt of the jokes her classmates made regarding her mother and her chosen "profession." Jewel had grown a rather large chip on her shoulder towards her mother because she felt that if her mom had just chosen a normal job, like bank teller, or secretary, then her problems would be solved. But no, her mother just had to be a fortune teller. But Gem hated to be called a fortune teller; she much preferred the term *seer*. Regardless of the laughter and pointed fingers, Jewel loved her mother. So in order to cope with the jeering, she escaped. She began reading at a young age and found that she not only loved to be able to escape into a story, but that she loved facts surrounding the story as well. The more she learned, the more empowered she felt. So what if she didn't fit the mold that her classmates said that she should—that society said she should? Big deal, because guess what, suckers, she knew every country, their capitals, their government types, and even their national religions. In her mind that put her a step above them simply because their meager minds could only come up with insults because of something they feared. But *her* mind held the secrets to all sorts of knowledge. Okay, so maybe they weren't really secrets since anyone could do a Google search on them and get the information, but that wasn't the point. The point was that Jewel had felt powerless, stuck because of her circumstances, until she discovered that she had a knack for learning. She found that anytime someone made her feel inferior she would become desperate to learn something new, almost as if by taking in new knowledge somehow pushed out any hurt a person had inflicted on her.

Surely with everything she had learned, all the knowledge she had acquired, she could figure out how to deal with the situation she now found herself in. Knowledge had never failed her; it couldn't fail her now. She wouldn't let it, because she wasn't ready to die, not when a new world with amazing possibilities had just opened up for her. In this new world she would no longer be the freak, and that was something worth living for in her mind. Perhaps Dalton was the answer to the question of how. When he was near she could feel her spirit stir, and instead of trying to slip further away, it reached for him. Maybe it meant that he would be able to accept her for who she was. She had read so many paranormal romance novels that spoke of soul mates, and she wouldn't deny that she had dreamed of such a thing for herself. Until recent events she never thought it would be possible, but the connection she felt to a man she had never even spoken to was something that she couldn't ignore, not when she now knew of the magical world around her. But even as her heart leapt at the idea of having a soul mate, of having a perfect counterpart, something whispered to her mind that it wasn't possible. *How could anyone really accept you as you are?* The voice didn't sound like her own, but yet it felt as though it was coming from inside of her. *You have buried yourself in your books to find acceptance in knowledge. Why do you need anything else from anyone else?* Okay, now she knew *that* couldn't be her because she had never *not* wanted to be accepted by at least someone. Everybody needed someone...didn't they?

—

I don't need her, Dalton thought to himself, knowing it was the biggest lie he had ever told himself as he paced back and forth within the cover of the forest. Every few steps he sent scathing looks towards Peri's home, growling low in his chest. "How dare she bind me from...," he paused. *From what? From the woman he adamantly claimed wasn't his mate? And yet he couldn't stand the thought of being kept from her. Still that didn't give his Alpha and Perizada the right to choose separation for him. It should be his choice. He should be the one to decide to torture himself mercilessly by denying himself the other half of his soul.*

After Dillon had left him standing there seething, Dalton had repeatedly thrown himself at the house only to be repelled time and time again. He knew it was pointless. He was no match for the power of the high fae, at least not when it came to magic. The physical pain of being thrown back from the barrier was much more tolerable than the hell he was living with inside of himself. For the first time in a long time he truly wanted something more than the loneliness he had wrapped around himself like a warm blanket. He wanted the light that a true mate would bring to him. He wanted a love that he knew he didn't deserve—wanted it with a desperation that scared even him. Dalton knew the only way that it would be fair to Jewel would be to bare his soul to her. He needed to come clean about his past, about what was done to him and his family, and about what he had done in the time after that. It wouldn't be fair to claim Jewel without her truly knowing him— knowing the things he was capable of. Only then would he know if she could love him.

The idea terrified him. It was hard enough to admit your weaknesses to a friend, not that he had any. The idea of revealing all of your secrets, no matter how ugly, to the one person who could rip you heart out was beyond frightening. He was drawn from his thoughts when he saw movement from the window of Jewel's room. His head whipped around and he moved closer as he watched Dillon and one of the new males step into the room. A low rumble built in his chest as the two wolves stepped even closer to her bed. The spell that Peri had put over the house made it impossible for him to hear anything. Admittedly, it might be a good thing that he couldn't hear them. When the tall wolf, he finally recognized as Gustavo, stepped even closer to Jewel, Dalton finally lost it in a haze of fury. He let lose a roar worthy of an enraged lion, and despite the spell, he knew Gustavo had heard him as the Spanish Alpha's head whipped around. Dalton knew his wolf was at the surface staring at the Alpha. Gustavo narrowed his own eyes, staring right back at Dalton, attempting to make him submit—it only made Dalton want to laugh. He would submit to no wolf who thought he had the right to get so close to his Jewel. Later he would evaluate the fact that he had mentally just called her *his*. Right now he just wanted to rip the other male's head off and Dillon's as well.

The Spanish Alpha took another step closer to the bed but his eyes never left Dalton's. He was testing him. Dalton shook his head slowly at the Alpha. *Not a smart move, old man,* he thought to himself. Up until that point he had been able to keep his wolf from taking over completely, but when Gustavo reached out and touched Jewel's cheek, Dalton's hold broke. Spell or no spell his wolf was going to get into that house. He had no idea what would be left once his wolf was finished, and at the moment his need to get to Jewel was stronger than his care for the safety of the others. *The Great Luna help them all,* he growled as he ran full force towards the window to his mate's room.

3

"There were days that I honestly believed being a blind seeing eye dog trainer for the blind was about as weird as it got. Man, was I wrong." ~ Heather

"Peri is producing lazy warriors these days." A small but firm voice had the group jumping from their reclined and seated positions. Elle was the first to her feet as she quickly looked around to make sure all of those in her care were accounted for.

Once she was sure the three healers were safe, as well as the others, she turned back to the bearer of the small voice. A pixie known to her as Dae, one of Ainsel's top warriors, was standing on a low hanging branch. Pixies often chose to stay in the trees when dealing with other species. Their diminutive frames, ranging from one to one-and-a-half feet in height, made them appear vulnerable to those bigger than them, but Elle knew they were powerful in their own right. She wouldn't let her guard down just because they were smaller.

"Why don't your comrades show themselves?" Elle asked him. She knew better than to believe that

Ainsel would have sent only one warrior out to confront them. He wasn't as old as he was because he was careless.

"You need not worry yourself with them, she-warrior," Dae told her. "They have no orders to attack—unless you first engage me."

"I really want that to be reassuring, but the last time we were confronted by a group of pixies, the males were cast into the *In Between*," she pointed out.

Dae's face scrunched up as though he was sucking on a sour lemon. "Yes, that was a nasty bit of business. King Ainsel has discussed the situation with both Perizada and Vasile. He will not go back on his word to assist the fae and the wolves."

"Then why is he hiding the veil?" Adam asked.

They watched as the pixie warrior glanced warily around the forest. "King Ainsel does not trust the human realm any longer. Volcan was once a very powerful sorcerer. There is no telling how far his reach is."

"He's been in lock down for centuries," Stella spoke up. "Surely, he isn't that powerful yet."

"Healer," Dae said as he bowed respectfully. "We are honored by your presence as well as the presence of your sister healers." He motioned to Heather and Anna. "But in response to your comment. Evil is like mold that begins to grow on one tiny weak spot on a single piece of fruit. It begins to quietly eat away at that piece until there is nothing left but rot. Then before anyone is aware, it has quickly infected the piece next to it and then the piece next to that one until all of the fruit has been covered. The only way to stop the mold from spreading is to get it away from any other fruit; otherwise, it will just continue to move on to the next piece. Evil, like the mold, will spread quickly."

"Okay, well, that doesn't sound ominous at all," Heather quipped.

"Considering we are the fruit in that analogy, could we please enter the pixie realm?" Adam asked Dae.

Dae made a motion with his hand and the group watched as a ripple in the air began at a spot just below the branch upon which the pixie stood. "By invitation of the King of the Pixies you may enter." He waved the group forward.

Elle started to move but Sorin placed a hand on her arm and the hard look in his eyes softened as he looked at her. "I will go first."

Elle didn't argue; she was learning that there wasn't anything she could say that would change the protective nature of her mate, no matter how powerful she was.

Anna followed Stella and Heather through the rippling air that was the veil between the pixie and human realms. Three months ago she had been sitting in the voodoo store, Little Shop of Horrors, attempting to avoid the crazies that came out after dark. Now she was entering a "realm" that was not her own where lived little magical beings no taller than the length of her shin. Her mother, being an American gypsy, had always believed in the mystical.

Anna wondered now, as she stepped into the cool air of the pixie realm, if her mother had known such creatures existed.

Her eyes widened as she looked around. It was obviously night time, but the stars in the sky shone so brightly that they had no trouble seeing the beautiful, lush foliage around them. Anna had thought that everything would be small considering the size of the pixies. But to her surprise, and to the surprise of her friends as well judging by the looks on their faces, the trees were huge. The flowers growing around them were as big as sunflowers, though they looked nothing like sunflowers. She felt as if she had just stepped into the pages of a fairy tale.

"Okay, is it me or does anyone else feel like the animals that are bound to be hiding just behind all those leaves will bust out in a song at any moment?" Stella mumbled.

Heather laughed. "I've only heard Disney movies, but I'm assuming that is what you're getting at?"

"Like good old Walt himself drew this place into existence," Stella agreed.

Dae motioned them forward, and Anna smiled as more and more little pixies emerged from the forest. Some were males and dressed in warrior type clothing. Others were obviously female, wearing dresses that shimmered as they moved. She realized as they flitted about that they had wings; she hadn't noticed that when they had been listening to Dae in the human realm. The wings fluttered so quickly that you could only see them if you looked very hard. Anna realized she had stopped when she looked down to see a little pixie pulling on her pants leg urging her forward. She glanced back up to see that the group was indeed further ahead of her now. She smiled at the pixie. "Thank you." And then she hurried to catch up with the others.

"Overwhelmed?" Crina asked her.

Anna chuckled. "A little. It's so beautiful it almost doesn't seem real."

"Okay, so blind chick moment," Heather broke in. "This is one of those times when I really wished I had some concept of what y'all are talking about. I can tell from your voices that it must look amazing."

Stella patted Heather's hand that was laying on her arm. "Console yourself with the fact that once we are battling the evil Volcan again, you won't have to see your death coming."

"Anyone ever tell you that your nurturing instincts suck just a bit?" Heather asked.

"Anyone ever tell you that it's the thought that counts, not the technique?" Stella asked, causing a sudden shout of laughter from the group.

"Touché," Heather conceded.

Anna smiled at the two girls and was thankful for their ability to take things in stride when at times she felt like the weight of the world was being dumped on their shoulders. Since they had begun their journey, the young healer had noticed a dull ache deep in her chest. At first she chalked it up to all the walking; she wasn't exactly in the best of shape. But the pain never abated. But the most troubling thing about it, and the part that made her certain that the pain wasn't physical at all, was a sudden desire to go back to Farie. It was like when she would forget something after having left her house, only she didn't know what it was, just that she was sure that she had forgotten something. Anna rubbed the place on her chest just over her heart as they continued on, all the while attempting to ignore the little nudges that urged her to hightail it back to Peri's.

She didn't know how long they had walked, their heads constantly turning this way and that as they tried to absorb their fantastical surroundings, when they came to a sudden halt. Anna nearly bumped into Crina who was in front of her. She stepped to the side so that she could see the holdup. Her eyes widened ever larger than before when she saw the sheer number of little bodies filling the trees, flowers, and ground before them. At the very front of the group standing on a large rock, she could only assume based on his confident posture, was none other than Ainsel, the King of the Pixies.

"Perizada, high fae of the council, ambassador to the wolves and trainer and keeper of the gypsy healers, has requested that we shelter you," Ainsel's voice boomed, surprisingly loud considering his size. "She has explained to me the circumstances and risks involved, and I have agreed to allow you to stay in our realm." He paused as he looked at each member of their group until his eyes finally landed on the three healers. "I do however have one request."

"Nothing is ever free," Heather muttered under her breath.

"I require the healers' assistance," he finished.

"What sort of assistance?" Sorin asked as he took a step forward so that he was standing in front of their group.

"The healing sort," Ainsel answered, his brow drawn together and lips pinched tight as if it should have been obvious.

"Does Peri know of your request? Elle asked.

Ainsel didn't meet her eyes as he answered. "Sort of."

"Sort of how?" Adam prodded.

To Anna's surprise the great pixie king suddenly looked a little like a child caught drawing all over the walls with a permanent marker.

"Sort of, as in, I might have tried to tell her when she was leaving but I don't know if she heard me."

Anna watched as Elle's eyes narrowed on the small king. She was sure that at any moment the fae warrior was going to skewer him. But to her surprise after several tense moments, Elle straightened and motioned for the king to lead on.

"We will discuss this request once you have shown us where we will be staying," she told him.

Ainsel seemed to think that was as good as he was going to get at the moment and nodded as he turned to face the direction they had been walking. Anna leaned over to Stella covering her mouth to help muffle her voice. "What do you think he wants with us?"

Stella shrugged. "To use our mojo somehow I suppose."

"I can tell you right now if he attempts to drain power out of us by drinking our blood, we are going to have our first ever pixie roast," Heather added.

"Did you know," Crina's voice broke in as she sidled up next to the girls. "Pixies have very good hearing?"

Heather smiled as she looked in the direction of Crina's voice. "Maybe they'll think twice about trying to use us healers then."

Crina laughed. "Maybe you're right, healer. You would make a good wolf."

"Come on now, let's not start talking cray-cray." Stella tugged gently on Heather to get her to speed up. "Don't you think it's enough that we have found out that we come from some ancient lineage and will one day be mated to a werewolf? Let's not go adding furry and *likes to hang head out the window* to our list of traits."

Crina held her hands up in surrender. "Okay, point taken. Too much supernatural makes a cranky Stella."

Anna laughed as Stella shot Crina an unladylike gesture. "You can take the girl out of the Bronx...," Anna said and laughed again when Stella shot her the same sentiment. She didn't miss the fact that Stella had been rubbing her chest in the exact location that Anna had been earlier or the fact that as soon as Anna looked at her, Stella dropped her hand.

Stella bit her tongue to keep from blurting out colorful expletives as the trees parted and her eyes fell on a tiny little town. It looked like something an architect might use while drawing up plans.

The homes looked like they had been plucked right out of a Thomas Kinkade painting with their charming little flower boxes and crooked chimneys. They were built close together with little picket fences connecting one yard to the next, and all around these little homes and yards flitted hundreds, maybe thousands, of tiny pixies going about their daily lives. A hard pinch had Stella gasping and turning away from the fairytale setting to look at Heather.

"Was that necessary?" Stella growled.

"I've been tapping your arm and saying your name repeatedly and you wouldn't respond. I had to make sure you were still conscious."

"I'm still standing," Stella pointed out.

Heather shrugged. "Okay, so maybe I just felt the need to pinch a black chick. Sue me."

Stella rolled her eyes. "If you weren't blind I might take offense, but since you don't even know what the difference in a black chick and any other color is, I'm letting it go as ignorance via vision impaired."

"Fantastic, so what is it that has everyone standing so still and breathing a little faster than normal?" Heather asked.

"The fact that you picked up on everyone's breathing is a tad creepy."

"If I told you I see dead people would it make it less creepy?"

"No."

"Perfect, now moving on," Heather said as she motioned with her hand in front of them. "What is it?"

"A miniature town," Stella told her as she turned back to look at the pixie village. "Everything is scaled down to fit the pixie's foot-tall bodies."

"Okay, so nobody bothered to tell the blind girl that the pixies were short. That would have been good to know had a fight broken out."

Stella laughed. "Exactly what are you going to do in a fight?"

"Well if I knew my enemy was only a foot tall, I would kick lower; it's not rocket science, Stel," Heather said dryly.

Stella shook her head at the girl who had fast become a close friend. She didn't know how Heather kept such a good attitude in her circumstances, but she was glad that she seemed to see the glass as half full. Stella was a glass is half empty kind of girl. She knew she was too young to be so jaded, but then life hadn't dealt her the best hand. She hoped that maybe Heather's positivity would rub off on her.

"I know you all are thinking that there is no way you could stay in any of our homes, and you would be correct," Ainsel shouted out above the noise of the zooming pixies all around them. "That is why we have set aside a specific place for you all to stay." He motioned to their left and the group started forward pushing past a curtain of foliage until they were in another clearing, minus the miniature town. It was simply a field, but above it the pixies had somehow fashioned a roof out of thick lush vines. It was beautiful, and rustic, and Stella immediately wondered where in the world they expected her to pee.

She described the area to Heather and in classic Heather fashion she blurted out what everyone else was thinking. "Where are we going to pee?"

All of the girls nodded in unison with Heather's question.

The pixie king looked at a female pixie who had followed them into the clearing. "We have set up separate bathing areas along with latrines." She motioned towards the other side of the clearing with her arms spread wide indicating that the separate locations were far apart.

Stella decided that if she had to relieve herself in a hole in the ground, it actually probably wasn't the worst place in the world she had ever peed—there's a reason her neighborhood back home smelled like urine in the summer time.

"I realize the accommodations are a tad primitive, but it's the only thing we could come up with on such short notice. Peri assured me that you all would be fine with the situation," Ainsel told them.

"She was right, King," Elle, who seemed to be their official spokesperson, told him. "This is fine; we've all stayed in worse conditions. Now, about your request...," her forehead dipped low as her brow drew together.

"I can let you all get settled," Ainsel said absently as he started to walk towards the vine curtain that would take him back to the town. "We will get it all sorted out."

Adam blocked his way as Elle took a step towards him, her mate at her side. "No, we don't like to have unpaid debt. Tell us why it is you need our healers. Please," she added as an afterthought.

The look on the king's face had Stella's curiosity peaked regardless of the fact that she was indeed tired, and not to mention the fact that for the last few hours she felt as though someone had been digging at her heart with a dull spoon. She didn't know what that was all about but it was getting old fast. And on top of that she was beginning to have this profound sense of loneliness, despite being surrounded by her friends and a few dozen pixies. She was doing her best to ignore the new developments as she stepped closer to Elle and Sorin. Heather, still attached to her arm, moved with her seamlessly as though she were simply an extension of Stella.

"This is going to be good," Stella whispered to Heather. "The look on old Ainsel's face is classic *I'm so embarrassed but if I don't tell someone I'm so screwed.*"

Heather grinned. "So sad that you had to waste that analogy on a chick who has no idea what kind of face that is."

"Too true, but you seem to appreciate the effort."

"My brother has gotten himself into a little bit of a bind," Ainsel began slowly. "He's young and heavily pursued by the females of many of the pixie clans."

"They have different clans?" Stella whispered to Heather.

Heather shrugged. "Who knew?"

"As you know," Ainsel looked at Elle and Adam, "different clans of pixies have different gifts. My brother had a misunderstanding with one of the wingless pixie females, and well," he paused, "I think it would be easier to explain if the healers saw for themselves."

Fifteen minutes later a large, human sized, wooden cart was pushed into the clearing by a gang of huffing and puffing male pixies with their wings beating the air furiously as they strained. It was completely enclosed with a door on one side to allow entry.

"I would ask that only the healers take a look at him. I would prefer to protect as much of his dignity as possible." Ainsel requested.

Elle turned to look at them. Stella met the fae's eyes and she could see the question there. *Do you want to do this?* Stella hoped her eyes conveyed her answer.

Do we really have a choice? Elle gave a slight shake of her head and Stella knew she had understood.

Stella took the first step towards the cart; Heather was on her left side while Anna was on her right. She attempted to describe the layout of the scenario unfolding before them to Heather, probably to ease her own nerves more than to help Heather in any way. As they reached the cart door Anna reached up to the latch and unhooked it. She gave Stella a wary look before slowly pulling it open just enough for her to peer inside. What she saw had her gasping and shutting the door as she quickly stepped back. Her hand covered her mouth as shock widened her eyes. Stella wasn't sure now if she even wanted to look, but she knew she had to. She pulled the door open and stuck her head in just a little. Her eyes landed on the king's brother as the air whooshed out of her lungs. "Oh, honey, that's just not right." She shook her head and pursed her lips. "That's just not right."

"I take it that I should be happy I can't see right now?" Heather asked.

"You might want to do a two-step or whatever it is you Southern girls do; that is how happy you should be."

—

"Does she belong to him?" Gustavo asked as he pulled his hand away from the cheek of the sleeping beauty. He watched as the large wolf outside repeatedly slammed his head into the window. Gustavo knew of no reason a wolf would act in such a manner unless another male was touching his mate.

"She isn't of age yet so there are no mating signs. But his pull to her and desire to protect her is, as you can see," Dillon motioned to the uncontrollable Dalton, "intense."

"If you believe him to be her mate, why are you allowing other males near her?"

Dillon's brow drew together as he continued to watch his Beta attempt to get into the house. "Because he has been denying it. Sally and I believe that Jewel will not begin to heal until she receives the blood and the pull of her mate. Sometimes a man has to be pushed to the breaking point in order to get him to see what is right in front of him."

"Unless you want one of us to die, I suggest you cease pushing him," Gustavo suggested as he took a step away from Jewel. The wolf outside stopped throwing his body against the house and began to pace like a caged animal, his eyes never leaving his mate. His nostrils flared as his breaths came out in great pants, and Gustavo could tell he was struggling to keep from continuing his assault on the house.

"He has been a member of my pack for a long time. I know how much he can take," Dillon told the other Alpha. "He still isn't willing to claim her, but he doesn't want anyone else to have her either. That isn't good enough for me. As his Alpha I want what is best for him. I need healthy wolves, not just physically healthy, but emotionally healthy as well. Damaged wolves don't fight the evil threatening the world; they are too busy fighting the evil inside of them."

"I hope you are right, my friend. I would hate to be the male that was standing here when that window finally breaks." Gustavo turned and walked quietly leaving the Alpha to stare after his wolf.

Gustavo bypassed the other males and headed for the quiet of the back porch. He had known the moment he walked into the young healer's room that she was not his. In fact he knew with absolute certainty that one of the healers in the pixie realm was his. He could feel her, well feel her pain was more accurate. She was beginning to feel the pull of the bond between them. The feeling would not yet be painful, probably just more annoying than anything else since they had yet to meet. He had felt it the moment he arrived in Peri's home. The instinct to find her was like a rock in the bottom of his shoe stabbing him at different times as it rolled around beneath his foot. It wasn't beyond his control, not yet at least. Just knowing she was there would be enough for now, and knowing she was safe helped. He stared up into the star covered night sky and at the full moon that was a constant reminder of their Creator. "Gracious, Great Luna," he told his Creator knowing she would hear him. "I hope that I will be all that she needs." Gustavo had never been worried about his ability to be a good mate to his female, but knowing that his mate was a gypsy healer, and a human who had no clue of their world until recently, changed things. They would both have to be willing to learn, and to be patient with one another, because they most assuredly had different expectations of what their relationship might be. He took a deep breath and let it out slowly. Deciding that worrying about his mate wasn't going to bring her any closer in the immediate future, he decided to just be happy that he had finally found her.

Gustavo knew it was a joyful revelation that he would have to keep to himself. The other males would only see it as a challenge if he spouted off that he was certain one of the healers was his. So he would just keep his head down and go on as though he was as clueless as he had been before he arrived. *I will be with her soon,* he told himself because he needed to remind his wolf to continue to fight the darkness. Soon her light would fill them and for the first time in a very long time he would finally feel whole.

—

"I should undo the spell just as he's about to plow into that window and let him tear into you," Peri said as she stepped up beside Jewel's bed. "When will Alphas learn not to meddle in the love lives of their wolves?"

"As if you don't enjoy meddling yourself?" Dillon glanced at her from the corner of his eye. He could feel her mate's eyes on him from the hallway and was not surprised that Lucian wasn't far from Peri. He rarely let her out of his sight if he could help it, which was probably a good thing.

"I suppose I have meddled once or twice."

Dillon chuckled. "Three thousand years old and it's only been once or twice. That's impressive."

"Most things are when it comes to me." A low growl rumbled from behind them. Peri turned her head slightly to look at her mate. "Really? You consider that flirting?" She shook her head. "One of these days, wolf, I'm going to just give into my wicked urges and turn you into a nice wall hanging."

"Do your threats really work on him?" Dillon asked.

"Depends on what you mean by *work*."

"Perizada, enough," Lucian growled as he took a step into the room.

She waved a hand at him. "Fine, I'll behave. But I did come in here for more than silly bantering." She nodded towards Dalton. "Are you going to continue to bring the males in here and let him beat his brains in?"

"If it means it will knock some sense into him, then yes. I do not want the binding taken down until he submits. When he is ready to accept what is, then I will let him near her again."

Peri shook her head and let out a huff of laughter. "Did it ever dawn on you that keeping her from him would only drive him further into the dark?"

"It's a chance I have to take. He wasn't going to stay and if he leaves Jewel will die." Dillon's eyes lit momentarily with the emotions of his wolf.

"She turns eighteen in a month and a half— October thirty-first."

"Let's hope it doesn't take that long for the fool to do the right thing."

This time Peri let out a bark of laughter. "You expect a half feral wolf with a past so demented that he won't claim his mate to make a smart decision? I don't know if I should think you're an optimist or an idiot."

"Lucian," Dillon growled.

Lucian grabbed Peri's hand and pulled her towards him. "Come, love, I'm sure there are other wolves here you would like to provoke."

"Oh, how well you know me," she sighed as they left Dillon to his thoughts.

Dillon watched his Beta pace restlessly outside the window, his glowing wolf eyes challenging him. The only reason Dillon wasn't putting him in his place was because he knew at the moment Dalton wasn't rational. All he could see was his mate out of his reach and other males close to her. He refused to let Dalton ruin not only his life but Jewel's as well because of ghosts he couldn't banish. He held the wolf's gaze as he called out. "Antonio, come!" Was it cruel to put Dalton through this? Probably. But it was also necessary if it would force him to claim the woman who had been created just for him.

Forty-five minutes and seven males later, Dalton was still pacing. Dillon wasn't surprised each time Dalton threw himself at the house when the males got close to Jewel. He would have been more surprised had he not responded that way. He nearly let out a breath of relief when the final male stepped into the room. It was Kale, the Beta of the Ireland pack, and the largest of all the males that had arrived. He wasn't as big as Dalton, few were, but he had a presence about him that filled a room before he even spoke. As soon as he stepped forward and was visible to Dalton, Dillon saw something shift in his Beta.

"What happened to the lass?" Kale asked. Dillon noticed that the Beta's Irish brogue became heavy when he was feeling protective. Usually the Irish wolf didn't drop his TH or Ts, having picked up on American dialect through traveling.

"She had a run in with Volcan and his pet," Dillon told him as he watched the wolf outside carefully.

Kale took a step towards her and leaned down to breathe in her scent. As soon as the Irish wolf's face neared Jewel's neck, where her scent would be strongest, Dalton lunged. Dillon felt the power hit the house just as the wolf's head slammed into the glass of the window. To Dillon's surprise a crack appeared in the glass.

"She is nah mine, even if she is nah of age, I feel nothing other than the care wolves feel towards healers." Kale's voice was cool and when Dillon looked over at him, he saw that his eyes were on Dalton as well. "There is only one reason a male would act in such a way. Is the lass his?"

"She isn't of age so the mating signs aren't there, but the pull is."

Kale's eyes narrowed and recognition dawned on his face. "Is that Dalton Black?"

Dillon didn't miss the anger that laced Kale's words.

"It is. He's my Beta," Dillon said as he looked back at his wolf. Dalton's eyes were glued to Kale's and Dillon wasn't sure that Peri's spell would hold him any longer.

"I hope that you are wrong. A lass as beautiful and pure as this one," he motioned to Jewel, "should nah be destined to belong to a monster."

"No offense, Kale, but that is *my* wolf you are speaking of. I know his past and he is not the man he once was." Dillon felt his wolf pushing forward as he sought to not only put Dalton in his place but also defend him from a possible threat.

"If you are okay with allowing their mating then you do nah know all there is to know about Dalton. Men like Dalton Black doonah change."

"What do you know of him?" Dillon growled. "You obviously have history with him, so what is it that you think is so unforgivable to condemn a man who has changed his life?"

Kale began to reach down slowly with his left arm, and when his hand rested gently on Jewel's leg, Dillon was shocked to hear, not a growl from an enraged wolf but the roar of a determined man. His head whipped around to find Dalton pounding on the window in his human form. His body shook from the bolts of energy being shot into his body from Peri's spell and yet he held fast. His hands began to bleed as they broke through the glass.

"What the hell is going on?" Peri snapped as she appeared in the room directly in front of Dillon. Lucian was by her side in an instant pulling her away from the man that was demolishing a window that he shouldn't be able to touch.

"How is he doing that?" Peri turned to Dillon. But Kale spoke before Dillon could answer.

"Do you see his eyes, Dillon? He is not sane. Anything good in him died when he chose to rape an innocent woman."

"GET OUT!" Dillon roared just as Dalton jumped through the broken window. Peri grabbed Lucian and Kale's arms and flashed them from the room a second before the raging wolf would have been on them. "DALTON, STOP!" Dillon pushed his power into the command and for a brief second he thought it wouldn't reach through the rage. But as soon as Dalton's hand rested on the exact spot on Jewel's leg where Kale's hand had been only moments ago, he calmed. The change in him was so immediate and so drastic that Dillon was afraid to speak—afraid to break the control that his Beta had finally gained.

Dalton's head began to rise slowly and when their eyes finally met Dillon saw the utter shame in them. Dillon grabbed a pair of sweat pants identical to ones that seemed to have been put in every empty location of the house and tossed them to Dalton. He let go of Jewel's leg long enough to put them on but returned his hand immediately.

"I know you did not do what Kale has accused you of." Dillon's jaw clenched tight as he spoke. "I have seen evil men, Dalton, and you are not one of them."

"Are you sure?" Dalton's voice was guttural with his wolf so close to the surface. "Are you so certain that you haven't been harboring a murder and rapist all these years?"

"YES!" Dillon barked. "Whatever happened, whatever Kale thinks he knows or saw, *I* know that you are not capable of that."

"You're wrong," Dalton paused. "I have killed."

"We all have. Hell, some of us, like you, are several centuries old, and we're predators. It's not possible to live that long and not kill someone. Not in the world that we live in."

Dillon waited for Dalton's response, but his Beta simply bowed his head until it rested next to his hand on Jewel's leg. He knew there was more they needed to discuss, but now was not the time. He turned to go but as he grasped the doorknob his Beta finally spoke.

"I did not rape that woman."

Dillon looked back at him. "I knew that."

"But I did kill her, and I would do it again. What does that make me?"

"It makes you a man willing to do whatever it takes to protect the innocent. Because I know that you would only have killed a woman if you were protecting someone from her." He could tell Dalton was surprised by his answer, and though Dillon did not know exactly what the circumstances had been, he knew that there were times when not even a woman deserved mercy.

—

Kale let out a shaky breath as his thoughts wandered back to that night so very long ago when he had run into Dalton Black for the first time. He hadn't now expected to see the wolf alive all these centuries later. Kale was sure Dalton would have wound up getting himself killed. Although he thought he understood the situation when he had rushed into that room many years ago, he now questioned himself. He remembered seeing Dalton with the female he had chosen for company, but he had not seen evil in the wolf's eyes.

While there were male Canis lupis that sought out female companionship from humans, it was not the norm. Most males saved themselves for their true mates. Even so, when a man did seek out relations with a woman, it wasn't usually done in such a crass way as seeking out paid females. That act alone told Kale that Dalton was battling some dark demons. For Jewel's sake he truly hoped that he was right in believing that Dalton wasn't capable of such an act. He knew Dillon would want to talk to him about the things he had said and he hoped Dillon had more information than he did that proved Dalton's innocence.

He made his way up the stairs intending to head towards the room that he had been given with his Beta, Banan, but as he passed the room where the healers had stayed, and where Kara was still staying, he caught a scent. He paused, raising his nose in the air and taking a deep breath. Nothing had ever called to him as the cinnamon smell did. He followed it into the room and over to one of the beds on the far wall. His wolf perked up as he recognized the scent as well. *Mate,* he told Kale. "Possibly," Kale responded though he didn't want to get his hopes up. He reached down and laid his hand on the blanket that covered the mattress and closed his eyes. He wondered what she looked like, wondered if she was playful or serious, tall or short. None of that mattered, of course, he just wanted her to be his. Kale tried to focus on the smell, clearing his mind and reaching for an invisible bond that he was sure had to be forming. Perhaps being in the location where his mate had been had triggered the bond. His breath caught as he felt a sharp pain in his head. He squeezed his eyes tight, attempting to fight off the pain. And as it abated he realized it was not his pain he had been feeling. There was no fear mixed with the pain so he didn't think she was in trouble. She was out there, and though Peri had said she was safe with the pixies it bothered him that she was in pain and he could do nothing to help.

As he stepped away from the bed and headed back for the door, not wanting to alarm Kara should she walk in, he felt an overwhelming sense of longing rush through him, and then it was gone. It was her; he knew it was, but he wondered if it was him she was longing for. As an American who knew nothing of their world, he knew she couldn't possible desire him as he did her, but he hoped once they met the mate bond would help her accept that he was hers, created only for her.

As he closed the door behind him he shook his head, irritated with his lack of control because of a smell. "Keep creeping around in girls bedrooms and sniffing their beds and she will definitely think you're a prize".

4

**"There is nothing I could ever do to be worthy
of your love. There is no amount of penance
I can pay, sacrifice I can make, or forgiveness I can beg to deserve you. But I need you.
Stay with me. I don't deserve you, but please
stay with me. I have nothing to offer you other
than what is left after all the world has taken.
Stay with me and I am yours. Heart, mind,
body, and soul, I am yours." ~Dalton Black**

His throat burned with the effort it took to hold
back the tears as he pressed his face closer to
her skin. Over and over he breathed her in, holding on to the reality that she was here with him.
No one was touching her or taking her from him.
She was here with him—where she belonged. He
hadn't changed his mind about her needing someone better than him. He hadn't suddenly decided
that he was the best thing for her; he knew the opposite to be true. What had changed was the fact
that after seeing those males near her, after seeing
them touch her and then realizing that if she was

not his then she would belong to another to love and touch, he knew that he could never give her up. Only death could take him from her and for that he was sorry.

His wolf rumbled deep inside of him with contentment that only the nearness of their mate could bring them. He had to fight the beast to keep from crawling up in the bed and wrapping them around her. *Closer,* the wolf growled, *mate, touch, closer.* He pushed his wolf back, attempting to make him understand that laying down next to a woman who did not know them was not an acceptable thing to do. His wolf did not care what was acceptable.

"Please forgive me," he whispered as he forced himself to relax his grip on her. She was so small compared to him, so fragile because of her humanity, and he never wanted to be the one to hurt her in any way, not ever again. He had hurt her. Maybe she didn't realize it, but by refusing her he had kept her from healing. For that alone he deserved to die. Who rejects their mate? What kind of male allows his mate to suffer when he could take it away?

His head snapped up and a snarl erupted from him as the door to her room opened. His eyes narrowed as Costin pushed around Sally as she attempted to enter the room.

"Costin, relax; he isn't going to hurt me," she told him as she tried to step around him.

"And you deduced that from the cuddly look on his face?" Costin avoided making eye contact with Dalton. *Smart wolf,* Dalton thought.

"No, because he knows I'm trying to help his mate. No male will hurt someone trying to help their woman, especially not a healer. Now move!"

Dalton stood slowly as the two approached the bed. His lip lifted as a growl grew in his chest as Costin neared his mate. *Too close*, his wolf told him and he agreed.

"Costin, you wouldn't want a male near me if I was injured. Step back."

"Will you let her check your mate?" Costin asked him.

Dalton gave one nod. "Only her."

"You will not harm her."

Dalton ignored the command because he knew the wolf was only trying to protect his female and he respected him for that.

"I will not harm your healer," he assured him.

He watched as Sally stepped closer and laid her hands gently on Jewel's head. The healer closed her eyes and was very still for several minutes. When her eyes opened she looked pained as her head rose to meet his eyes.

"Are you going to take care of her now?" she asked him and he did not miss the accusation in her tone. The insinuation that he had not cared for her up until that point stung, but he deserved it.

"She is my mate."

"So glad you finally decided to pull your head out of your—,"

"Sally," Costin growled.

She turned to look at him, her eyes full of innocence. "What? I'm just stating the truth." She turned back to him and began spouting off orders. "She will need your blood. I know you have given her a little in the past, but she will need you to be a tad more generous from now on. She needs a connection to this life, something positive. The pain and torture she endured has caused her mind to retreat and her spirit has followed. It's a protection mechanism that some people seem to have. I've been doing some research on it, but human doctors don't understand it and don't have any treatment for it. But we aren't human are we?" A single brow rose as her lips quirked up in a small smile. "We are something more. Give her something to live for. At first I didn't think that she could hear us, but every time I use my magic on her to check on her I can feel that she feels me. It's as if she is aware even though she is unconscious. Because of that, I believe she can hear us. Tell her about yourself, about your Creator and how the Canis lupis came to be. Tell her about the incredible love she blessed her wolves with in having a true mate." Sally paused, her head tilted to the side as she studied him. Suddenly she reached across the bed and laid a hand on his arm. Normally he would have jerked back, but the warmth that flowed into him froze him in place. Her face softened and her eyes filled with tears. Her mate had his arms wrapped around her waist, and Dalton could tell he wanted to jerk her away. He didn't blame the young wolf.

"You can't change your past, Dalton Black," Sally said as she pulled her hand away. "You have no control over the future. What you do have is the *right now*. You have this moment and that is all you have. You are promised nothing more. That is what our lives are, a collection of moments. You can make those moments worthy of the life your Creator gave you by selflessly giving them to someone else, or you can hold onto those moments using them to wallow in things you can do nothing about. What are you going to do with this moment? Who will this moment be for?"

Dalton didn't hear the door close as they left. He was too busy staring at the woman who was going to change his life forever. He pulled a chair over to her bed and took her hand in his. The warmth of her skin against his was a marvel to him after having despised touch for so long. He knew, as he threaded his large fingers through her smaller ones, that he would always want her touch, always welcome it and crave it. His eyes were drawn to her face as he heard a soft sigh, one that cried of relief, hum through her lips. Dalton leaned in close to her, his lips brushing her ear as he spoke. "This moment and every moment after is yours."

"You should be careful of the promises you make, Dalton Black, especially when making them to your true mate."

Dalton stood slowly at the sound of the Great Luna's voice and turned to face her. He kept his head bowed as he answered her. "I take my oaths seriously, Great Luna." He felt the warmth and good-ness in her flow over him and drive him to his knees. Who was he to stand in the presence of his Creator?

"You are my child," she answered his thought. "I have waited for you to turn to me for a very long time. I have watched you be hurt by the evil in the world and watched you be hurt by foolish choices you have made. I know everything about you; noth-ing is hidden from me. The path you have taken is not the one I laid out for you, but it is not too late. You must make things right with me in order to be what she needs. You claim you are not worthy of her because of your indiscretions; you profess that you desire to be something more than what you have been. Listen carefully, my child. I, and only I, can make you something more. Your *moments* as you called them belong to me, for I am the one who created you. Only if you seek to right your relation-ship with me and learn my ways, will you be able to truly change." He heard her step closer and then felt her hand on his head. "I am your judge, but I am also your deliverer. I am waiting. It's time you came home."

Dalton quaked with the weight of all he had experienced and done in his long life. His spirit felt crushed under the guilt of his transgressions. He had used and abused so many people and things instead of turning to the one who could truly give him relief and heal him. "I confess to you that I know and accept responsibility for my iniquities, against you, against myself, and against others. It is killing me, devouring my insides and tearing my soul. I can't handle it anymore and I refuse to make Jewel be the one to have to try to hold me together. Please forgive me. I don't know how to be the male you destined me to be, and I don't know how to be the mate to one so shattered when I myself am just as broken if not more. I need your help." His hands trembled at his sides as the tears he had never let fall finally flowed.

Dalton sat at the feet of the Great Luna and wept as one who had finally realized he could no longer survive alone. The separation from the only one who could make him clean, unblemished, was too much. He knew from lessons as a child that their Creator loved them deeply and desired a relationship with them, but she would not force it. She chose them, but they had to respond to her prompting.

"I forget your past. Your transgression are wiped from my mind and you are forgiven, Dalton Black. You will face much more evil in this life. You will be reminded of things that you should no longer dwell on. These reminders will attempt to drag you away from me. But you are mine. You do not belong to the darkness. I have given you my light. I have given you a true mate who is a constant reminder of that light. You will fail one another. You will make mistakes but you must be willing to forgive as I have forgiven you. You cannot do this alone, but I can do it through you. Stay with her and protect her from those who would harm her. Shelter her from the storms that are coming. Remind her when she forgets that you are by her side. Your place as her mate should be an example of my place as your Creator. For her, you will sacrifice. For her, you will deny yourself. And for her, you will forsake all others. Let nothing separate you for I have brought you together. You will become one."

Dalton knew she was gone before he ever looked up, but he could still feel her presence. She lived inside of him now and a deep, abiding love that filled the cracks that had shattered his heart. For the first time in centuries he felt as though the weight of the world was lifted from his shoulders. The constant pressure on his chest that kept him from taking in a full breath had finally eased. He knew that he still had the consequences of his choices to deal with. He knew that he was a different man than he would have been had he made different choices, but he also knew that he wasn't beyond hope as he had always thought. He let out a deep breath as he stood and returned to the chair next to his mate's bed. He took her hand once again in his and braced himself for the memories that would flood his mind as he bore his soul to her, the only one other than his Creator that would ever be able to erase the pain inside of him.

Jewel needed to know him if she was to be with him. She had a right to all of him if they were to become one and he would give her nothing less.

The moonlight streamed into the otherwise dark room as Dalton reclaimed the seat next to Jewel's bed. Her chest rose and fell with her slow breaths, and her skin shimmered like pearls under the glow of the moon's beams. She was completely oblivious to all that had happened. Even after confessing to the Great Luna, he still felt as though his very presence would contaminate her. Yet he knew now that he could not stay away. Even had he wanted to, his wolf would have never allowed it.

"You shouldn't be stuck with me. If the world was a fair and just place, you would have someone gentle and kind, not scarred and bitter," he confessed to her. His deep voice, though whispered, still seemed too loud in the quiet room. "And yet, little dove, I cannot let you go. I cannot allow someone else to have you." Dalton leaned forward, resting his elbows on his knees and folding his hands together as he let out a slow, deep breath. There was so much she needed to know so much that he needed to confess, and he didn't know if he would be able to look into her eyes and tell her. It was a copout, but he knew the only way he would be able to tell her about his past was if he didn't have to see the disgust in her eyes as he spoke.

"I was born Dalton Roan Black," he began, "in 1764 to John and Cybil Black. I couldn't have asked for two more loving parents. Like most werewolf mates, they only had one child. We were members of a small pack in a village just outside of Salem, Massachusetts. Back in those days, large packs in North America were rare. Owing to the superstitions of the people during those times, we were mistrusted and hunted in larger cities. It was much safer to live in small communities. We had to be careful and not come across as too different, or odd. Anything that was different was perceived as evil, so it was just our family and three others in our pack." He paused as memories of his childhood flashed in his mind—fishing with his father, baking bread with his mother, running in their wolf forms with their pack under the light of the moon.

"Everything was good in my life until the witch hunts began. We were all paranoid, but we thought we were staying under their radar. But one night while we were sleeping, witch hunters captured my father, mother, and me. We woke up chained in an underground cell. If ever there was something I wish I could forget, Jewel, these memories are it." His jaw tensed as he told her about how the men talked about torturing him and his family in order to get a confession of witchcraft out of them. As he described the torture that he endured at the hands of Gwen and her goons, his hands fisted into the sheets on her bed as his body relived the pain all over again. He didn't want to taint his mate with such filth, but he also didn't want any secrets between them. So he told her of the many times Gwen had attempted to seduce him, only to then punish him for his lack of response to her. Dalton revealed things to Jewel in the quiet of that room that he had never shared with another. It was like opening a metal door, its hinges corroded with decades of rust and age, as his mind delved into the bowels of misery he had kept locked away.

"I wished for death," he whispered, his voice thick with emotions that he never showed anyone. "Every night after Gwen left me, my skin crawling from her touch, I begged the Great Luna to take me and end my torment. But I woke every morning still alive. I began to feign being weak so they would quit giving me so much of the drug that they thought suppressed my so called magic, and eventually I was able to call my wolf. I escaped the physical prison they held me in, but I was no longer the man I once had been." Dalton's jaw clenched as he struggled with how to continue. How would he tell one as pure and innocent as Jewel about the abhorrent things he had done in an attempt to forget his past? His head turned at the sound of footsteps coming down the stairs, and he knew he had just been saved from humiliating himself until another day. He stood quickly and leaned over her, blowing gently on her face and neck. "Keep fighting, little dove, I will not be far," he whispered before turning and leaving through the window just as quietly as when he had entered.

—

Jewel tried to move as the words spoken by the deep voice penetrated her mind. She knew that voice belonged to a male named Dalton. She had heard Sally discussing him with Costin. The despair and loneliness that laced his words broke her heart. He was convinced that he was beyond forgiveness and beyond repair. But what he didn't realize was, if a person even bothered to think such things, then it was not too late. It wasn't until forgiveness and repair were no longer in someone's vocabulary that they needed to be worried about being lost forever. But then if they were at that point, they generally didn't care.

"I can hear you!" her mind screamed at him. *"You aren't the sum of your past; don't let it conquer you."*

She wanted to comfort Dalton and to remind him that he was no longer trapped in that evil prison, and Gwen, whoever she was, could no longer hurt him. But she knew that would be a lie. Memories, though they might not be able to physically harm the way the reality does, could still continue to damage the soul. It was painfully apparent that Dalton was still battling his memories, and they were still wreaking havoc on him. She didn't know why he had chosen to share his pain with her. He spoke to the others that had been in the room of her being 'his', and she didn't know exactly what that meant, but she knew that whenever he was near she didn't feel so lost.

Unfortunately, right now, she *was* lost. Her mind had retreated as far away from consciousness as possible in order to escape the torture she had endured at the hands of an evil woman. Jewel had tried to be brave, tried to endure just five minutes more, but she had failed. She had simply wanted the pain to end. Now she was stuck in her own body, unable to communicate or move. She could hear everything going on around her, but could do nothing to let them know. Sally was so broken over not being able to help her and it tore Jewel up inside. Her only comfort were the times when Dalton, with his wonderful, deep, rich voice, came to her. He was sad, miserable even, and yet she craved his company. As he left her now, his words lingering in her ears, *keep fighting, Little Dove, I will not be far;* she wanted to beg him to stay.

"Please don't go," she pleaded. She was afraid that if he never returned, she would never find her way back.

—

"He's been here again," Costin said quietly as he and Sally entered the room where Jewel lay. Two weeks had passed since the confrontation between the other males and Dalton. Costin had not been fully convinced that the male was ready to accept his mate, not at first. At first he thought it was more that Dalton couldn't stand the other males being near her, which to Costin was understandable. He hated it when other males, friend or not, were too close to his Sally. It was a wolf thing, as he had told his mate many times; it would never change. But Dalton had returned every night since, and though Jewel, according to Sally, had not moved any closer from the depths she had retreated to, she did look better. Costin could smell Dalton on her, all the way from the other room, which told him that the Beta had been giving her his blood as Sally had instructed. He could only imagine how difficult it must be to share something so intimate in a house full of other males and with a mate that was totally unaware. Awkward.

"He's doing what is best for her," Sally responded to his thoughts. "How can it be awkward to do something that you know could save your true mate's life?"

"You know how intimate sharing blood is," Costin said with a wicked glint in his eyes that brought a bright blush to her face.

"Yes, but he is doing it in the context of healing, not, not...," she stumbled.

"Not what, Sally mine?" he asked as he slowly stalked her.

She held up her hand to stave him off. "Behave, Costin," she warned. "And you know exactly what I mean."

He shrugged noncommittally. "Perhaps, but it so much fun to see you get so embarrassed over our love life."

"If you don't behave there will be no love life to get embarrassed over."

Costin's grin widened even further. He shook his body in a faux tremble. "Oooo you know I love it when you threaten me. Keep it coming, baby."

Sally couldn't help but laugh at him, which was one of his favorite sounds. "You're such a pervert. Now get out perv so I can tend to Jewel's cleanliness."

Costin's grin fled and a frown took its place. "I don't like leaving you in here alone; can't I just turn my back?"

"If Dalton came in here and undressed to get a sponge bath, would it be alright if I stayed as long as I turned my back?" she asked sweetly.

Costin snarled at her, but she wasn't the least bit intimidated, nor would he ever want her to be. "Fine, I'll go. But I don't like it."

"Noted," Sally said as she shut the door behind him.

Dalton heard the door close to Jewel's room as Sally's mate left. He didn't blame the male for not wanting to leave his mate. Dalton hated leaving Jewel but he wasn't in control of his wolf enough to be around males he didn't know, or others that he did know and didn't like. He let out a low rumble. He was usually more patient than this, but when it came to being near Jewel, he found that his patience ran very thin.

He could hear Sally's movements, but knowing that she was going to be bathing Jewel and tending to her needs, he refrained from looking in. He desperately wanted a glimpse of his mate. It had been nearly twenty-four hours since he had seen her last. Needless to say, he and his wolf were more than ready to lay eyes on her.

"You can come in." Sally's voice came from just inside the window. He was surprised that he hadn't realized she had moved closer to him, or that she had opened the window, but then he seemed easily distracted as of late.

"She deserves privacy," he said as he stepped back so that he could look at the healer.

"I'm not going to strip her naked, Dalton." She sounded exasperated with him as she stepped back giving him room to enter. He simply stared at her, not moving any closer. She let out a sigh. "I will keep her covered. She relaxes when you are near and when she hears your voice. Come in and wash her hair, or is that somehow improper?"

The look in Sally's eyes made it very clear that she wasn't going to let up until he did what she asked. Like the other males, Dalton found that it was very hard not to acquiesce to a healer's request. Letting out his own growl of irritation he jumped through the window effortlessly, his tall frame causing Sally to have to tilt her head back to look up at him. He found it interesting that she wasn't afraid of him. There weren't many who were not intimidated by him, and most of those were very powerful Alphas.

Unable to stay away from her any longer, Dalton turned from Sally and moved silently towards Jewel. His heart beat painfully in his chest as her scent overwhelmed him. He wanted to touch her, wanted to run his fingers through her hair and bathe her in his own scent. But he didn't like an audience so he kept his hands to himself.

"Here," Sally said from beside him as she handed him a basin of water that had steam rising off of its surface. She laid a washcloth across his arm and held out a bottle of shampoo. "I've laid a towel on the floor to absorb the run off so don't worry about that; just make sure you rinse it well or it will irritate her skin. Redhead's tend to have very sensitive skin to anything with chemicals in it." That was all she said to him as she went about gathering things and humming to herself.

He stood there for several more minutes when he finally realized that Sally had no intention of saying more nor allowing him to avoid his appointed task. He grabbed a small table and pulled it toward the end of the bed where her head lay. The headboard had been removed to make it possible to sit behind her. Taking a chair he sat down and stared at the beautiful tresses that framed her face. Her hair was shorter than what he thought he would have wanted on his mate, but then the cute bob suited her.

"Males have been killed for less than touching a female's hair," he told Sally as he took the brush she had laid on the table and began to gently run it through Jewel's hair. He could have told her that her mate would probably attempt to kill him if he tried to touch Sally's hair because like many other forms of touch between mates, touching each other's hair was sacred, intimate, and reserved for only one another. He could have said much on the subject, but he made it a point to only speak when there was no other option. He felt that he owed Sally for caring so diligently for his mate, and so for that he would make an effort. He felt like a whole sentence was a pretty good effort.

Sally let out an un-lady like snort. "Why am I not surprised? Was it something that involved one male breathing in the general direction of another's true mate?"

That was all either of them said as Sally began her ministrations and Dalton finished brushing Jewel's hair and began to pour water onto it until all of the strands where wet. As his fingers massaged the shampoo into her hair, he found that he very much like the pomegranate smell of the soap that blended so well with her already sweet scent. He realized in that moment as he cared so intimately, regardless of what Sally thought, for his female, he wished he could speak through their bond. He wanted to share with her just how beautiful he found her. In a world where all he had seen for so long was black, grey, and shadows, for the first time in centuries he was seeing color, and it radiated off of her.

Dalton longed to tell her how her scent called to him and his wolf and that he couldn't wait for the day when he could wrap her in his arms and keep her safe from all of the evil in the world. It didn't surprise him that he was willing to actually speak so much to his mate, for her he would do much more than that. He was about to tell Sally that he would need more water to rinse her hair, but when he forced himself to look up from Jewel, he saw that Sally was gone. He looked over at the bowl and found it was full, and there were two other bowls that had been added. He rinsed her hair, careful to keep the water from running down onto her face. Once he was sure there was no trace of soap left, he gently wrung the locks out and then dried them with the towel Sally had placed beside her on the edge of her pillow.

After once again brushing her damp hair, Dalton found himself remembering something his father had taught him long ago. As he ran his fingers through the short locks his mind jumped back to that evening in the quiet of their home, sitting by the fire talking as they always did.

"One day you will have a mate, Dalton, and it will be your privilege to care for her," his mother told him as his father brushed her hair. The affection which his father and mother showed one another was nothing they ever kept from him. They were very open about their touches and words of love. Every night Dalton's father would brush his mother's long locks as they sat in front of the fire and then braid it until it was like a golden rope down to her waist.

"What if she doesn't like her hair braided?" Dalton asked when his father had motioned for him to come over and learn what seemed a complicated task for his large hands.

His mother laughed quietly. "Every woman likes her mate to tend to her hair. It is special and a right that only he has."

"I can only teach you so much when it comes to caring for your female," his father said as he undid the plait he had just finished and then handed Dalton the brush. "And this is one of them. Your true mate will be pleased to find that you can care for her in such a simple, yet very considerate, way."

Dalton's mind returned to the present as he found himself trying to separate the strands into three sections, but Jewels hair wasn't quite long enough for a braid. That didn't matter to him. If all he did was brush her hair for her, or run his fingers through the silky strands, that was enough for him. Dalton stared down at her and wondered if Jewel would be pleased that he could braid her hair. Would she want him to touch her in any way at all after everything he would share with her? Though he had been back every night since the confrontation, he had yet to share any more of his past with her. Instead he found himself reading to her. Sally had begun leaving books beside her bed as a not so subtle hint, especially since the first time she had done it, she had also left a note on the top that had read, *she loves to read…why are you still staring at the books, dummy? Read to her.* Dalton had frowned at the piece of paper, but then he figured it could have said something much worse considering the healer didn't seem to like him much at the moment.

So he had read to her. The first book had been *Alice in Wonderland,* which he found to be ironic considering Jewel had been taken from her life in the human realm and thrown into the figurative rabbit hole that just happened to lead to his world. The next book was *A Wrinkle in Time,* which was again about humans being made aware of a seemingly alternate world that was going on around them while they were completely oblivious. By the third book, which was *Harry Potter and the Sorcerer's Stone,* he was catching on that Sally was trying to make a point. Jewel might be his mate, but she was also very human and very new to this world. Though it was no surprise to him to have a true mate that he would claim to be his forever, it would be very surprising and probably overwhelming to her once she woke up. If she woke up.

He put down the hairbrush and pulled his seat around so that he was sitting next to her in his usual spot. When he looked over at the table where Sally usually left the books he found a note, once again, on top of the stack. He picked it up and felt his chest tighten as he read it.

One month. That was all it said.

He knew exactly what she was referring to. He had one month until Jewel turned eighteen. One month until the bond that was supposed to be between them would open, creating a connection that they would share with no other. One month and he would know if she would reject him or accept him. He longed for it but at the same time feared it. He wondered if once the bond was open he would be able to look into her mind and see why she was so far from him. Would he be able to somehow call her back to him? Dalton knew the other message Sally was trying to convey to him through the note was that once the mental bond was open Jewel would have admission to his thoughts and his memories, no matter how dark they might be. Essentially, Sally was saying she can either find out because he chose to trust her with the information, or she can find out through her right as his mate to have access to all of him.

Beneath the note there was only one book. Dalton shook his head with a bitter laugh as he read the title. How fitting, he thought, as he picked it up and leaned back, getting as comfortable as someone his size could in a small chair. He needed to tell her his story but not that night. On that night he wanted one more chance to just be Dalton, the male he had become before he would have to show her the Dalton he had once been.

He opened the book and began. "*Beauty and the Beast*, by Gabrielle-Suzanne Barbot de Villeneuve. "Chapter 1, A Tempest at Sea." In a country very far…"

Jewel's mind was still trying to catch up from Dalton's hands being in her hair as Dalton's voice filled her mind. He had washed her hair, something so simple, and yet for him to serve her in such a way, to treat her with such reverence, brought tears to her eyes, or at least she thought it did. She wanted to hug Sally for asking Dalton to help do the usual tasks of taking care of her, and though most girls probably would have been embarrassed, logically she knew it had to be done. She couldn't very well lay there in her own filth, so who better to do it than the person who continually assured her that he would take care of her? He was obviously taking his oath very seriously if he was willing to wash and brush her hair. A thought popped into her mind then. She wondered if it bothered him that her hair was short. Though what she read was fiction, it seemed like in all of her love stories the heroine had long flowing locks that the hero could run his fingers through. Then she wondered if she would grow it out for him, if that's what he wanted? She had never considered whether or not she would change things about herself for a man because she honestly believed no man would ever see her in a romantic light.

The rich tone of his voice drew her from the thoughts of his hands in her hair. He was reading to her again and it was one of her favorite fairytales. Her mind immediately flipped through the catalogs of information that she knew about the book. Beauty and the Beast was originally written in French and later translated to English and there had been multiple adaptations done. The one Dalton was reading was the original French version. She had read it many times, but it had never sounded as good as it did right now.

Jewel had no sense of time in the place her spirit had retreated to, and so when he finally read *The End*, she didn't know if it had taken him all day, all night, or a combination. She could only imagine how boring it must be to read to her every time he came to see her. She enjoyed hearing the stories that she had read many times. There weren't many classics that she hadn't read. But though she appreciated his effort, what she really wanted was to hear more of his story.

He had begun telling it quite a while ago, but since then he had not shared any more with her. The shame she had heard in his voice when he spoke of his past was no doubt the reason he kept silent. Jewel was beginning to wonder if he would ever tell her. She had heard him speak to Sally, and even a man named Dillon, about her being his mate. This triggered a memory from her time in the dark forest where she, Kara, and Heather had been held prisoner by the evil fae woman. Heather had told them that werewolves existed. After traveling with a woman who claimed to be a fairy, by disappearing and then reappearing in a different location, Jewel didn't doubt werewolves might exist. She wondered what the ramifications of such a revelation meant for her as a gypsy healer, but looking at it from a logical point of view it made sense to her that perhaps the werewolves had more in common with natural wolves than being fury.

For instance, she had read that wolves in the wild had a mate, only one, for the duration of their lives. Natural wolves lived in packs with a specific hierarchy—with an Alpha at the top and then the rest found their place according to who was strongest. She had heard Dillon say that he was Dalton's Alpha, which she deduced to mean that werewolves did indeed have a similar system to natural wolves. She found herself quite fascinated with the information and often forgot that it wasn't a book she was reading, but reality—her reality.

So after all of her knowledge had been exhausted on the matter, she began to have questions. Had Dalton *chosen* her as his mate or was there something magical about it like her being a gypsy healer? If he chose her, on what criteria had he based his decision? They had yet to even meet, so it wasn't like he had a plethora of information on her. Furthermore, if he had not chosen her, but instead was somehow magically stuck with her, how did he feel about it? Was their mating simply a pairing of a compatible female and male in order to procreate and keep the werewolf numbers up? Or was it something deeper? She so badly wanted to speak and to ask all of her questions. Jewel loved information, loved learning, and it drove her crazy to have so many variables dancing around with no way to solve them.

With his reading done she knew that he would now tell her goodbye and leave her to herself and her thoughts. She knew she couldn't expect him to just sit there all of the time staring at her unmoving form, but she dreaded when he left. She felt his breath on her neck as she always did before he left. The only time it was different was when he gave her the warm liquid that Sally claimed to be his blood. Jewel didn't believe that, however. Blood would never taste that good or make her feel so connected to another. She figured it must be symbolic in some way, which is why Sally likened it to blood. This was not one of those times. Instead he blew on her gently as if blowing on a wound to stop the sting and then whispered to her the same words he said every time.

"Keep fighting, Little Dove. I will return."

Then he was gone and she was still there stuck in darkness, lonely, and scared that she might never find her way back. She was beginning to grow cold, lost in her conscious as she was, and the only time she had a measure of warmth was when Dalton was with her.

Something had been growing inside of her during the times when she was alone. Fear. Fear that he would not come back but would leave her forever. Even if she was his so called mate, how could anyone want to have to care for an invalid when they didn't even know that person? He had no ties to her. In truth she was no one to him so why wouldn't he tire of reading to her or caring for her mundane needs? Why not retreat any further away from the pain that would surely come if he deserted her?

"You will not stop fighting, Jewel," Sally's voice pierced through the thick fog of panic, and Jewel felt the healer's warm hand on her forehead. She knew that Sally couldn't hear her thoughts; she had tried speaking to her, even yelling to no avail. But when Sally touched her and used her healer abilities she was able to pick up on Jewel's emotions. Every time Dalton left the healer came to her and gave her what felt like a mental slap in the face. It was necessary and Jewel appreciated it. She didn't like being led by her emotions. She wanted facts, truths that told her what was or wasn't.

"He will be back. He never goes far, and if he didn't leave and go clean up, the stench of him would begin to make you want to hurl. And that would suck seeing as how you can't move."

Sally definitely had a way of putting things in perspective. The cool air hit Jewel's forehead as Sally moved her hand, but she didn't leave.

"I know you can hear me, Jewel," Sally told her. "I don't know how I know that, but when I do my healer mojo thing I can sense it. I'm hoping that once you turn eighteen, the bond between you and Dalton will open, and he will be able to speak with you and you with him. That would make life a tad easier when it comes to figuring out how to bring you back." Sally sounded tired and Jewel felt bad that she was constantly having to tend to her. "From what the girls have told me about you, I imagine it's driving you crazy not to be able to ask about all this mate talk. And since men are about as helpful as an armless postman about sharing information of any kind be it sensitive or simply facts, I don't imagine Dalton will give you a whole lot. So if you have some time and don't have any place to be...," she chuckled.

Ha, ha, Sally, funny girl, Jewel thought dryly.

"Then I am going to tell you the story of the Canis lupis. This is a fairy tale—the likes of which you have never heard. Disney has nothing on the lupine. Seriously, if they turned our lives into one of those reality shows, the ratings would be off the charts, if for no other reason than werewolf men are, how would an intellectual like you put it?" Jewel listened as Sally made a 'hmm' sound as she considered her own question. "Okay how about the males of the Canis lupis species genetically gravitate towards a level of attractiveness that humans can't even begin to fathom."

Jewel snorted a laugh in her mind. *Or you could just say hot, with a double t. But who am I to judge?*

"Once upon a time, in a land far, far away, like another realm actually," Sally began and Jewel realized that this story might have quite a lot of side commentary that most fairy tales did not. Again, who was she to judge? She was, after all, lying in a comatose state unable to join the rest of civilization in the journey called life. If Sally's fairy tale, which was apparently true, contained a good bit of cliff notes, then she would happily listen.

"A goddess known as the Great Luna created a race by joining humans with wolves." There was a pause. "Okay, so that didn't come out exactly the way I wanted it to. I don't mean she had like wolves, you know, *joining* humans as in the biblical sense. That totally was not what I was going for…"

If ever Jewel wanted to do one of those face palm things, now would be the time.

5

"Living in the Bronx of New York City does something to a girl. You have to become hard in order to survive. There is no room for weakness because the weak become prey, and prey die. I have seen some very questionable things where I am from, but none so questionable as the tragedy before me, nor any as hilarious." ~ Stella

"Is there anything you can do to help him?" the pixie king asked the three healers. Stella knew that he could see in their faces that they didn't have a clue how to help his brother, but like any fool wishing for the unattainable, he asked anyway.

"Put him out of his misery?" Stella finally spoke up. She saw Heather nod from the corner of her eye and Anna made an mmm-hmm sound.

"Kill him?" Ainsel asked and his voice jumped an octave.

"What I have found in my work with animals is that sometimes the merciful thing to do is put them down," Heather added gently.

"Can't you just put him back right?"

Stella bit back her laughter because she could see that the king was obviously distressed over the matter. But really, it was his brother's own fault he was in such a predicament. He was a womanizer and apparently he had fiddled with the wrong woman. It always amazed her how surprised someone acted when they were caught in a crime. What were they expecting—a slap on the hand and twenty minutes in time out? Ainsel's brother had finally been brought to task over his promiscuous ways but was not expected to suffer the consequences.

"Even if we could, it wouldn't be right." Stella folded her arms across her chest and met the king's gaze. "Sometimes you have to practice tough love. If you constantly get your brother out of trouble, how will he learn?"

"Okay, now I'm just dying here," Adam said from somewhere behind the three girls. "What could possibly be so bad?"

"Shh," Crina scolded her mate.

"Have you talked with Peri about it?" Anna asked. "Isn't she someone you respect, whose judgment you would trust?"

Ainsel shook his head vigorously. "Peri, of all, cannot know."

"I think I agree with him on that one," Elle said as she stepped up next to Anna. "Peri isn't known for her discretion."

"But she might be able to help him," Anna pointed out.

Elle shook her head. "Whatever was done to the king's brother is obviously humiliating. Peri would never give mercy to a male who had earned his disgrace."

Sorin, having taken the role of leader in their little group, pushed away from the tree he had been leaning on and walked towards the king. "They have given you their answer; now what say you? Shall you still grant us sanctuary, or do we need to be on our way?"

Ainsel looked once again at each of the healers; his eyes stopped on Stella and she knew he was hoping she would have a change of heart. He needed to get used to disappointment, she thought to herself.

When he realized that there would be no help from them, his shoulders slumped slightly in defeat. "I gave Peri my word that I would allow you to stay here. I will not go back on that."

Sorin gave the king a slight bow and then motioned for the group to follow him. He led them back to the clearing that had been prepared for them, and Stella braced herself for the questions that were about to bombard them. She really hoped she could answer them before she started laughing, but the odds of that were not looking very good as she felt her shoulders begin to shake with the effort to keep herself composed. Anna was having the same level of success as her own laughter bubbled out of her.

"Okay," Adam said as he glanced at Elle. "Barrier?"

"Yep," Elle nodded and they both worked their magic to create a sound proof, but unseen, wall around them.

"I'm with Adam on this," Crina said as she stepped closer to the now giggling healers. "What did you all see? Sorry, Heather, no offense."

"None taken," Heather said around her laughter. "Honestly, I'm sure it would be funnier if I could imagine what they had described to me," she pointed to her eyes, "but I can't help but laugh with these to yahoos cracking up."

Stella held up one hand to Crina and the others waiting to hear what they had seen in the carriage while she clutched her stomach with her other hand. She took several deep breaths attempting to compose herself. When she, Anna, and Heather were finally letting out composed sighs, she wiped the tears of laughter from her eyes and pulled her shoulders back.

"So," she began with a clap of her hands. "Ainsel made it clear that his brother has a little bit of a problem thinking with a part of his anatomy that should not be used for thinking. From what I can gather based on what I saw was that whatever woman who last befell under his charms decided enough was enough. I'm thinking the conversation went something like this. *I heard you been sniffing around a whole bunch of other pixie behinds. I told you; I don't play that. If you want to act like a dog sniffing every tail that is lifted in your face then perhaps your nose should be replaced with something more suitable. After all, it isn't your nose that the ladies need to look out for.*" Stella wiped the smile from her face as she looked back at the blank faces staring at her. She was waiting for the moment when the light bulb would go off. She didn't have to wait long.

"Mother of pixie dust!" Adam grinned. "Are you telling me that the offended pixie put his," he pointed to below his belt and then up to his face. "On his...where his...,"

Anna and Stella were nodding as they listened to Adam talk through his revelation.

"Oh, that is too much!" Elle laughed and Sorin had to help hold her up as the convulsions that had rocked the healers before suddenly rolled through her. Sorin wasn't laughing. He actually looked like he might be in pain, no doubt thinking about how Ainsel's brother must feel stuck in such a state.

"No wonder the king was freaking out," Crina giggled. "That would be like one of us walking around with a big boob on the front of our face."

Adam's laughter stopped like a water faucet had been turned off. He straightened up and frowned at his mate. "What would be wrong with that?"

Crina slugged him in the arm and Stella could tell she hadn't held back any of her werewolf strength as Adam rubbed the offended spot.

"Do you feel scarred for life?" Elle asked Anna who, though she was legally an adult, at times seemed so innocent.

Anna shrugged and as she often did surprised them with her answer. "I won't ever be able to look at Mr. Snuffleupagus from Sesame Street the same again." That brought another round of laughter from the group.

"So are we really not going to tell Peri about this?" Heather asked after they had finally pulled themselves together.

Stella saw Elle shoot Adam a look, one that her brother had sent her many times when he was trying to get her to read his mind. But then Elle and Adam weren't humans, maybe they *could* read each other's minds.

"I think that for now we should keep this little morsel to ourselves," Elle finally said with Adam's nod of agreement endorsing her. "I'm not saying we will never tell her, but I'm thinking it should wait until we no longer need the pixies to save our bacon."

"Good point," Heather agreed.

"Well," Anna breathed out as she took a seat on a log that had been positioned to be a chair. "I don't know about you all, but that totally taps out my *what the hell* quota for the month, and quite possibly the year, and that's saying something because I'm from New Orleans. People in the Bayou take weird to a whole new level. And honestly, I'm kind of disappointed that there is still three months left in the year. I mean what could follow that?" She motioned back towards the direction they had come from.

"I have to agree," Stella nodded as she took a seat next to her. "I thought having two crazy white chicks magically appearing in my dressing room at the club was my *what the hell* moment of the year. Who knew it could be beat."

"And by a pixie with a penis on his face at that," Heather added.

"Say that three times fast," Adam joked as he too took a seat and pulled Crina into his lap.

"If Sally were here she would no doubt dub him PP face," Elle chuckled.

"When this is all said and done, we should get him a personalized license plate, PPF, maybe as a Christmas gift or something," Heather grinned.

"Yes!" Anna laughed. "He could attach it to the front of his carriage."

"What does it say about us that we, thirty minutes later, are still laughing about this?" Stella asked.

Heather stepped in the direction of Stella's voice, shuffling her feet until they hit the log the two others were sitting on. "I think it says that, perhaps like the rest of the American culture, we have an unhealthy fascination with penises."

"Or faces," Anna added.

"What about those of us who aren't American?" Adam asked.

Heather shrugged. "Not my problem that you haven't discovered what disturbing qualities are running through the populace of your race, but I suggest you figure it out. It will come in handy when you have to one day blame someone for the things about yourself that you're sure couldn't possibly be your fault."

Adam's brow rose as he looked at the blind healer. "What happened to your silver lining, half glass full attitude?"

"Adam, it is all fun and games until a pixie ends up with a penis on his face where his nose should be." Heather started to laugh along with everyone else at Stella's clever quip—the girl was full of them, but a sudden stab of pain in her head had her gasping instead of laughing. For a split second she saw a bright flash, she actually *saw* something though it was so fast and so painful that she didn't care to try and evaluate it at the moment. Her hands flew to her head as she squeezed her eyes closed gritting her teeth.

"Heather," Stella's voice sounded as if it were coming through a tunnel. "What's wrong?"

She held up a hand to her friend and took several deep breaths. Finally the pain left, just as quickly as it had come, but in its place was something she could only describe as a yearning, a hunger so ferocious that her heart began to beat faster and her palms began to sweat.

"Did the pixies spike the drinks they gave us earlier? Because I'm beginning to feel like one of those cry baby drunks." Heather finally released her head and sat up a little straighter taking several deep breaths.

"You looked like you were in pain," Anna offered.

"That would be a correct evaluation. But it was more than that; I saw something, as in like for a second there wasn't only darkness. It was just a flash that had me cringing away."

"It was something bright then," Stella told her.

"If you say so," Heather said as she rubbed her chest.

"Okay wait a second," Anna said in a voice that was unusually sharp. "You just rubbed your chest. Why did you do that?" There was an urgency coming off of her that had Heather wanting to stand and pace, but she remained sitting. She found that sometimes going against her immediate instinct kept her out of hot water.

"And you," Anna continued. Heather assumed she was talking to Stella because her voice had changed directions. "You were doing the same thing earlier, rubbing your chest. Why?"

"Woaw, I'm feeling a little pressure that if I answer this wrong she's going to go all voodoo doll on me," Heather muttered as she leaned closer to Stella.

"Anna, why are you asking about them rubbing their chests?" Elle asked her voice coming closer to the three of them.

"Because I was rubbing *my* chest and have been periodically since we started our little journey. There's been this, this I don't know how to describe it other than an ache in the same place that Stella and Heather have been rubbing. And I feel this strong need to go back."

"Go back?" Elle asked. "To...?"

"To Peri's," Heather answered for her, completely understanding the need.

"I've felt the same," Stella finally admitted. "But along with those wonderful things, I've also felt this sorrow, I don't know why."

"It's the mate bond," Sorin's voice joined theirs.

"But we aren't mated," Anna told him, though he obviously already knew that.

"Your mates must be among the males that are at Peri's now, which is what Peri had thought would happen. Maybe because they have gotten closer to you the bond is beginning to tug a little."

"I would totally be okay if it decided to tug in a little less painful way," Heather said as she once again found herself rubbing her chest.

"Is this going to get worse?" Stella asked.

"I would like to tell you no, but it seems like in the past year as more and more wolves have been finding their true mates, what we had always considered usual, or normal hasn't been the case. So it might worsen, or it might just stay the same until you finally meet him."

"I'm going to go out on a limb here and say that we won't be that lucky."

"So we really are going to have mates?" Anna asked after several minutes of silence. Heather noted the excitement and hopefulness in her voice and her heart echoed those sentiments. After hearing all of the girls' stories, their pasts and pains, she knew that it was well past time for them to have something positive happen. If it came in the form of a huge, handsome, dominant werewolf, so be it, who was she to complain?

—

Volcan stood staring out into the barren realm of the draheim. He felt like a sewer rat since he had had to take up residence in a cave in this forgotten realm. But it was his only option at the moment. He had to rebuild his coven. He was patient. He had not become as powerful as he once was by acting rashly. A roar in the distance drew his attention back to the fact that living with animals that humans would have considered dragons was definitely something that would have to be a very short term solution. The draheim weren't known for their hospitality, and he was sure that soon enough they would pick up on his scent. Judging by the appearance of their landscape, it did not look like they had been eating well, not in a long while.

He didn't think he would be stuck here much longer. The young healer that he had fed on was now filled with his essence. He had literally fused himself into her blood. He just needed the link to be opened and then he would be able to siphon her power, power he would need in order to once again create witches. As soon as the bond between her and her mate opened, he would have access to her. During the battle in the dark forest he had seen how the grey wolf had stood over her body protecting her from not only the enemy, but everyone. He was no fool. That was mate behavior. It was only a matter of time. He just had to be patient and keep from becoming the draheim's dinner. That would definitely put a damper on things.

—

"It's been over two weeks, Perizada," Dillon said as he and the other wolves practiced fighting off her magical attacks in the forest outside of her home. "When are we going to make a move?"

"I've learned a thing or two in my three thousand years on this ball of dirt," Peri told him as she threw a particularly nasty fireball at Kale. "When your enemy is not making ruffles, it means he is more than likely somewhere attempting to figure out his next move. Now, while he is making his plans, we too are planning. And one of the things that we need to decide is if, when, and how to go on the offensive."

"Yes," several of the males spoke up interrupting her, which earned them each a power bolt to the chest knocking them on their backsides.

"Or," Peri continued, "do we wait to see what his move will be? I have been going through the archives of the fae, attempting to see how Volcan came to power the first time. I want to know exactly who helped him and who was loyal to him. And I want to know if they are still loyal. While you lot have been snoozing away like dogs lying in the sunshine, I've been going out and doing my own surveillance. Right now all of our people are safe. The other healers are hidden, and Volcan doesn't know that we have obtained help from the other packs. I want to keep that upper hand. If I send you barbarians out into the world like bulls in a China shop we lose the element of surprise."

"Why don't you send one of us to check on the señoritas?" Gustavo asked attempting to sound innocent.

"Nice try, Casanova," Peri said as she flicked her hand at the Spain pack Alpha sending him flying into a tree. He stood as a growl slipped out. It was quickly cut off when Lucian stepped out from the shadows of the trees, his eyes trained on Gustavo. "Relax wolf," Peri, said to her mate. "Posturing doesn't bother me. It's not like he could get within five feet of me anyway. And if he ever wants to meet the other healers, he will play nice. Won't you?" she asked the Alpha as a single brow rose on her elegant face.

"Knee jerk reaction," he told Lucian. "Perdón."

"It is in our nature to want to take action," Lucian spoke to the group after giving Gustavo a nod. "We are hunters; we seek out prey. When we feel like those who are ours are in danger, our patience runs thin. What we must not do is give into the need to do *something* for the sake of doing *something*. There must be purpose behind every decision. That is the only way to guarantee success. For all of her flippant attitude and sharp answers, my mate cares deeply for those who need protection. She will not do anything to jeopardize the safety of the healers or anyone else. If you need more reassurance than my word, then contact Vasile. He trusts Perizada and that is good enough for me."

The males, one by one, nodded.

"It is good to have a level-headed wolf with us," Drayden, Alpha of the Canada pack, admitted.

116

Peri tsked her tongue at the Alpha. "There is no such thing as a level-headed wolf."

"What would you call your mate then?" Kale asked.

"Depends on the day, or hour. On a particularly difficult day it might be a minute by minute change in description. I can assure you level headed has never been one of those descriptions." She tapped her chin thoughtfully. "But if you wanted to know what he gets called most," she paused when Lucian let out a deep growl. A twinkle of mischief danced in her peridot eyes as she said, "lucky."

"You call him lucky?" Nick, Drayden's Beta asked.

"Let me guess," Dillon chuckled. "It's because he's mated to you."

"Good guess but no, I call him lucky because I've yet to turn him into a rug. I have a feeling some of you will not have such good fortune."

Ciro, Alpha of the Italian pack, leaned against the side of the house, taking a break from the sparring while the others spoke to Perizada. He found that the exercise was helping to curb his restlessness, though it didn't remove it entirely. Like Dillon, Ciro was ready for some action. He had come to help defeat Volcan, and to find his mate. He wasn't about to be modest and say that he only came for the noble reason of assisting. When he had received the call from Vasile asking for him to join Perizada and the others, he knew. Like a clear bell ringing out in his mind, he knew that it was just *right* that he go. The words had barely left the Romania Alpha's mouth and Ciro knew that one of those healers was his. Once he had arrived in Peri's home, the pull he felt in his gut confirmed that he was getting close. His wolf was pacing inside of him, itching to phase and run for the pixie realm. He had a feeling it wouldn't go over well if he tore through the veil and burst into their land, spouting off that he wanted to see his mate. He would wait. It helped that he was pretty sure the pull he was now feeling was the mate bond. He liked knowing that the connection was already forming. So yes, he would wait, but he didn't know how much longer his patience would last. Alpha males weren't exactly known for their forbearance when it came to their mates.

—

Dalton was beginning to feel like a creeper as he stared into Jewel's window—especially since the one who held him captive wasn't even legal according to human laws. He had one week left. One week until his little dove turned eighteen and then their bond would form and he would finally be able to talk with her—at least that was his hope.

He had yet to tell her anymore about his past. He honestly didn't know why he was stalling. Waiting to tell her would not make the truth any less horrific or make her any more accepting of him. He needed to just rip the bandage off fast and get it over with. The problem was that it was a big ass bandage. He knew that if he didn't tell Jewel everything himself, then there was a chance that she would hear it from someone like Kale who had known him for a very long time. Though the information Kale thought he knew was indeed false, it still would feel like betrayal if the information, true or false, did not come from her mate.

Footsteps behind him and the scent of magic on the air alerted Dalton that he had company before he heard her speak.

"You could stay with her all of the time, you know," Peri said as she stepped around him so that she could see him and the window at the same time. "You don't have to keep leaving."

Dalton felt the words like a knife to his gut. *Keep leaving,* two little words, and yet when spoken in regards to how he had been treating his mate, they felt as heavy as a steel beam.

"Hmm," Peri continued. "Who would have known that even the stoic Dalton Black could look like a kicked puppy if just the right buttons are pushed? Granted, I know what to look for, anyone else looking at you would still see the mask you keep in place. It is very subtle, but it gives me hope that you feel some depth of emotion, more than just a mate wanting to claim what is his. Perhaps Sally is right and there is hope for you yet."

"I do not like the way they smell—so close to her."

He saw her brow raise from the corner of his eye. "Okay, you're still back at the very first sentence I spoke. So you are referring to the fact that I said you could stay with her. You're saying you can't because...," she drew the word out prompting him to finish for her.

"Control," he bit out not liking the fact that Perizada was very good at working people to do what she wanted. He didn't like being a puppet. He didn't like explaining himself, and he knew the only reason he was saying anything at all was on the off chance that Jewel could hear or someone took it upon themselves to share with her what he had said or not said.

"The bane of every male werewolf," Peri agreed. "The constant battle to keep control of a beast who is a predator and fiercely protective."

Dalton didn't respond. He didn't know what she wanted him to say, and to be honest he didn't really care. Since the moment he had laid eyes on the fair skinned redhead, she had become his world. He had tunnel vision and she was the only thing he cared about. For all he knew the world was crashing down around them with Volcan at the center of the storm and all he could see was Jewel.

"Has Sally told you about her times with Jewel after each time you leave?" She paused but when she realized he wasn't going to respond she continued. "She does her little healer stuff and looks inside of Jewel. Sally said that every time you go what she feels in Jewel is something that she would compare to a panic attack. Sally said she can feel her anxiety rising and can feel her soul become restless and fearful."

This got Dalton's attention. Finally he pulled his eyes away from the window of Jewel's room and met Peri's gaze. He knew that his wolf was peering out and his eyes would be glowing. It was all the control he could manage. He was lucky he wasn't walking around with canines showing and claws lengthened. Peri held his gaze for longer than most wolves could but when she finally looked away he knew it wasn't an act of submission but rather a willingness to humor him and his dominance.

"Why didn't Sally tell me this?" he asked and failed at keeping the gruff sound from his voice.

"Have you looked at yourself in the mirror lately? You aren't exactly the picture of a warm fuzzy puppy. I mean seriously, man, nothing about you screams, *please come talk to me, I'm so nice and won't bite your head off at the first chance.* If anything, you pretty much look like one of those deranged purple minions from that movie Despicable something or other. Have you seen that movie—total riot? But alas, I digress. So what it all comes down to is Sally didn't say anything to you because you've been acting like a complete ass."

"You could have just led and finished with that one sentence," he informed her through tight lips.

"Flamboyant descriptions are my specialty. I try not to hinder my talents by accommodating other people. Bad habit to get into."

Dalton was tiring of the female before him and just wanted her to take her opinions elsewhere so that he could go spend time with Jewel. He was just about to say something to that extent but Peri beat him to it.

"Just consider for a minute what she needs and not what makes you comfortable or uncomfortable. None of the males other than Dalton and Costin have entered the room since they found out that she was your true mate. If you're going to be hard up about it, I can strip the scents from the room."

A single brow rose on his face as he looked at her.

"Oh, good grief," she groaned. "Why did I even offer? Fine, give me three minutes and consider this your Christmas present for like the rest of your life."

Dalton watched as Peri disappeared and then reappeared in Jewel's room. He heard her whispering words with her arms outstretched and saw a soft glow emit from her form. True to her word, three minutes later she gave him a slight nod and then left Jewel's room. Dalton didn't hesitate to hop through the window. His nose tickled at the lack of smell. It was as if nothing existed in the room at all. Though he was glad he couldn't smell the males, it disturbed him to be able to see Jewel across the room but not pick up her sent. She smelled like the ripest pear, sweet and edible. His wolf wanted him to phase so that he could rub against her bed, covering her in his scent. Dalton voted against that, thinking that to a human that would probably be a little disturbing. His wolf told him he didn't care. He wanted their mate to smell of them so others would know she was theirs.

The sun was beginning to set and the room grew dim as he took a seat next to her. He leaned forward and pressed his nose against her neck breathing deep. Suddenly everything was right in his world as her scent filled his lungs. It was driving him mad not to be able to look into her eyes, to hear what her voice sounded like, to know what she tasted like. For the first time in his life he actually craved the touch of another. He had watched other wolves, mated pairs and pack members, be openly affectionate and had never had any desire to join in. He didn't hug his pack mates as some males did in brotherly affection. He didn't shake hands or pat others on the back. He kept his distance at all times, and others seems to sense that because everyone who knew him, or came near him, instinctively gave him a wide berth. It didn't hurt his feelings; it was the way he wanted it, until now, but only with her. The thought of anyone else touching him, even in the lightest of touches, made his skin crawl.

He took her small hand in his larger one and threaded their fingers together. Her skin was soft as silk, and though it was no longer smooth or without blemish because of the horror she had endured, she was still utterly beautiful. His thumb brushed across her hand reverently as he treasured the gift of being able to touch her.

"Peri told me that Sally can feel your anxiety when I leave. I hate that you feel that way, but honestly I'm a little relieved to know that though you are not conscious, perhaps you need me as badly as I need you," he admitted to her. "Every time I get up to leave you I have to force my legs to move. Everything in me screams at me to stay, to never leave your side, and yet I still hear that voice that tells me you deserve so much better than me. But if you want me to stay, if that truly is what you want and need, I won't leave you. I will stay for as long as you will have me." Dalton watched her face carefully as he spoke to her. He knew he shouldn't expect a reaction, but he couldn't help but hope for something, anything that told him she could hear him. But there was nothing.

He let out a deep sigh and leaned forward resting his elbows on his knees still holding her hand in one of his. "Only a week until your birthday. I know that I can't wait any longer. I have to tell you the rest of my story." Dalton had just promised her that he wouldn't leave her, and yet he had no idea how he was going to sit in that chair after he shared all of his secrets with her. How could he stay in her presence after he poured out all of his filth? He felt like his mere presence would taint her.

"I wandered the forests for over a month in my wolf form after breaking free from Gwen and her demented friends," he began and steeled himself for the emotions that he knew would crash into him like a hurricane against the shore. As the words poured from him he found himself pulled into the memories, reliving them whether he wanted to or not.

—

Dalton wasn't sure how much distance he had put between himself and the hell hole in which he had been held captive. His wolf had taken over, and when he had burst forth into the fresh night air, he had phased and started running and only stopping when he had to drink water or risk collapsing. A few times he had picked up the scent of other Canis lupis, but he didn't stay in their territory long enough to warrant alerting them of his presence.

As he traveled alone he found his thoughts swirling inside his head, mixing with the thoughts of the wolf. He was angry, but that was nothing compared to what his wolf felt. His wolf was enraged at having been so easily subdued and at the mercy of mere humans. He was a predator, and not just any predator. He was the best of two species and yet he found himself despising his human half. He didn't want to be linked in any way to people who could do such horrible things to someone else just because they were different. The more he thought about it, the angrier he became and the more he succumbed to the darkness that lived inside every Canis lupis male.

When he finally allowed himself to rejoin civilization, there was nothing civilized left in him. Violence reigned in his heart, and chaos filled his mind. There was no peace anywhere inside of him, not even when he slept, which was only a few hours a night and only in fits and starts. His wolf paced restlessly, craving blood and carnal pleasure to sate the anguish and growing emptiness inside of him. He sought out the companionship of women, something that Canis lupis males, at least honorable ones, never did. An honorable wolf saved himself for his true mate not only because she was the only one who deserved to share such intimacy with him but because the males of his species knew how painful it would be if their true mate had lain with another. But there was no honor left in him. He never forced a woman and was never physically violent with them, but neither did he care for them or treat them kindly or with respect. He took what he wanted and left them feeling used and discarded. They were only human after all; they didn't deserve his compassion or care.

Dalton never stayed in one place too long—one because he didn't like being around people, and two he usually wound up killing one or two people in every town he came across. They were never innocent men, but even though they were guilty of some atrocity or crime, the violent death they met at his hands was probably too extreme of a punishment. But just as with the human women, he didn't care because they were just human men. They were nothing to him but judgmental, evil people who preyed on anyone weaker than them. He figured he was just giving them a taste of their own medicine. Only slightly different because when he killed them, it was always in his partially phased form. He enjoyed the terror he saw in their eyes when they realized that there was no way they would survive against one such as him. Dalton was a big human, but he was an ever bigger wolf. He lived that way for decades and decades. Destroying evil men, seducing easy women, regardless of their single status or lack thereof, and ignoring the laws of his own kind. He traveled from territory to territory, avoiding packs and slipping through the hands of Alphas who had heard of his violent ways.

—

Drawing himself out of the memories he had plunged into as he told Jewel about his past, he let out a deep breath. "A month ago when Dillon allowed the males from the other packs to see you, I don't know if you heard the wolf named Kale accuse me of raping a woman. I need you to know that though I did terrible things, I was never capable of something so disgusting and vile. I would take no pleasure in taking what a woman would not give freely." He didn't add that he had no problem finding woman more than willing to give him whatever he wanted. He was extremely attractive like all the males of his species and women were drawn to his dominance. "I was traveling in Colorado at the time; the pack there was and still is under the rule of an Alpha named Dillon Jacobs—my Alpha. I didn't know that he was aware of me being in his territory, and he made sure his wolves didn't alert me to the fact that he knew. Dillon is a patient hunter and he wanted to learn all that he could about me. As I found out later, Dillon had a habit of taking in damaged wolves and sheltering them, rehabilitating them. I don't think he realized that there was no rehabilitating me.

"I was at a brothel, one that a lot of supernaturals frequented—though not usually wolves. It was my usual place to be if I wasn't hunting. I met a woman there and she was alluring, more so than any I had come across. There was something familiar about her, but I couldn't place it. I chose her as my companion for the night," Dalton paused. He was dreading going into details, but he didn't want any secrets between them.

"Once we were alone and things began to progress, she whispered something in my ear, something I had heard so many times before many, many years ago. Her voice changed to one I recognized and when I pulled back to look at her, I saw that it was Gwen who was lying on top of me. I would like to say that I stayed calm, but my wolf took over. I called her some choice names and pushed her off of me rather violently. When she realized that she once again would not have me, she pulled out a knife from her stockings and cut a shallow line on her throat. I was dumbfounded by what she was doing. I just stood there, unsure of what was happening. She then tore the front of her dress exposing herself and mused her hair. Then to my surprise she started shrieking and screaming like a mad woman. I just realized what she was saying when the door flew open and a large male who smelled of wolf filled the doorway. Gwen was screaming that I raped her, tears were streaming down her face, and she was attempting to hold her dress together as if she hadn't been the one to tear it in the first place. The wolf, who I learned was Kale, the Beta of the Irish pack, started after me, and I phased and jumped through the window before he could get his hands on me. I knew I had to get out of there before the Alpha found out. Violence against women in our culture is punishable by death. So I ran again. This time I stayed in the wild, once again avoiding human towns. I had once again been shown just how conniving humans could be, and I wanted nothing to do with them." He paused to collect himself as the anger he felt so many years ago resurfaced. He didn't want to feel those emotions, especially since his mate was human. He never wanted her to feel that he couldn't care for her because of her species. He knew now that he could not judge an entire race by a few that chose to give in to evil.

"A year past. But because the Fates have a sick sense of humor, I ran into Gwen again. By then I had deduced why I had not been able to recognize her. She herself was practicing witchcraft, probably drafted into service by one of Volcan's people. The night that I found her I just happened to be near a town and had heard the cries of a woman saying someone had taken her baby. I don't know why I felt the need to help her, but my wolf and I couldn't imagine anyone hurting a child, something so innocent and helpless. When I picked up the unmistakable stench of black magic, I followed it and found Gwen clutching the child with one hand and a knife in the other. She was going to sacrifice the child as an initiation into a coven. I couldn't believe the depth of her depravity. I made myself known to her. As usual, her desire to possess me overcame her. She practically dropped the poor child on the ground. I told her that I realized that I did indeed love her and had just been too scared to admit it. I asked her to come to me, to take me. It took everything in me not to choke on the words. I would rather have my heart carved from my chest with a rusty saw blade than touch her. But it got her away from the baby. As soon as she was close to me I struck, and I killed her, quickly. I killed a woman, but I didn't know what else to do. There was no coming back for her. Once she sacrificed that child she would have been lost to the darkness, if she hadn't been already.

"What I didn't know was the mother and some other townspeople had witnessed the encounter. Soon, news of what I had done had spread through-out the region. I was still on the edge of the Colorado border at that time. Naturally, as local Alpha, Dillon learned of my actions. He sought me out and con-fronted me. He basically told me that he would no longer allow my behavior to continue in his territory, or in any other. But if I was willing to save a child then there must still be something worth saving in me. He gave me a choice—he would either destroy me or I could become a member of his pack. He didn't want to know of my past. He didn't want to hear about why I had become who I was. He simply wanted me to choose from then on to no longer be that man. I asked him to give me a few days to think about it and he said, 'No'." Dalton chuckled at the memory. Dillon was a true Alpha. He did not bend when it came to the health and safety of the ones he cared for. "He said if you have to think about it, then I might as well destroy you now. So, I went with him. It was hard joining a pack again. I was continually challenged by the other males at first, each attempt-ing to assert his own dominance. Eventually I fell into my place in the hierarchy. Up until recently I was Dillon's third, but our Beta was killed in the battle against Volcan and that evil female fae. So now I am his Beta."

"And now you know." He realized how tight he was clutching her hand, like a life line to the present to keep him from falling into the depths of his dark past, and relaxed his grip.

"I hope that you can forgive me. I have disrespected you so many times. I disrespected all of those females and I became judge and executioner of men that should have faced the law not my beast. I will never be the man I was before my parents were murdered, and I was tortured and molested at the hands of a mad woman. I don't know if I can be the male you need, but I want to try. If you will give me a chance, I will do everything in my power to keep you safe, protected, cherished, and loved. I don't know if those emotions even exist in me anymore, but I honestly don't think I can survive any longer without you."

"Before I saw you my future was nothing but a black hole that I was forever falling toward. I had nothing to live for. I have been carrying my guilt and shame on my own, by choice. I was unable to allow anyone in for so long and I was ready for it to be over. I never dreamed the Great Luna would give me a true mate, not after all I had done. But apparently, like Dillon, she sees something in me worth saving." Dalton knew that was the most words he had said in his entire life and suddenly he was just out of steam. He felt exhausted, as if he had been once again running through the forest without stopping. He felt raw and bare before Jewel even though she was not awake. It was worse than being naked and vulnerable. He wanted so bad to get up and escape her judgment, but he had promised her that he wouldn't go.

"I wish I knew that after all of that you still wanted me here," he told her honestly. Dalton wasn't good at being vulnerable. He didn't like the helpless feelings it brought on, but for the first time in his life, he needed the approval of another. "I will be honest, little dove. If you chose me, if you give yourself to me, then I will never let you go. I've told you my past, I've shared with you things I would never and have never told another soul, and I could understand if you wanted to walk away. But if you don't, if you declare me yours, and accept my claim on you, I will never be able to walk away, even if you changed your mind and decided you made a mistake. Can you accept that? Can you handle a male who has never had anything to call his own, has never had another love him, and if he is given those things, will hold onto them with every fiber of his being?"

He didn't want to scare her, but just as he needed to be honest with her about his past, she deserved to know the depth to which he would go to keep her if she made herself his. She needed to know that all males of his species were possessive and protective. He didn't know if he could control those instincts toward her. He was honestly afraid he would smother her, and she would grow to hate him. At least if that happened, she won't be able to say she wasn't warned.

Dalton stood and moved until he sat next to her on her bed. He still held her hand in his and with the other arm he leaned across her and braced himself above her. Leaning down until his lips were nearly touching her ear he whispered to her. "Choose me, Little Dove. I don't deserve you, but I want you, I need you." Dalton swallowed hard when he felt her hand tighten on his. He pulled back quickly and looked down at their entwined hands. She was squeezing his so tight that her knuckles were white. He could hear her heartbeat increasing and her breaths growing shallow, and his heart nearly broke when he saw tears fall from her closed eyes and streak down her white cheeks. He wiped them away gently with his free hand whispering to her softly. "Shhh, I hear you. Relax my precious, Jewel, I won't leave your side. I'm taking that as your surrender. The Great Luna help you because you are stuck with me now." Dalton pressed a firm but gentle kiss to her forehead and smiled when he heard a sigh escape her and her hand loosened on his. He sat there for several more minutes with his eyes closed, breathing in her scent, absorbing the feel of her soft skin in his hand, and reveling in having the right to touch her. The world could be burning down around them, Volcan might have taken over and unleashed his evil, but all Dalton could focus on was the most precious thing he had ever seen. He had come to help, to protect their race and the humans from Volcan, but he knew that nothing would come before Jewel. He would protect her and destroy the world if need be in order to keep her safe with him.

6

"I'm just going to say it, I think we are doomed. Honestly, I've got a bunch of males trying to sniff my healers, I've got a Beta on the verge of either destroying himself or taking his mate and running, and a group of my people hanging out in pixie land getting kicks off the kings brother's debacle. Hope you weren't counting on us to save the world, because if you were, you are so screwed." ~Peri

"Have you had any leads?" Lucian asked his mate. Evening had fallen hours ago and Peri was still restless, unable to sit still for longer than a few seconds. He watched as she paced back and forth in their room. Her shimmering white hair was free of its usual twist that she kept it up in, and he couldn't help but notice how alluring she was, even in her agitated state.

"Focus," she snapped at him, obviously having picked up on his thoughts.

"Make yourself a hag and then I might be able to." Lucian was proud of himself for quickly picking up the sarcasm Peri often threw at him, and he knew that she enjoyed their verbal sparring.

"I'm afraid there is just no way to ruin this perfection; you're up a creek."

"What creek?"

She rolled her eyes at him. Obviously he had not understood her reference. He would have to ask Sally what it meant. His mate wouldn't explain it because she got too much joy out of seeing him at a slight disadvantage to her. He humored her because it made her happy.

"I'm missing something," she finally answered his first question. "Volcan wouldn't have just gone into that field with no backup plan. He had to have known that there was a possibility that he would be thwarted, especially because of Lorelle's indiscretion."

"What do you mean a backup plan?"

"I mean that he knew there was a possibility that he would lose possession of the healers. Because of that possibility, he would have set up some sort of contingency plan, some way to ensure he still could benefit from them."

Lucian agreed with her. Any good strategist always had multiple plans, because the first one usually did not play out the way it was supposed to. But, like Peri, he felt as though he was missing something. "It feels like it should be obvious," he told her.

She nodded as she stopped her pacing and faced him, her arms crossed in front of her chest and lips pulled tight in a thin line. "Exactly. Ugh!" she growled. "I hate it when something is staring me smack in the face and I can't get it to just reach out and slap me."

There was a light knock on the door and then Costin's head popped in. "I'm sorry but all I heard was just reach out and slap me and honestly my curiosity got the better of me."

Lucian could hear Sally behind him. "Shut the door, you dork, or Lucian just might kill you."

Peri's eyes narrowed on the young wolf, well young in comparison to Lucian, and she took a step toward him. "In what universe would you ever think that your curiosity was any concern of mine? There is only one reason that I am letting you walk away, Costin of the Serbian pack, and that is because I like your mate and don't want her to die. Now, shut the door. If you want to leave your head in the doorway while you do it, feel free."

Costin's eyes danced with playfulness. Lucian was convinced the Beta had no self-preservation instincts.

"Wow, you really should have been born a she-wolf. I've never met someone who more adequately embodies the term bit—," Costin was cut off as he growled and his head was jerked back and the door pushed closed.

Lucian smiled. He had seen Sally's small hand with a handful of her mate's hair. He liked that one. She was unassuming, but underneath she was strong as steel.

"I honestly don't know how he has survived for sixty years," Peri said as she turned back to look at him.

Lucian reached out his hand, beckoning her to him. He had given her the space she seemed to need but he was done with not touching her for the day. "If it will please you, beloved, I'll be sure to be extra hard on him tomorrow during our sparring."

Peri stepped into him and he wrapped his arms around her, pulling her between his legs to his chest. His forehead rested on her stomach and he purred as her fingers ran through his hair. He was convinced there was nothing on earth better than her touch.

"Just make sure to not break anything that would take too long to heal. I don't need injured wolves when we make our move."

Lucian nuzzled his face against her causing her shirt to rise up enough for him to press his lips to her warm skin. For his wolf, there was nothing better than skin-on-skin touch with their mate and he felt the beast sigh in contentment. "As you wish," he whispered against her.

The room was suddenly dim and Lucian couldn't help the smile that stretched across his face. His female was powerful, an Alpha in every sense of the word.

She placed her hands on either side of his face and slowly tilted it until he was looking into her pale green eyes. "And what is it you wish, wolf?"

Lucian knew his eyes were glowing as his wolf perked up at the tone in Peri's voice. It was more than a question; it was a challenge to pursue her, hunt her, and claim her. Yes, his mate was powerful. He loved that, but he loved even more that in his arms she became just a woman, his woman in need of him and only him. Before he could answer she flashed from the room. He knew where she would eventually end up, but he would humor her and follow her trail. The hunt was on and the reward would be well worth the time and energy.

———

Nick watched as the young healer, Kara, walked along the edge of the forest. He had noticed she tended to slip out of the house alone in the early evening. He had told himself that as a Beta, nearly as dominant as an Alpha, his instinct to protect was off the charts and that was why he had been sure to follow her and keep an eye on her from a distance. Her human senses would never be able to pick up on his presence, not unless he wanted her to notice him. But he didn't, since she was only sixteen and he knew that it would not be appropriate for them to be alone together out after dark.

"Dammit," he growled to himself not for the first time. "What are you doing, Nick?" It also wasn't the first time he had asked himself that question. His answer was always the same, *I'm protecting a healer who is defenseless.* He wouldn't lie; he had noticed her beauty. She was small with sandy brown hair streaked with blonde. She had a diamond stud in her nose, cute as all get out, and she had the most compelling blue/green eyes he had ever seen. Even though he noticed these things, he didn't see her the way a male sees his female, and he was very glad of that because, once again, she was only sixteen. He kept reminding himself of that and the fact that if he was attracted to her in that way then he needed the bloody crap beat out of him.

He knew another reason he felt the need to protect her was because of the haunted look in her eyes that said she had seen far too much ugliness in her young life. Kara was very mature for her age and sometimes he did forget how young she was. She held herself in a way that made it clear she could and had taken care of herself. Nick had shamelessly listened to her and Sally talk. They didn't discuss anything personal, not really. It was more things regarding the current challenges they were facing. Kara frequently made comments on how she wished she could help Jewel and that she wished it had been her who Lorelle had hurt instead of Jewel. This spoke volumes to Nick about her character. At sixteen she felt the responsibility of one much older, and Nick found that he wanted to remove that burden for her.

His steps froze as he watched her kneel down and sit back on her heels. She pulled at the strands of grass around her and, after several moments, looked up at the night sky. Kara's strong voice and the confidence with which she spoke was just one more sign that she had fended for herself for too long.

"So I hear that you listen when your wolves talk to you." He realized she was talking to the Great Luna. He knew he should leave and give her privacy, but his feet stayed firmly planted.

"I don't know if that means you will listen to me or not. I'm not a wolf, but according to Sally I will one day be mated to one. I'm going to jump out on a limb here and hope that you are listening." She paused and Nick watched as Kara let out a slow breath and brushed the hair from her face.

"Jewel needs your help. I'm willing to take her place if that is what it takes. It's not like my life has been some grand event. I have no family. There is no one back in my realm that is missing me right now, so it really doesn't matter if I live or not, or if I'm in a coma for the rest of my life. But Jewel has a mother, and from what we can tell she has a mate. She's smart and has so much to offer. She has more knowledge in her little pinky than I do in my whole body. Now if you need someone who can carry two trays loaded with food and drinks then I'm your girl, but otherwise I am pretty useless. That's really all I have to say; please just consider it. If I could do this for Jewel, then at least I could say that I have done something that actually matters."

Nick heard the underlying plea. Kara felt that if she took Jewel's place then she might actually matter. It twisted his gut to hear such pain in her voice. He turned to follow her back as she walked towards Peri's home. Nick admitted that he was impressed with her selflessness, but what he couldn't admit was that he was steadily begging the Great Luna not to grant Kara's request. If for no other reason than that she was a gypsy healer, precious to their race and each of them deserved to live. But also because she had a mate out there somewhere. Even though it would be two years before they would ever know, he would need her. If Kara died she left her mate to face his darkness alone until it finally consumed him.

Nick hated to see Jewel, also a healer, so badly hurt. He wanted her to get better and wanted to see Dalton become whole because he had found his true mate. But even though he wanted those things, shamelessly he wanted Kara healthy, alive, and safe even more.

—

"Okay, regardless of the fact that I can't see all the cool little pixie people, and their beautiful realm, I know you guys have to be as bored as I am. And by bored I mean I'm thinking of banging my head repeatedly against the closest tree just to break up the monotony. I mean, seriously, other than this need to plow back through the forest all the way to Peri's and jump in the arms of some man I don't know, my life is not all that exciting at the moment."

Anna nodded. "Agreed on the whole needing to make a run for it. However, rest assured, Heather, being able to see hasn't improved the quality of our time spent here. If anything it's made it a tad more disturbing. Since you cannot see, you've missed the looks the little pixie men are giving us. You haven't seen them eye you up and down like you're a piece of apple pie."

Stella laughed. "Heather, I wish you could see Anna's face. You would think this chick hadn't lived in New Orleans her whole life. I *know* they have some interesting folks down there on the bayou. But the way she keeps shooting nervous glances at the curious pixies, it's like she's never been out of her house."

"Curious?" Anna balked. "They are a tad more than curious, Stella. I mean that spike haired one asked if he could see if my *excreters* were larger than his head."

"Wait, where was I when this happened and what are excreters?" Adam spoke up as he took a seat next to Crina.

Heather and Stella were laughing so hard they could hardly speak.

"Apparently that's a pixie term for breast," Elle answered for them."

"Oh that is awesome!" Adam threw his head back and laughed.

Anna shook her head with and grumbled. "You wouldn't think it was awesome if it was your excreters he was asking about." She turned from the laughing bunch and looked at Sorin who, though he wasn't laughing, did have an amused expression on his handsome face. "Sorin, how much longer will we have to be here?"

"And where is Peri?" Stella added as she wiped the moisture from her laughter from her eyes. "I thought she said she would be checking in with us."

And when she does show up, how about you ask her if she knew all along that we would be getting the jitters for men we've never met?"

"She has been here," Elle answered for her mate. "Or rather I should say she has stopped in once."

"We've been here a month and she's only stopped in once?" Heather asked having composed herself as well.

"Well, she couldn't look Ainsel in the face after I told her about what happened with you girls and his brother," Elle told them. "I also told her about you three, and she seems to think some of the males back at the house are having the same issue."

"How did she respond to that? Is she convinced that any or all of them are potential mates to us?" Stella asked.

"From our experience with the Great Luna, Peri was pretty sure that at least a couple if not all of you would find your mates among the males that Vasile sent to help. The Great Luna is rebuilding her race, for whatever reason she needs the Canis lupis to be strong and the fastest way to make that happen is to have mated pairs. That means she isn't just going to let five gypsy healers go around willy nilly unclaimed," Elle explained.

"So why is Peri keeping us apart then?" Anna's eyes narrowed.

"Because sometimes Peri seems to think she knows what's best even…,"

"Even if she's as wrong as pixie with a penis as a nose," Adam finished for her.

Elle pointed at him, "Exactly."

"Okay, so the healers are having mating pains, the males are pining for them, and here we sit surrounded by pixies gone wild," Crina growled. "Did she know when she decided to pawn us off on these little beings that they were such perverts? I mean the king's brother has a—,"

"We know, we know," Adam chuckled. "Let's not rehash it or I'll just start laughing all over again."

"Peri's only thought was to keep you all safe," Sorin spoke up, "even if it meant a little discomfort because of a new mate bond, and perverted pixies"

The group was quiet for a few minutes before Heather spoke up again. "I take it back. I am not bored. Just keep those little male pixies a coming. Who knows what they'll say next."

"Should we tell her what they asked about her?" Anna whispered just as Stella started shushing her.

"Anna," Heather said slowly. "What is the stripper trying to hide from me?"

"Dancer," Stella corrected dryly.

"You say Texas; I say most awesome state on Earth—same difference." Heather waved her off. "Now, Anna, what did the little blue men say?"

"They aren't actually bl—,"

"Not the point," Heather cut Elle off.

Anna let out a long sigh. "Why do I always get stuck having to repeat things that should never be repeated?" When nobody responded she finally answered. "First, they asked if it was difficult for you to see. I thought they were being wise guys so I said, 'I guess, why do you ask?' Then they said, 'Well, how can she see through her undergarments?' Naturally that got Stella and I a little more curious. You were actually gone to the restroom at this point, so we asked them to explain what they were talking about. They asked if a spell was put on you by a jilted lover like the king's brother."

Heather's head tilted to the side as she considered Anna's words. "I don't get it? What kind of spell would have been put on me?"

"Well, they thought perhaps your eyes had been taken by one of your many lovers because you couldn't keep them to yourself."

"And where exactly would my jilted lover have put my eyes?" Heather asked with a raised brow as she attempted to keep the humor out of her voice.

"I thought the same thing, but don't worry I didn't have to ask; they offered that info right up," Stella commented.

"Why don't you tell her?" Anna nodded helpfully.

Stella laughed. "Oh no, you totally got this one."

"Ugh," Anna groaned. "Fine, they said that your lover must have taken your eyes and placed them in your excreters so that you would only be able to see him."

Heather's laughter bubbled up through the trees as she threw her head back. For a moment she was even able to ignore the constant twinge in her chest. "They think I have eyes in my—," she couldn't finish her sentence because she was laughing so hard.

Twenty minutes later Elle and the other girls were sitting around the fire roasting a dinner of wild rabbit given to them by the pixies. A wide smile stretched across Crina's face.

"I was thinking..."

"Never a good sign," Elle muttered.

Crina ignored her. "Heather, why don't we play a little joke on the pixie male population?"

"I'm listening," Heather said and leaned towards the she-wolf's voice.

—

Dalton looked at the clock for the tenth time in the past ten minutes. He knew it was the tenth time because each time he had looked at it only a minute had passed since the last time, and that was ten minutes before. He stood and began to pace the room as he had been doing off and on for the entire day. He was restless. The week had been dragging and now here it was mere hours until October thirty-first. A thought occurred to him as he took three long strides and pulled open the door to Jewel's room. Sally was sitting in a chair in the hallway reading a book, which was where he saw her the last time he had pulled the door open.

"Does it just have to be on the day of her birth, or will it be at the specific time of her birth as well?"

Sally turned the page of her book and answered without ever looking up. "Don't know."

Dalton shut the door with a frustrated growl. That same monotone uninterested tone of voice had laced Sally's response to every question he had posed to her. She really didn't like him. He could live with that; as long as she took care of Jewel and kept her healthy, he could live with just about anything Sally could dish out. He resumed his pacing, glancing down at Jewel every few minutes and up at the clock every minute in between glances.

"You are driving everyone here crazy," Peri snapped as she flashed into the room. "I can only imagine what Jewel must be feeling with your huge, lumbering self stomping around in here like it's a freaking parade. Go kill something and then come back when you are calmer."

"I don't want to leave her."

"Take a number at the back of the, *I don't give a flying flip what you want,* line, and then go and do what I told you to anyway. You aren't making the clock move any faster. You're making the other wolves edgy, which in turn is making my wolf edgy, and if there is one thing I can't stand worse than werewolves, it's edgy werewolves."

Dalton glared at the fae for several minutes before finally turning toward the window. He pushed it open and jumped through it landing soundlessly on the ground. As he turned to tell Peri to keep the other males away, he was met with the window slamming shut in his face.

"One of these days, fairy," he growled low under his breath as he headed towards the forest, phasing in midstride allowing his clothes to tear away from his body. He hated to admit that she was right. He needed to run—needed to kill something. The waiting, wondering if when she finally turned eighteen their bond would snap into place, was enough to drive even a sane wolf over the edge and he was far from sane. Sanity was a ship that had sailed past him in the dead of night, and his second chance at catching it was lying unconscious and beyond his reach.

Dalton ran, allowing the cool, fall air to cleanse his lungs as he took in deep breaths. It rippled through his fur stroking his skin as it separated the strands. It felt as those it had been months since he had communed with the forest, but it had only been days. He hated to leave Jewel's side, but he needed to collect himself. He usually had much better control of his emotions, and it was driving him a little bit crazy that he couldn't seem to get a handle on himself.

He had no idea how long he had been running or how far he had gone when a thought that was not his own entered his mind.

"He's gone. He said he wouldn't leave and yet I can't feel him."

Dalton's steps faltered as the feminine voice caressed his soul. He felt her presence all the way to his marrow, and for the first time since his parent's death he didn't feel empty. He phased back into his human form as his knees crashed into the hard ground. Rocks and dirt bit into his bare skin but he ignored it. His mind was too focused on the fact that he could feel his true mate. He could sense everything about her. He knew she had a headache. He could feel her heart racing as she struggled with her need to be close to him.

"Jewel," he whispered hoping not to frighten her.

There was a pause and then her voice was back. *"Dalton?"*

"Yes. You know who I am?"

"Where'd you go?" she asked, ignoring his own question.

"I needed to stretch my legs," he told her. Not wanting to admit that he was nearly clawing the walls like a deranged cat waiting to see if their bond would open. *"How do you feel?"*

"A little confused and a lot scared, and oddly enough what stands out above those two emotions is frustration."

"I'm on my way back."

"Good," was all she said in response.

Dalton stood and took off at a dead run, once again phasing into his wolf. He felt a howl rising in his throat as his wolf raged to get back to her. Dalton knew he was going to have to get control of himself before he entered her room or the combination of her scent and their bond being open would push him over the edge to claim her.

When he reached her window he half expected to see her sitting up on the side of her bed. Her voice in his mind was so full of life that he had nearly forgotten that she was still unconscious. But as he peered in, simultaneously, throwing on the clothes Peri had no doubt left for him—the shirt was pink and the sweat pants were an awful teal color—he saw that she was lying just as still as ever.

Dalton pushed the window open and climbed silently through. Her pear scent washed over him and his wolf purred in satisfaction. *Ours*, he thought and Dalton agreed, *yes she is ours.*

"Dalton?"

His eyes snapped to her face at the sound of her voice in his mind. Her flawless skin called out to him. He wanted to touch her, to feel how soft she looked, and to let her warmth seep into the cold places inside of him.

"I'm here," he told her as he pulled his usual chair up next to her bed. *"I keep expecting you to suddenly sit up and open your eyes,"* he admitted.

"I don't know if that will ever happen." The doubt in her voice had his insides twisting. He felt helpless, unable to take care of his mate, to give her what she needed. *"How long have I been this way?"*

"Over two months now."

"You have been with me the whole time." It wasn't a question.

"Not the whole time." Dalton felt the guilt of his unwillingness to claim her knocking on the door of his conscious not for the first time.

"What does it mean that I am your true mate?" Jewel asked him. *"Sally has been talking about it but I want to hear it from you."*

He drew in a deep breath and took one of her hands and entwined their fingers. It still baffled him that he longed for her touch. He craved it like a starving man craved a morsel of food and his wolf would not be denied.

"I am a Canis lupis, a grey wolf."

"A werewolf?"

"Yes. I, along with others in my species, was created by the Great Luna." Dalton explained how the Great Luna decided to join the spirit of man and wolf together to create their race. He told her of how important family was to their Creator and how she had preordained each of them to have a true mate. *"You are the light to my darkness,"* he told her gently. *"I have lived over three centuries and never found any who complete me the way you do, and I could live for three thousand centuries and still never find another such as you. Jewel Stone, you were created for me, and I was created for you."*

"You have no choice in the matter?" she asked.

"Who is the clay to question the potter?"

"But you did question," she challenged him.

Dalton couldn't help the small smile that played on his lips. Jewel was right; he had questioned the Great Luna. He had wondered why she would give him a mate at all, especially one so innocent.

"Can you blame me?" he asked her.

Jewel could feel the heat from Dalton's hand in hers and wished that she could command her own hand to flex and grab onto him so that he could feel how badly she wanted him to never question his

Creator again. She wanted him to understand that he had value and that his past did not dictate his worth. Though she had only known Dalton a short time and in that short time their conversations had all been one-sided, something deep inside of her knew that he was hers. It felt so primitive and animalistic and yet it also felt completely natural.

"Do you feel like I belong to you—like I am yours?" she finally asked him after several moments of silence.

"Yes, but I do not expect you to understand that since you are human."

"Do you want me to be yours?" She needed to know if he truly wanted her or was he just accepting his fate?

She heard him chuckle and when he spoke, it was out loud. "I didn't think that I would ever want a true mate. Not after…," he paused.

"Gwen," she finished for him.

"Yes." His whispered word in her mind was painful even for her. "You heard everything didn't you?" He asked her and she knew he was referring to all of the horrific things he had endured and done.

"Yes."

This time he spoke to her mind. *"As you can imagine, my past has left deep scars on me. I didn't know if I would ever be able to truly move on."*

"And now?"

"I still don't know."

They were both quiet for a time after that. Jewel simply took comfort in the feel of his hand in hers and the presence of him in her mind. Having this bond or whatever it was between them helped her to not feel so alone.

"You will never be alone again," his voice broke through her thoughts.

"Do you hear all my thoughts?"

"Yes, but I will try to give you your privacy. It's just hard because the only way for me to know if you are okay is to stay in your mind."

"It should bother me, but I'm so tired of being all alone in here," she confided. Jewel felt his hand tighten and then felt his lips on her forehead. *"I've never been kissed before,"* she admitted as she felt herself drifting off to sleep. Though she had slept off and on, this was the first time she hadn't minded.

Dalton knew it was foolish to feel so relieved over the fact that his true mate, who was in a coma-like state because of the violence committed against her, had just admitted that no other male had ever kissed her. The wolf in him wanted to howl his victory into the night, but he settled for simply smiling at his now sleeping mate. He had felt how tired she was, and though all he wanted to do was talk to her, to hear her voice in his mind, he was also driven to care for her needs and what she needed then was rest.

The door opened behind him but he didn't bother to turn. His Alpha's scent filled the room before his voice did.

"Based on the fact that you aren't pacing like a caged animal, I take it to mean that the bond opened?" Dillon asked as he stepped up on the opposite side of Jewel's bed.

"It did," Dalton confirmed.

"How did she respond?"

For a moment the question threw him because he hadn't considered the fact that Jewel hadn't been freaking out over being able to speak to each other through their minds. Most humans would have found that more than a little odd. But then, Jewel was no longer just human. She had recently found out she was of gypsy healer decent, werewolves existed, and a dark sorcerer was determined to drain all of the blood from her body. So maybe speaking mind to mind with a male who claimed to be her mate wasn't exactly shocking.

"She didn't act like it was anything out of the ordinary," Dalton told him.

"It might be a relief to her," Dillon said as he looked down at her.

"What do you mean?"

"She's been laying there for two months only able to communicate with herself and even that is limited. I imagine she can tell her hands to move all day long, and yet still they lay there limp and useless. So now having you to talk to, it's probably quite comforting."

He hadn't considered that. How horrible it must feel to be trapped inside your own mind. She can think and can reason, and yet she can't get her own body to obey her. His wolf would probably be driven mad if they were in such a state.

"Sally wants to talk to you," Dillon said interrupting his thoughts.

"I'm not stopping her from coming in," he told his Alpha, though he still didn't take his eyes off of Jewel.

"She doesn't want to disturb Jewel's rest." Dalton's head snapped up at his Alpha's words. What he knew Dillon was really saying was that Sally didn't want to talk within Jewel's hearing. He gave a curt nod and then leaned over Jewel placing another soft kiss to her hair.

"I will stay with her," Dillon told him. "She will be safe."

Dalton nodded as he met his Alpha's eyes briefly before he turned and left the room. He found Sally in the living room of Peri's home. It was the first time he had left Jewel's room using something other than the window since he first arrived. He appreciated the fact that none of the other wolves were around. He wished that he had more control, but the fact was that until Jewel bore his mark his control would be sorely lacking.

"Dillon said you wanted to speak to me." He took a seat across from the healer just as Costin came in and sat down next to his mate. Dalton gave Costin a brief nod but then focused back on Sally.

"So, you are true mates?" she asked with a small smile. It was the first time she had smiled at him.

"We are," he answered.

"Not to rush things, but have you been able to look into her mind and maybe get an idea as to why she won't pull back away from the oblivion she seems hell bent on slipping into?"

Dalton shook his head. "I didn't really get that far. We talked briefly and then she fell asleep. She is tired."

"I would imagine so. Finding out that you are true mates with a werewolf and that you each have open access to each other's minds can be quiet overwhelming," Sally said as she leaned into Costin. He wrapped an arm around his mate and pressed a kiss to her neck, right where his mark was. Dalton felt a twinge of jealousy. He wanted Jewel to have *his* mark, wanted her to bear the evidence that she was taken, branded on her. The need was so strong that Dalton had to force himself to remain seated.

"She took all of the information rather well," Dalton told her.

Sally nodded. "I'm happy for you, Dalton."

His brow rose as he met Sally's brown eyes. "Really?"

She rolled her eyes at him. "Just because I was pissed at you for being a stubborn, flea infested fur ball doesn't mean I don't want the best for you. I'm a healer. Even when I may not like it very much, caring for the wolves is my job, and that includes you."

"Thank you." He paused. "I think."

She laughed as she stood up pulling her mate with her. "You men of few words are so weird. I know you need to be gentle with Jewel. Her mind is fragile whether she realizes it or not, but I need you to see if you can find out why she is resisting or why her soul is resisting. I keep trying to draw her back but she keeps just enough space between us that I can't bring her back to consciousness."

"I had hoped that the bond opening would be enough," Dalton told her, but his eyes met Costin's.

"The need to be everything for your mate can be overwhelming," Costin said, obviously having understood Dalton's frustration. "You will have to come to terms with the fact that you will not always be enough."

With that they left him sitting in the empty living room surrounded by every male Canis lupis's nightmare—to not be enough for his female, to not be able to fix her.

7

**"The greatest power evil has over the world
is the silly notion that evil can only go where
it is invited. That is like saying a termite has
to be invited to devour the wood of your
home when really all that is necessary to
let him in is a tiny opening." ~ Volcan**

The power that flooded his blood was all the confirmation Volcan needed to know that his plan had worked. Jewel Stone was his. The bond that existed between true mates was open, and that meant that he too had access to her. He had been patient and once again that patience had paid off.

"We will be together soon, Jewel, or should I call you Little Dove?" Volcan closed his eyes and pushed his essence into the bond, seeking out the depths of the healer's mind. She was strong, powerful, but she was also human which meant she would be easily manipulated by her emotions. All he had to do was find a weakness, one area to exploit, and she would be his.

—

Peri tried to keep a straight face. She knew that she needed to be the mature one, the diplomatic one. But when she flashed into the pixie realm to find Heather bent forward with her shirt unbuttoned, holding it so that nothing could be seen, she just lost it. The others around her—Adam, Elle, Crina, even Sorin—were laughing so hard she was sure at any moment she was going to see pee flowing down their legs.

"What is she doing?" Peri leaned in close to Anna who was wiping her eyes.

"Oh crap! Peri, you scared me." Anna jumped as she turned to look at her.

"You're watching a blind chick bend over the ground with her shirt held open while she mutters, *'Where is that blasted button?'* And *I'm* what scares you?"

This only brought another round of laughter from the human girl. Peri crossed her arms as she waited for the healer to gain her composure and then raised a brow at her as if to say *I'm waiting.*

"The pixies think that one of Heather's lovers had a spell cast on her to take her eyes," she finally told her.

Peri's eyes narrowed as she looked from Anna to the blind woman in question and then back to Anna. After several more moments a wide smile spread across her face. She remembered what Elle had told her had happened to the king's brother, and it dawned on her why the pixies would have drawn this conclusion with Heather.

"And where did they think her lover has put her eyes?" Peri asked.

Anna was biting her lips so hard that Peri was sure at any moment there would be a hole where part of her lip should be. "In her chest," she finally busted out and into a fit of giggles.

Peri felt a nudge from her other side and turned away from the giggling Anna. Elle was standing there with a wide, Cheshire cat grin. "Tell me that isn't hilarious?" she said and nodded toward Heather.

"So I take it all these pixies watching seem to think Heather is looking for her button with her breasts?"

Elle snorted and nodded. "Oh come on, you know it's a riot."

"What would be hilarious is if Heather suddenly stood up and directed her chest at one of those male pixies over there and covered up one breast and said this is me winking at you." Peri had to steady herself as Elle leaned on her grabbing her stomach as she laughed. So maybe she should have been a bit more mature in handling it, but then a blind chick acting like she was using her breasts as her eyes was pretty freaking hilarious.

Peri shook her head at the group and grabbed Elle's hand and flashed them to a different, quieter section of the realm. When Elle finally collected herself she stood up straight and let out a long breath. "So, any news?"

Peri chuckled. "Aside from the fact that we have a healer with winking breasts?"

"Nope, that is exactly the news I was talking about. There can't possibly be anything more important than a blind gypsy healer who can see using her excreters."

"Her what?" Peri choked, trying to swallow at the same time she spoke.

"Apparently, that is what the pixie call the female chest."

"Okay, well, just when you think you've heard it all," Peri said shaking her head. "The only news I have for you is that it's official, Dalton and Jewel are true mates."

"She's awake?" Elle's eyes widened.

"Unfortunately not, but Dalton has confirmed that their bond has opened. Jewel turned eighteen today."

"Well that's a good thing, right?"

Peri shrugged. "It's a thing, good or not is left to be seen. I still think that Volcan has an ace up his sleeve that I've somehow missed."

Elle's brow narrowed. "You think it has something to do with the mate bond between Dalton and Jewel?"

"I have no idea. I don't see how it could because regardless of how brilliant that psycho is, he couldn't have predicted that Jewel would be Dalton's mate."

"You'll figure it out," Elle encouraged. "You always do."

"Yes, well, while I'm off saving the world, you and the three burritos be sure and entertain the pixies for me."

"Speaking of the healers—and it's the three *amigos* by the way—they have been feeling the pull of the bond and it's getting stronger. They don't complain about it, but I catch each of them at different times cringing or looking off longingly towards the direction of the veil. Should we be concerned?"

"It's not going to kill them if that's what you're worried about. But I can't promise that it won't get worse before it gets better."

"When will it get better?" Elle asked.

"Well, let's see, they're in pain now because they're separated from their true mates, and later they will be in pain because their true mates are possessive, domineering, arrogant butt heads." She tapped her cheek thoughtfully. "So never I guess."

"Has anyone ever told you that you are just a ball full of warm fuzzies?" Elle asked sarcastically. "And you can't fool me, old friend, I know how you really feel about your mate."

"It is not my job to go around making everyone feel like their crap doesn't stink or that world peace is actually a possibility. It's my job to keep everyone alive. And how I feel about my mate doesn't change the fact that male werewolves might be better off as rugs in our homes. I'm just saying." Peri winked at the warrior. "But yes, I adore him. Tell anyone that and no one will ever find your body."

"Warm fuzzies, Perizada, warm fuzzies," Elle laughed as the high fae flashed.

—

Jewel could feel him. She didn't know how she knew it was him, other than the warmth and wholeness that flooded her from his nearness.

"It seems like forever since I last saw you," Dalton's voice penetrated the deep slumber she had fallen into.

"It can't have been that long," she told him and was shocked to see that in her mind's eye he was there standing before her. *"Is this a dream?"*

He chuckled and the sound sent ripples of pleasure down every nerve ending in her body. "That was a new feeling," she thought. It was something she had read about in her many romance novels, but not anything she had experienced firsthand—until now.

"You know it is not. We are talking through our bond."

"But how can I see you. It's as if you are really here before me, like I could just reach out and touch you."

"Why don't you?" His sultry voice dropped an octave and Jewel was pretty sure she had just swooned for the first time.

"How?"

"Our mental bond can be used for much *more than just words,"* he told her.

Jewel was pretty sure that if she could blush while in a coma, then she had done just that. The implication of his words was loud and clear.

He took a step closer to her and another until he was standing less than three feet away. He was huge, at least a foot taller than her five-foot-four inches. She had to tilt her head back to look up at his ruggedly handsome face. It was the first time she was seeing him, and she couldn't understand how one such as him could have picked her. He had dark brown hair that was messy in all the right ways. His cool, pale blue eyes seemed to see straight into her soul, and she felt more vulnerable than if she were naked before him. His strong jaw and high cheekbones were too hard to be considered beautiful; he was masculine in every sense of the word. He seemed so capable as he stood there with his shoulders back and his muscles bulging in his dark shirt and jeans. He was everything she never thought she could have, not her, with the strawberry locks that she kept short, just below her ears framing her face.

She was just plain Jewel, nothing nearly as glamorous as her name, and yet the male before her claimed to be hers. She was pretty sure that it must all be something she had concocted in her comatose state. Her reality would never be one so full of excitement and well, truth be told, utter sexiness.

"*You find me to be sexy?*" he asked her as his head tilted ever so slightly to the side. His lips quirked up in a crooked smile, and she was pretty sure that if she never tasted those lips she would die of disappointment.

"*Interesting,*" he murmured.

"*I thought you were going to try and give me some privacy,*" she scolded.

"Yes, well that was before I realized how fascinating your thoughts would be."

"Are you shameless?"

He laughed. *"When it comes to you, apparently, yes I am."*

Well, she thought, what was she supposed to say to that?

"I want to touch you," he told her and again she was taken aback by his forwardness. The need in his eyes was completely unmasked, and she wondered at his ability to be so open with her. Wasn't he afraid of rejection?

"You need me just as much as I need you; why should I be worried you will reject me?" He held his hand out to her and it took all of her limited self-control not to throw herself in his huge arms.

Jewel placed her much smaller hand in his and let him draw her closer until there was no space between their bodies. She could feel every hard muscle against her softer form, and her heartbeat began to become erratic. She was actually afraid she might pass out. She didn't even know if that was possible, but whatever altered conscious state this was, it was real—very, very real.

"Relax," he purred into her ear. His warm breath caressed her neck and she felt her eyes drifting closed as a soft moan escaped her lips. How appalling, she thought. She didn't want to come across as some loose floosy. But then if he kept pressing his lips to her neck like he was currently doing, she just might climb up him and plaster herself to him.

"How am I supposed to relax with you doing that?" she asked through breathless pants.

"Jewel?" Dalton's voice suddenly seemed stronger, less sexy, and very full of concern.

She opened her eyes and was surprised to see confusion and shock in his face as he held her tighter to him.

"Did you say my name?"

"It's time for me to go; I'll be back, Little Dove." And just like that his physical form vanished. But she could still feel his warmth, just as she had so many times as he stood vigil by her bedside.

"Are you alright, love?" Now his voice was out loud instead of just in her mind, and she wondered how he could sound so different from one breath to the next.

"I'm fine," she told him, attempting to bring her quivering voice under control. She was completely embarrassed at her response to him. If this was how she responded to his mental presence, what would she be like when she was finally awake again and standing before his Adonis form?

"Sally wanted me to talk with you about why—,"

"Why I can't seem to wake up?" she finished for him. She didn't want to sound defensive but she knew she did. *"I don't know. The logical part of my brain knows that the suffering, the pain, is over. But...."*

"But there is a part of your brain that doesn't want to let go of what happened, and because of that it's just safer to stay where the pain can't reach you."

"How can you know that?"

"Direct access, love," he reminded her.

"Okay, that might get a little more than annoying."

"You have the same access to me."

Jewel had already considered that, but there was a part of her that totally understood the whole *can't unsee* concept. She was afraid that she would hear or see something in his mind that she would never be able to unhear or unsee. Jewel was a sponge when it came to information, and she knew that once it was in her mind it was there for good.

"I will never hide anything from you, Jewel," Dalton told her, speaking out loud again. "I am who I am and I'm not proud of the things I've done. I can't change the past; all I can do is strive to be different. I wish that there weren't things in my past that will hurt you, but they are there, and sooner or later you will have to face them."

She knew that, she just preferred that it be later rather than sooner. *"I know that you can't change your past, Dalton, and I don't expect you to. I just want to make sure that I'm really ready to know, you know what I mean? It's one thing for a person to tell you something, it's a whole different thing for me to experience it through your memories."*

He was quiet for a few moments and she wondered if she had hurt him. That was the last thing she wanted. The idea of hurting him was abhorrent to her.

"You didn't hurt my feelings, Jewel." He sounded amused, as if she didn't have the ability to hurt him.

"That's not what I'm saying either. You above all else have the ability to destroy me."

"Gee, Casanova, you really know how to make a girl feel special."

Dalton couldn't put his finger on it, but something about Jewel was off. When he had returned from talking with Sally, he had noticed that her skin was flushed and her heart rate was sporadic. Although those two things in and of themselves peeked his interest, what really stirred his wolf was his mate's scent. It had changed, albeit subtly. He had forced himself to stop and take several deep breaths to be sure, but on the third breath he was sure he was scenting her pheromones. His little dove was turned on. He couldn't imagine what on earth had her in such a state, and when he had tried to enter her mind, he had found himself unable to get in. He didn't want to alarm her so he had tried to sound calm, and when she didn't elaborate or offer up any information on what had happened, if anything, he hadn't wanted to push her.

As interesting as this mystery was, he knew what was really important was finding out why she wasn't waking up. He wanted to complete the Blood Rites. He had a feeling that would bring her back, but then he didn't want to push something so incredible permanent on her, especially when she barely knew him.

"What if I never wake up?" she asked him after several minutes of silence.

"I won't let that happen. I have too many plans for you," he teased. He felt her embarrassment, but he also felt the beginning of interest.

"Do you have any suggestions for me to try?"

Dalton hesitated before he answered. He didn't know how she would respond to the answer he was about to give her, but he figured it was worth a try. *"I haven't given you any of my blood in a while."*

"That was really your blood?" Her voice rose in his mind and for the first time since all of this began he felt fear in her. *"Is that hygienic?"*

"Werewolves don't carry diseases if that is what you are worried about."

"Why did it taste good? I mean, that's not normal."

"A lot of things that humans find weird are perfectly normal for werewolves."

He imagined if she could she would shrug as she murmured in his mind. *"Good point."*

"We're true mates; that means everything about the other one appeals to us. Our scent, our taste, and our touch are all hypersensitive between us."

"So you think that if you give me your blood, it will help me come back?"

"I think the pull that we have for one another is going to help, and when we exchange blood it makes our bond that much stronger," he explained. He almost felt guilty for the nearly euphoric feeling that was building in the deepest part of his soul at the thought of sharing something so personal with her. He wanted her blood, but he needed her to understand the severity of the consequences before he took it. He

didn't know if she was listening to him or just sub-consciously picking up on his thoughts, but her next question was right up his line of thinking.

"Have you had my blood?"

"No." He felt the sting in his words on her feelings and felt like an ass for being so short with her.

"You don't want it?"

She couldn't possibly understand how her question would affect him, and so he forced himself to swallow the growl that rose in his chest. *"I want your blood more than anything. To be able to have such a claim on you, to have your scent running through my veins so that every wolf who comes near me will know that I belong to you and you belong to me, is intoxicating. I want to know what you taste like and to know that I am the only male that will ever have that privilege nearly drives me to my knees. But there are consequences to me taking your blood since you have already had my blood."*

"What consequences? Will I become a werewolf?"

Dalton smiled. If Jewel were a wolf her coat would probably have a red tint to it; she would be lovely. *"No, Little Dove, werewolves are born, not made. There is a ceremony that is performed between true mates called the Blood Rites. One of the ways true mates lay claim to one another is through marking each other with their bite. I will bite your neck and leave my mark on you and take your blood into my body. You will then bite me, though your mark will not remain visible. You will also take my blood into your body, as you already have, and my scent will be in you forever. No wolf will ever be near you and not know that you are mine."*

"Why doesn't my bite stay on you?"

"There is another way that mates lay claim to one another; we gain markings. The males of our species have tattoo like markings on their body indicating their rank and place in the pack. When we find our true mate, those markings change. My markings have changed. They now climb up my neck and down my right arm. You too will have markings that match mine somewhere on your body." Dalton was tempted to look for those markings, but he would have to be patient and wait for her to wake until he could see them. *"The other important detail is once the Blood Rites are complete, our fates are tied to one another. If you die, I will follow and if I die,"* he paused hating to think of a world without Jewel in it, *"you will follow."*

"Wow, you guys really take this claiming stuff seriously."

"We might be a little on the possessive side, and as I've expressed to you before, I might be a tad more on the extreme side because of my history."

"Some of the books I read have males like you in them. I never thought men like that really existed," she confessed to him.

"Are you glad that you have one such as that to call your own?" he asked her, not sure if he really wanted to know her answer.

"Will you ever break my heart?"

"I would sooner rip my own heart from my chest," he told her truthfully.

"I honestly can't believe that I can call you mine. You are way out of my league."

Dalton didn't like that she didn't think she was worthy of him. The truth was she was worth far beyond him or what he could give her. But he was selfish and not willing to give her up. *"You're wrong there, Little Dove. It is you who are out of my league. But I'm afraid you are stuck with me."*

"I suppose I will just have to make do," she teased him.

Dalton sat down on the side of her bed and leaned over her, pressing a kiss to her forehead. *"I suppose you will,"* he whispered through their bond. Then he bit into his wrist and held it to her lips. *"Drink please, Jewel. Drink and come back to me."* Her lips wrapped around his arm, and he bit down on the inside of his cheek to keep from moaning like an idiot. He didn't want to scare her with the intensity of his desire for her so he tried to block his emotions from her as she drank from him. He could feel her soul drawing closer to his, filling him, and beckoning his own to her. It was intimate as hell, and he found that he could become addicted to the feeling—to her.

"I should be totally grossed out by this; I know that and yet I feel like a druggy hoping for my next fix." Her voice was breathless even in his mind, and he couldn't wait to hear it sound like that out loud. He felt the rush of the act flowing through her, and then suddenly she was exhausted. It poured over him and he felt himself slumping forward having to catch himself so that he didn't lie down on top of her.

"Sleep love, I will be here when you wake," he told her gently.

"Will you come visit me again, like you did before?"

Dalton was caught off guard by her question, and it took him several moments to answer. By the time he asked her what she meant, Jewel was already sound asleep. What had she been talking about when she said come visit like he did before? Maybe she had dreamt of him and she thought it was real. He wasn't sure, but as badly as he himself needed rest, he needed to know what she was talking about. He closed his eyes and slipped into her mind. He was prepared to wait to see if perhaps his answers would come through her memories or dreams. Part of him felt like he was invading her privacy, but at the same time he was driven to keep her safe no matter what—even at the expense of her personal space.

Dalton sifted through her memories and felt himself growing sad as he realized just how much of her time in her short life had been spent alone. She was every bit as scarred as he was, just in different ways for different reasons. Perhaps the Great Luna did know what she was doing when she destined them to be true mates. He wanted to replace all of those lonely memories with new ones filled with love and acceptance. There was nothing more that he wanted than for his mate to feel as precious as he knew her to be. He didn't have a clue how to be what she needed, but he would figure it out; no other outcome was acceptable.

—

Dalton didn't know how much time passed before he found the memory. He was standing with her in what appeared to be the dark forest and he was holding his hand out to her. This was obviously a dream of some sort; he'd only spoken to her by her bedside. She seemed hesitant at first, but once she took his hand she suddenly surrendered herself to him. His shoulders tensed as he watched himself kiss her neck. Why was he becoming jealous of her dream? Perhaps, she had unknowingly plucked a picture of his appearance from his own mind and then dreamt of him. Since that was probably the answer, why on earth did he want to rip his dream self off of Jewel and beat himself to a bloody pulp? Suddenly he, the Dalton in her dream, looked up at him. He and the dream Dalton locked eyes and a wicked smile spread across the apparition's face. And just before the real Dalton was pushed from her mind, he saw one of the black eyes of his dream self wink at him.

"What the hell?" he growled as he shook his head. He rubbed a hand across his forehead and down his face as he tried to calm his churning insides. Something wasn't right. The Dalton in Jewel's dream wasn't him. It couldn't have been. Because if she had taken an image of him from his mind, then she would have dreamt of him with pale blue eyes, not black obsidian ones. As he stared down at his mate's sleeping form, he could smell his blood in her as it flowed through her veins. It somewhat calmed him and his wolf after having watched another man, though appearing like him in every way save the eyes, paw and kiss on their mate.

"Why do you look like someone just snuck tapeworms into your spaghetti bowl?" Peri's sharp tone pierced the quiet room. He had gotten used to her sudden appearances and didn't jump at her intrusion. Rather he became mildly annoyed at her willingness to sneak up on an unpredictable beast.

He could retort at her descriptive and disturbing question, but he didn't make a habit of engaging others in meaningless conversation. Instead he simply answered the real question she was asking, what was wrong?

"Something isn't right with Jewel."

"You're a little slow on the uptake if you are just now figuring that out."

He ignored her sarcasm because ultimately he knew that Peri cared, no matter how flippant she sounded. "I just saw myself in her mind's eye, but she should not have known what I looked like," he explained. He didn't go into the details of how intimate the encounter had been. That was not for Perizada to know and he would never want to make Jewel feel as though he had revealed private matters about them.

Dalton looked up to see Peri walking towards the window staring out into the forest. She was beautiful and young looking despite her age, but in that moment as the moon's glow illuminated her face, he saw how tired the high fae truly was. The burden of being one so powerful could not be an easy load, and he found that he was glad that the Great Luna had seen fit to give Peri a mate. Lucian was a formidable male; he would be able to bear anything that his female could not on her own.

"Did she say it was a dream?" Peri finally spoke.

"No, she thought that it was me coming to her through the bond. It wasn't."

Peri nodded as her eyes narrowed. "That clever, clever son of a fairy," she growled.

Dalton watched in surprise as the space around the fae began to pulse with a soft light and her form seemed to grow. As she turned to face him, he saw the power that she kept so dutifully caged as it unfurled before him. He didn't fear her, but he could understand how others would.

"Perizada," Lucian's deep voice rumbled from the doorway.

"I thought he was trying to figure out his next move," her voice shook with indignation. "I thought we had thrown him off his proverbial game. I couldn't have been more wrong." Her eyes shifted to Jewel's sleeping form. "He was just laying low, biding his time until he had way to access what he wants—what he needs."

"What are you talking about?" Dalton stood up slowly, his protective instincts firing on all cylinders.

"Some powerful beings can use a mate bond, Dalton, especially in one who has no clue how to protect it." Peri's words crashed into his chest like a battering ram.

He looked down at his female and then back up at Peri who was still glowing. "Volcan." His voice sounded dark even to himself. "He's using our bond?"

"You have to shut it down." Her voice was hard as steel as she met his eyes, and even with his wolf peering out of them, she didn't back down.

"It's not a damn machine, I can't just shut it down."

"Then it has to be broken."

"No. I just got her." Dalton took a step towards Peri just as Lucian stepped in front of his mate.

"Then you will lose her." Lucian's voice was cool as he looked from Jewel to Dalton. "If he has access to her mind through your mate bond, then he has access to her soul and to her power. He will use her against us."

Dalton felt as if every ounce of air had been shoved from his lungs as Lucian's words sunk in. What they were asking of him went against every instinct he had. He understood their reasoning, but something felt wrong. Something inside of him was telling him not to allow their bond to be broken. He didn't even know if anyone other than the Great Luna could do such a thing, and he knew there was no way he could ever get those words to leave his mouth in order to ask her to do it. His eyes dropped to Jewel. *Ours*, his wolf rumbled in his mind. *Yes*, he agreed. *We will protect her. We will not let the sorcerer touch her.* His wolf was so certain, so sure of his ability to take care of their mate. *I will not allow the bond to be taken from us.* He was surprised to hear the complete confidence in his beast's words and Dalton believed him. The control that his wolf seemed to have over them both was powerful, and he knew that he would fight him with everything in him if Dalton pursued having the bond between he and Jewel severed.

"Dalton, did you hear us?" Peri's voice drew his attention away from his wolf.

"I will not let the bond be severed. Jewel is mine, she stays with me, connected to me."

The light faded from around the fae, and the weariness that Dalton had seen in her only moments ago returned. Peri placed her hand on her mate's arm as her weary eyes met Dalton's. She flashed them from the room, her final words trailing behind her. "Then you doom us all."

8

"He's coming for me. I can feel him even before I see him. There is a darkness in him. I can feel it. Something inside me knows that I should be afraid, that I should run from him. But then he touches me and I'm lost. Nothing matters but him. I want nothing more than to make him happy, to give him everything that he wants. But as I look in his black eyes I know deep down that it's not enough; I am not enough." ~Jewel

"You came back." Jewel soft voice filled the small room. She looked around and saw that she was in some sort of study. The walls were lined with books and on the far wall was a hearth with a warm fire glowing in its bowels.

"I will always come for you," Dalton told her as he took a step towards her.

"Where are we?"

Dalton looked around the room and then back to her. A warm smile stretched across his sensual lips. "A room I designed for you. You like books, like to escape into them?"

Jewel nodded and felt the heat of her blush on her face.

"This is one of the rooms in the home I built for us. I want you with me. You belong with me." His voice shook with the intensity of his emotions.

When Jewel looked up into his dark eyes, she expected to see desire, but what she saw had her taking a step back. In that moment, as their gaze held, she didn't see the man who had been coming to her night after night, speaking with her, pouring out his soul to her. No, what she saw was something dark and sinister and it wanted her.

"Do I scare you, Little Dove?" he asked her as his lips twitched up in a sardonic smile.

Jewel shook her head. "No."

"Then why do you back away from me?"

She turned her head, gazing around the room. "I simply wanted some space to explore the room you made for me." She kept him in her peripheral as she began to slowly make her way around the room. She knew it wasn't real and yet when she reached out a hand to touch the spines of the books on the shelves, she could feel the roughness. It seemed so very real and not just in her mind. As she pulled one of the books off the shelf and opened it, she lifted it to her nose and took in a deep breath. As the scent of the pages hit her, she realized just how powerful the mind truly was. The book felt tangible, and even smelled like dusty old pages, even as she told herself over and over that it wasn't.

"Do you like it?" His rich voice warmed her insides and she had to remind herself that this was not Dalton. His breath on her neck had those thoughts disintegrating, and when his lips touched her skin, she nearly dropped the book she held.

"It's lovely," Jewel whispered. She fought the urge to lean back into him, but she lost that battle as soon as his arms wrapped around her from behind and drew her into his strong body. She laid her head back against his chest and closed her eyes. The book slipped from her hands when his teeth grazed the tendon in her neck. Jewel gripped his hands that were pressed firmly against her stomach and bit her bottom lip so hard that she tasted blood. *Not real,* she told herself.

"Isn't it?" Dalton murmured in her ear. "I assure you we are both real, my love. Do I need to convince you?"

He released her and Jewel had to clamp her lips tight to keep the protest from leaping out. She didn't want him to stop touching her. Thankfully she got her wish when he turned her to face him and cupped her face gently in his large, warm hands. His tongue slipped out and moistened his lips, and she found herself leaning closer to him as she followed the motion. Dalton's warm chuckle at her obvious desire had her attempting to duck her head but his hands prevented her from moving.

"I'm glad that you want me," he told her gently as his thumb ran lightly across her bottom lip. "I want you and I'm not ashamed of that. I want to taste you,

Jewel." He leaned down closer to her mouth, and she could feel his breath on her as he continued to speak. "I want to explore every inch of your mouth, and when I'm done, I want to start all over again."

Jewel was speechless. No one had ever expressed such desire for her, and no one had ever sparked such longing inside of her. She was trying to think of reasons why she shouldn't let him kiss her, especially not as thoroughly as he just described. But as his fingers sank into her hair, and as he drew her lips to his, her mind went blank. His lips grazed her softly at first but then he let out a low growl and pressed them more firmly to hers. She needed to breathe and as she parted her lips to do just that, Dalton took advantage and his warm tongue swept into her mouth like a thief stealing any willpower she might have had left. She leaned into him, pressing her body shamelessly against his. His hands left her hair only to grab her hips, pulling her impossibly closer. Jewel was pretty sure he no longer just wanted a taste; he wanted the whole dang meal. She felt his tongue outlining her gums and then sweep across the roof of her mouth, and a shudder worked its way down her.

"Dalton," she breathed out as he nipped her bottom lip only to return full force, invading, claiming, and marking her mouth as his domain. She knew she needed to stop things because, regardless of whether this was happening only in her mind, she still wasn't ready to go further. As one of his hands trailed up from her hip along her rib cage, his thumb brushed lightly against the side of her breast until he was cupping her jaw and tilting her head to the side. Jewel was pretty sure she was going to pass out.

"You taste incredible," he breathed against her neck and then ran his tongue from her collar bone up to just below her ear.

"We should stop," she heard herself whisper breathlessly and even she heard the lack of conviction in her voice.

"Do you have somewhere else to be?" he teased.

She giggled nervously but it turned into a deep, husky moan as his teeth sank into her flesh. It wasn't hard enough to break the skin, but she knew it would leave a mark, or if it had been real it would have anyway.

"I won't take anything you don't want to give me, Jewel," Dalton told her as he released her skin. He licked the small wound and pressed a warm kiss there. "What will you give me, Little Dove?"

Jewel's head tilted back as Dalton's nose skimmed along her neck and down around her collarbone and lower still.

"I have nothing to give," she murmured. "I'm broken, lost in the safety of my mind. I'm not what you need. You deserve more." Jewel hadn't expected those words to leave her mouth. The thoughts had been slowly forming in her mind over the past few days as Dalton sat with her and talked to her. How could she be any sort of mate, or whatever, to him? He was strong, a powerful being made by a Creator who had plans for him, and she was a teenage human who had been sucked dry, literally, by a dark fae. He had his own wounds and she was in no place to help him deal with those things. He needed a healthy, strong woman who could help him bear the burdens he had carried for so long on his own. Jewel knew she would just be one more added burden that he didn't need.

"That's where you're wrong, Jewel Stone," he said in a much different tone than the sultry one he had been using. "You have so very much that I want and need. And I have what you need. I have seen the things you endured in your mind. I have seen how those humans treated you, shunned you, and left you alone. I can make you strong, Little Dove. I can make you powerful and knowledgeable about things you couldn't even imagine. You need me, love. Let me give you what you need. Let me have what I need."

Her eyes snapped open as she looked up at him, and for an instant it wasn't Dalton standing there holding her. The black eyes that stared back at her held no affection for her. His pale skin was stretched too thin across his bones, and the sharp angles in his cheek bones just accentuated his emaciation. His lips had a bluish hue to them and were no longer plump and full but rather thin and severe. She blinked and the disturbing male was gone and Dalton was once again looking down at her. Jewel tried to control her reaction as her brain raced to catch up to what her eyes had just seen. Suddenly she knew that it was imperative that she wake up. Maybe she couldn't regain consciousness, but she could get out of the sleep induced state.

"WAKE UP, JEWEL!" she screamed inside of her head. She squeezed her eyes closed and mentally cried out to her Dalton. *"DALTON! Please hear me.*

Dalton stared down in shock as he watched a red mark appear on the side of Jewel's neck. As he leaned closer he saw the outline of teeth.

"Bloody hell!" he snarled under his breath. What was going on? What madness had invaded the darkness his sweet Jewel was already enduring?

"Jewel, wake up, Little Dove. It's not me; please hear me, whoever you are with, it's not me." He reached into their bond searching for her, and just like before it was blank, as if a cord connected to him stretched out into the darkness forever. She was just gone.

"DAMMIT!" His hand came down hard on the side table causing the wood to split under the force of his anger. He felt helpless. What kind of mate was he if he couldn't protect his female? How on earth would she ever trust him, rely on him, if he couldn't take care of her? His wolf paced restlessly inside of him. He wanted the flesh of Volcan between his teeth. He wanted to hear his cries as man and wolf tore tendon and muscle from bone until all the life left his evil body.

Dalton's head whipped around when he heard Jewel whimper. He was at her side in a single stride, cupping her cheeks in his hands. Her skin was flushed and her lips trembled. He had no idea what she was going through, no idea what Volcan was doing to her. All he could do was stand there like a helpless human and watch as his mate was invaded, violated by a mad man. *Great Luna, hear me, please bring her back. I can't lose her, not when I've just found her.*

"DALTON! Please hear me." Her voice flooded his mind as he felt the bond snap back into place. His heart pounded painfully in his chest as her emotions crashed into him. He sensed fear mixed with curiosity and, of all things, lust. *Dammit all,* he thought, *why on earth did he feel lust pouring off of his mate when he hadn't been the one touching her?* He forced himself to ignore his heated jealousy and listen to her as she rapidly poured information into his mind.

"Dalton, it's Volcan. At first I thought it was you. He made me think it was you. Oh my, the things we...and what I told you...and where you...holy crap, it wasn't you; if I could be sick right now, I would be puking," Jewel admitted.

Her voice shook and even in his mind her fear came through loud and clear. He now understood why she had been so shy with him; she had been talking with him, or so she thought. She had been using the bond to feel and smell and taste him, but it wasn't him. The thought made him want to puke as well. The thought of her sharing anything intimate, whether it be words or touch with another, enraged him to a new level. He had to tell himself and his wolf that it wasn't real and it wasn't her fault. He was in no way angry with Jewel, but when he got his claws on Volcan, there would be nothing recognizable left.

*"He's calling to me. Even now, he keeps telling me he wants me, that I'm his. "*she continued. *"He keeps telling me that he can make me strong and that I will never have to endure ridicule again. "*

Dalton wasn't surprised that the sorcerer had found a weakness in Jewel and was feeding it and tempting her with acceptance, power, and knowledge. All things that anyone who had gone through as much as Jewel had would find appealing.

"He's using the bond, Jewel. Somehow, when our bond opened, he was able to access it. You have to shut it down, " he urged her, though it was the last thing he wanted her to do. He still didn't feel like it was the right thing to do, but he didn't know how else to protect her, and he didn't want Volcan's hands on his mate, mentally or otherwise. Jewel was his and he wouldn't share her in any capacity, nor would he have her first experiences being tainted in such a vulgar way. *"I need you to listen to me. I'm going to teach you how to build a wall in your mind between you and me. You will need to make it high and strong so no one can get through. "*

"Wait, hold on. Maybe, I can help. You all don't know where he is? He got away, right?" She paused but quickly continued; her words only continued to stir his wrath. *"Maybe I can find him if I pretend to be accepting of his offers. Maybe he will lead us right to him. "*

Jewel had barely finished speaking when Dalton growled deep and with a deadly calm. *"NO. "*He said it not only through their bond but out loud in the room where his mate lie motionless. He had never been harsh with her, had never growled at her out of anger, but the idea of her putting herself in danger where he could not protect her, even her spirit, was enough to push him over the precarious edge he balanced on. *"You will not! He is powerful, Jewel. I do not know what he is able to do through the bond. I can't protect you from out here. Please, I know that in this modern time women do not obey their mates, but I am asking you to obey me in this."*

"It's not that we don't obey, Dalton," she began not even acknowledging what he had said. *"We've talked about submission and the beauty of it when it is done out of love and sacrifice."*

"Little Dove," Dalton cut her off.

"Yes?"

"Submit to me in this." It was a command, one that would have been obeyed immediately if given to any wolf other than an Alpha.

"I don't know if I agree with you on that being the best course of action—statistically speaking." Her voice began to take on that teaching quality that at any other time would have him grinning like an idiot because he truly was enamored with her love of learning. But not in that moment. *"The chances of you finding Volcan are nearly non-existent. From what I've overheard, you all don't even have a general direction to follow. But with me being able to talk to him, I increase the statistics by at least 30 or 40%. If we are going to be smart strategists then we must look at every available option."*

"Then consider me a dumb ass because you continuing to allow Volcan access to our bond is not an available option."

"Can we compromise?" she asked hopefully.

"No."

"Please?"

"Still no."

"What if—"

"Hell will freeze over, global warming will suddenly make sense, and the oompa loompas in that book Charlie and the crappy factory will be the governing body of the United States, which they will have renamed Loompa Land, before I agree to continue letting that evil prick use our bond to entice you to him."

"Well, those aren't very good odds." Her voice was as calm as his, but lacked the death threat that his was laced with.

"Glad we are on the same page."

"Dalton."

"Build the wall, Jewel, strong and high," he reminded. *"You are mine and I will not share any part of you, not even your thoughts."*

Dalton began to show her in her mind how to build the wall, but he got the distinct impression that she was just humoring him as she acted interested in what he was explaining.

Several hours—and many unladylike words by his mate—later, Jewel was able to build a formidable wall between them. In fact, Dalton was surprised at how well she was able to block him.

"I will still be here with you, and I'll talk to you even though I won't be able to hear you," he told her as he took her hand in his.

"I still think you should give my idea some consideration."

"I did consider it and just as quickly determined it not to be the best course of action," he said matter-of-fact like.

"Soooo," she drew the word out and he waited for her to say what she was already thinking. *"How long will I be here, stuck like this unable to communicate with you?"*

Dalton could hear the frustration in her voice and he couldn't blame her. He was frustrated too. But until he could figure out their next move, this was all he knew to do. *"I don't know, Little Dove, but I will do everything I can to bring you back."*

—

Kale cleared his throat as he and the other males processed what Peri had just told them. He still had mixed feelings regarding Dalton, but he would never wish ill on another wolf's mate. Dillon had spoken at length with him about his Beta's past, and Kale was beginning to see that he had been fooled by the female he had caught with Dalton. His mixed feelings no longer stemmed from the idea that he had done something with a woman against her will, but from the darkness that cloaked the Colorado Beta. Kale had a gift that not many knew about—something passed down to him through the magic of his Irish people. He could see the auras that surrounded people, and Dalton Black had the darkest one he had ever seen.

"Do we have a plan?" he asked Lucian and Peri.

He waited as Peri paced the room. She was as restless as a wolf needing to hunt. He found it interesting that Lucian was so calm. The beast lived inside of the man and yet his mate was the restless one.

"Dalton is working up something in his mind," Peri answered. "But I have a feeling that if we don't keep an eye on that wolf, he's going to attempt to handle this on his own. He was a lone wolf for a very long time."

"He won't do anything that will hinder him helping his mate," Lucian said in the same calm, even tone he always used.

Kale motioned to the other males in the room. "And what would ya have us to do then? Surely we aren't just going to continue to sit here and do nothin." He knew that his accent was coming on a little thick; it usually did when he was frustrated. It didn't help that the bond was getting stronger, and he was worried about the discomfort his mate must be in.

"I'm working on that Beta," Peri narrowed her eyes at him. "I realize patience isn't a strong suit of your race, but you are just going to have to figure out how to have some. In case you mutts hadn't noticed, I don't particularly like moving at a snail's pace either. That said, there is more on the line than just a healer's life, and therefore, we will move as fast or slow as need be."

"Can he truly turn the gypsy healer into a witch? Gustavo asked.

"After the year I've had Rico Suave, I wouldn't be surprised if he could turn *me* into a witch." Her head snapped around and her eyes bore into Costin's. Kale noticed the male was biting back a smile.

"Not a word, pretty boy," Peri growled at him. He held his hands up in surrender, though the smile was out in full force.

"Then we wait for your instructions," Drayden, Alpha of the Canada pack, spoke up. "We came to help, in whatever form that may take. If that happens to be waiting," he shrugged, "then we wait."

Peri looked around the room and then her eyes landed on Kale. "Why can't you all be more like him?" She pointed at the Canadian Alpha.

"He's Canadian," Banan, Kale's third frowned.

"And what, you don't like Canadian bacon? What did it ever do to you?" Peri rolled her eyes.

Drayden simply chuckled. Kale had noticed over their time together that for an Alpha, Drayden was extremely laid back and even tempered. It was almost like he was a walking contradiction.

"Fine," he finally said as he leaned back, the chair creaking under his mass. "We will wait. In the meantime, Sally," he addressed the brown eyed healer. "Why don't ya tell us about the other lasses?" Kale did not miss the way Gustavo and Ciro both leaned forward in their chairs. They had been as edgy as he had been, and he was beginning to suspect that perhaps they too were dealing with a mate bond. He looked back at Sally and watched her eyes widen as she turned to look at Peri. Kale had to bite back his smile as the other males stared her down. They had all been chomping at the bit to ask about the other healers, but there weren't many who would test the prickly fae.

Peri shrugged. "It's not like they're going to have some divine revelation on which one is their mate if you describe the girls. Just keep it to the minimum, you know what I mean." Sally nodded and then turned back to Kale. The apprehension was gone and he could tell from the genuine smile and sparkle in her eyes that Sally cared deeply for the other girls.

"Well, where to begin?"

"How about with the blind, seeing eye dog trainer?" Peri offered helpfully.

"The what?" "Excuse me?" "Blind?" Nick, Gustavo, and Banan all spoke at once.

"I thought you said to keep it to the minimum?" Sally said through gritted teeth.

The fae's eyes gleamed as a smile tugged on her beautiful face. "Well, how were you planning on describing her to the males? Were you going to say and then there's Heather, she likes long walks, reading with her fingers, and teaching her four legged eye balls to keep from walking their humans into oncoming traffic?"

"Lucian," Sally whined. "Please do something with her."

He stood and wrapped an arm around her waist while whispering something in her ear. Kale was surprised to see the outspoken fae blush. He chuckled inwardly as he watched Lucian lead his mate from the room. "It's always the quiet ones," he thought to himself.

Sally's soft voice drew his attention back.

"Okay," she said a little breathlessly. Her eyes widened and her lips stretched in a wide smile as she rubbed her hands together. "So, any questions so far?"

"Why do I have a feeling that these are not going to be like the healers from long ago?" Ciro, the Italy Alpha, asked not unkindly.

A nervous laugh bubbled out of Sally. "We have a saying in the South, '*raising kids is like being pecked to death by a chicken.*' "

Ciro tilted his head in a wolflike gesture. "Forgive me, but I do not understand the significance."

"You will if one of these healers turns out to be your mate. Just remove *raising kids* and replace it with *being mated to a gypsy healer of the twenty-first century.* I suggest you get your game faces on, gentlemen." Grinning from ear to ear Sally leaned back and winked at her mate who was laughing under his breath.

Just about that time Dalton came storming out of Jewel's room. His hair looked as though he had been running his hands through it repeatedly as it stood in disarray. The dark circles under his eyes was testament to the fact that he rarely slept, but kept constant vigil over his mate. He had at least five days' worth of stubble on his face, and Kale was pretty sure he was wearing the same clothes that he had been from at least three days prior. The males in the room stared at him wide eyed as he strode single-mindedly through the room to the front door. It was rare that he ever left through anything but the window. But even rarer was the fact that he was speaking.

The entire trek across the room he never once acknowledged that there was anyone around him. He simply muttered under his breath, with tense shoulders and hands fisted at his sides. "Damn obstinate, stubborn female will be the death of me."

The door closed with a finality that slammed the room into silence.

"See," Sally said breaking the hush, "Case in point. There is a male who found his mate, who happens to be a twenty-first century gypsy healer. Now, can you fur balls actually tell me that he didn't look like he'd been pecked to death?" Their faces paled as they looked back at the door and then back to Sally, who was laughing. "And just think his chicken isn't even conscious. She's successfully pulling off unconscious death pecking. It does not get any less like the healers of long ago I'm sure. I suggest you put on your big girl panties and put any notions of meek, quiet, passive females behind you. If you don't, you just might end up with a boot, voodoo doll, or stripper pole up your butts." Coughs of surprise went around the room as Costin gave up trying to hold himself together and belted out a laugh.

"Is that another Southern saying?" Kale asked her as a single brow rose.

She smiled and her voice returned to the sweet one they were all used to. "Something like that. Now, are you ready to hear more about the other healers?"

Suddenly all the males stood at once, Kale included. "Actually, I think we have some training left to do, donna we Banan?" he said as all the others nodded their heads in unison.

"Aye, that we do," Banan answered. "And I tink we also have some, uh, repairs on the, uh, stuff, for fighten in such to get done."

"Exactly," Drayden spoke up. "Repairs."

Sally's eyes narrowed. "Go on then. Run while you can."

Kale was the last one out of the room. As he closed the door behind him, he heard Costin speaking and he paused, leaving the door cracked just a bit.

"You enjoyed that way too much, Sally mine."

"No, I just want them to be prepared. You know as well as I do, Costin, these girls aren't the type of American girls that other cultures picture when they think of us. They picture picket fences, perfect little families with two point five kids, soccer moms with mini vans, and dads that play catch and attend backyard tea parties. Those males need to know that the females they will take as true mates are damaged goods. I don't say that to be cruel, but Costin some of them have true horrors in their pasts. I'm scared of how they will handle taking one of these very dominant, bossy, possessive men as their mates. They're fragile. They all put up good fronts, even Heather. But deep down each of them has wounds as deep as the Grand Canyon, and each of those males that finds one as his true mate is going to have to be willing to scale the walls that they've built around their hearts."

It was quiet for a moment and then Costin spoke.

"You have a way of putting situations into words that speak truth into a person's heart. I'm so glad that you're my gypsy healer."

"What if I was damaged when you found me? What if I had Stella's past or Anna's? What if I had been blind since birth like Heather, unable to ever understand the things that you get to see and experience?"

"I would reach through the fires of hell to get you. If you weren't ready to let go of those dark things that put you in that hell, then I would walk beside you until you were ready to."

Kale walked away before he could intrude any more on their private moment. His mind was focused on the things Sally had revealed about the healers. *Damaged goods*, with wounds as deep as the Grand Canyon, she had named them. His wolf howled inside of him at the thought of their mate being one of these females. Not because he wouldn't want her, but because he had not been there to protect her. Sally thought that the males would have a hard time adjusting to the needs of the healers because of their past. But that's not what they would truly struggle with. Rather, they would blame themselves that they hadn't been around to keep them safe, sheltered, and loved.

"We will heal her," his wolf spoke to him.

"Aye, and what aboot us?"

"She will choose us; we belong to her."

Kale agreed. He was the other half of her soul. And as soon as she met him, she would feel whole again—even if she didn't now realize something was missing. It would all click. That was the beauty of the mate bond. There was no guessing game, no wondering if she will say yes, or wondering if he can make her happy. He would make her happy because it was in his DNA to do so. He couldn't not try to make her happy. And like all the males of his race that lived for centuries without their true mates, he was growing restless. He was ready to be there for her and to start their lives together. He needed his mate, and if what Sally said was true, it sounded like she needed him just as much.

—

Gustavo considered Sally's words and, knowing that one of the healers was his, felt a small amount of worry pierce his confidence. He had been around women and watched them evolve over the decades, but he didn't date so it wasn't like he knew what a modern day female would expect in a relationship. He muttered a few curses in his native tongue as he felt the bond tighten. He couldn't yet reach through it to her, but it was definitely getting stronger. He drew on his wolf's sureness that they would be enough for their mate, that they would keep her safe, and they would make her happy. The wolf didn't worry about the things he had no control over. He had absolute faith in the fact that their true mate was the other half of their soul. She would bring light where darkness had begun to take over. She would fill the empty places in him, and he would give the same gift to her. *Only us,* his wolf told him. *No other can be for her what we can.* The wolf's words centered him and, as he had many times before, he found himself thankful for the creature's simple primal instincts.

—

Nick didn't see her as he came around the corner of the stairs. Kara plowed right into his chest and he quickly grabbed her waist as she started to teeter back. Had his reflexes been any slower she would have taken a backwards dive down the stairs. Her eyes were wide as she looked up at him, and he found himself wondering what she saw. Did she assume that he was your typical biker because of the shaved head and biker boots? Granted, he did ride a motorcycle so he guessed that did sort of make him a biker.

"Are you okay?" he asked her as he gently pulled her back up the stairs. He didn't release her hips until she looked down at his hands. That had him pulling them back as if she'd burned him.

"Yeah, I'm fine. Thanks for the catch," she said as she smiled and straightened her shirt.

"If I hadn't been in my own little world, I wouldn't have plowed into you, and you wouldn't have nearly plummeted to your untimely demise." *Stop flirting with her!* he yelled at himself. She was sixteen for goodness sakes.

"I hardly think it would have been my demise, but you probably did save me from a nice knock on the head. I'm Kara, by the way. I know we've been like living in this house for a while together, but then Peri hasn't exactly encouraged friendliness." She held out her hand to him and for a second all he could do was stare at it. He was actually afraid to touch her skin. Just as she started to lower her hand, he grabbed it and shook it, probably a little rougher than necessary but he was trying to ignore how perfect her hand felt in his.

"Hi, Kara." Now he knew he shouldn't say her name out loud because he practically purred it. Could he act any more like an infatuated teenager? "I'm Nick, as you already know." He smiled at her and loved that she blushed. *No, you don't; you didn't even notice that she blushed because you don't notice sixteen year olds that blush,* he thought to himself.

"How old are you?" he suddenly blurted out, still shaking her hand like an idiot.

She laughed and the way her face relaxed and all of the sorrow melted away made him want to be the one to make her laugh for the rest of her life. *No, it doesn't. You don't want to make her laugh, you don't like the way her eyes crinkle on the sides as she smiles, and you haven't noticed that she meets your eyes when she speaks to you. SIXTEEN!*

"I'm sixteen, but I'll be seventeen in a couple months."

"You seem older."

"I've been told that before," she admitted.

Nick knew he needed to walk away. Seventeen in a couple of months was certainly better than sixteen, but it still wasn't legal. He needed to just let her be, and if she was to be his then in a year and two months he could claim her.

"Um," she said as she glanced around him. "So I sort of need to go to my room, and you sort of take up a lot of space."

He laughed at that. He really wasn't that big. Six one was actually short compared to most of the males in his pack. But she was small, not just short, but her frame was petite as well. That must be why he wanted to protect her, because she was small, and it was in his instinct to protect those smaller than him. Okay now he was just reaching.

"Right, okay I'll just...." He stepped to the right just as she stepped to her left. They both smiled as they nearly bumped into each other again. Finally he grabbed her waist, picked her up effortlessly, and turned—putting her on the floor behind him. Her room was only a few feet down the hall. And he didn't know that because he had been following her scent or anything weird like that.

"Nice bumping into you," he said and smiled and then turned away from her hoping he didn't really sound as nerdy as he thought he did. *Nice bumping into you, really, Nick?* He hurried down the stairs deciding that a run was in order. "Man, it's going to be a long year and two months," he muttered under his breath.

—

Kara closed the door behind her and leaned her back against it as she closed her eyes. She let out a deep breath as she remembered Nick's hands on her waist. She could not deny that it wasn't the first time she had thought about Nick. At first she had chalked it up to the fact that he stood out to her because of the shaved head and black obsidian glass eyes. He was striking to be sure. But over the months her fascination with him was bordering on obsessive. She couldn't believe that he hadn't noticed her staring at him or subtly following when he would go to a different room or even outside to practice with the others. She usually had a book with her so perhaps she was good at pulling off the, *I'm just a teenager lost in my paranormal romance don't mind me,* look. She knew it was just wishful thinking that he would be her true mate. No one like Nick would want someone like her. Not to mention he probably didn't even see her as potential mate material because of her age. Nope, Nick probably wasn't her true mate. And that would be a damn shame because she certainly couldn't ever imagine someone else's hands on her hips or even her name sounding the way it did when he said it. She glanced out the window as she heard the back door slam and saw Nick shedding his shirt. He was about to run as a wolf. So maybe he wasn't her mate and she should give it up; but there was nothing wrong with enjoying the view, right? His head turned back and looked straight up at her window. The piercing black eyes met hers, and before she quickly backed away, she could have sworn she saw something that looked like longing.

—

That is interesting, Ciro thought as he saw the exchange between the young Canadian Beta and the even younger healer, Kara. Maybe he wasn't the only one feeling a pull toward his mate. It would be odd if Nick was feeling drawn to Kara since she wasn't of age, but not impossible. For himself, his mate bond was still growing. He had noticed how restless Kale and Gustavo were, especially in comparison to Drayden and Banan, and was beginning to have suspicions that they too had begun to feel a mate bond. Ciro wondered if Peri had truly thought it through when she took the females to the pixie realm. Had she considered what she would have on her hands if three dominant males began to feel the bond of a mate they had waited centuries for and yet couldn't get to? His own wolf was ready to leave. The wolf's allegiance was to his mate first and to the pack second. So the wolf didn't understand why they were still here instead of seeking out their mate. But the man knew that as long as she wasn't in danger, they could continue to cooperate to keep the peace. *Peace is overrated,* his wolf growled. Ciro laughed and, in this instance, would have to agree with his wolf.

9

"What is my life coming to that I can't even feel safe in my dreams? Sleep used to be a time that I could escape into worlds my mind built but now it seemed it was a cage." ~Jewel

Volcan slipped into Jewel's mind once he felt the wolf leave her presence. He was surprised at how well the bond he had created with her was working. He could virtually feel her emotions, which made him aware of what was going on around her, despite her unconscious state. Now that the bond was open between her and her true mate, he was able to see completely into her mind. All was laid bare to him—every weakness, every fear, every dark thing that he could twist to his advantage. To his surprise, the things that made Jewel Stone tremble had nothing to do with being pretty, popular, or wealthy. When he looked deep into her soul, Volcan could see that what she feared most was the unknown. A lack of knowledge to her was just as detrimental as a lack of food.

He waited a few minutes longer to make sure her mate was not going to return and then he slipped into her mind.

"Did you miss me?" he asked using Dalton's voice.

"I'm not sure that I can miss someone that I don't really know." Her voice was cool and reserved.

"What has changed, Little Dove?"

Jewel stood once again in the study that Volcan, masquerading as Dalton, had created through the mental connection. She watched as Volcan moved towards her. He looked just as he had before, like her mate except for the eyes. She knew that it was important that he didn't find out that she was on to him.

"What do you mean?" she asked as nonchalantly as she could.

"When I came to you before, you could hardly catch your breath for need of me. So I ask again, what has changed?"

Jewel decided that a grain of truth might make the lie more convincing. *"Perhaps, I don't like needing someone so much."*

He chuckled, sending a shiver down her spine. It wasn't the shiver that she got when her Dalton chuckled. *"No, I imagine you don't. If you don't need someone, then what is it that you need? Everyone needs something, Jewel."*

"Perhaps, I have everything that I need," she challenged.

"If that were true then I would not feel the emptiness or the raw wounds that you still nurse when no one is looking."

Jewel didn't like that he could see so much of her. Her pain was her own and she had no desire to share it with someone like Volcan. She was carefully keeping a wall around the thoughts that she knew she had to keep safe. Even though she had no plans to use the mental wall in order to block Volcan out completely, she could use it to keep him from knowing some things. Apparently, she wasn't able to keep him out of her memories and out of her current thoughts at the same time. He had been making himself at home in her past.

Before she could respond he continued. *"As your mate I feel your wounds, love. I feel all those times you felt rejected, unwanted, unnoticed, and powerless. It angers me to know that you felt so helpless and I was not there to do anything for you."*

Jewel heard the words, but unlike when her true mate spoke such caring things to her, there was no passion in Volcan's voice. The words were hollow.

"But I'm here now," he said as he took a step closer to her. *"I can make sure you never feel helpless or powerless again."*

She felt a tremor of need flow through her at his words—not need for him, but need for the things he promised—and it sickened her. She felt dirty all of a sudden, pretending that he was her mate when she in fact knew he wasn't somehow contaminated her. She thought she could keep up the pretense but she couldn't. The temptation was just too great. She would just have to figure out another way to help

Dalton and Peri find Volcan. She made a split second decision then.

"I know who you are," she admitted to him. His brow rose in surprise. *"Please take off Dalton's face."*

His eyes narrowed on her, but to her surprise he didn't argue. One minute it had been Dalton standing before her, and the next it was a tall, thin male with white hair and pale skin that appeared to be stretched too tight over his skeleton. His lips had a blue hue and his eyes were so dark she felt as though she were falling into a black hole. Okay, so now she totally understood why he didn't approach her as himself. *Faaareak*, she thought.

"Volcan," she said, her voice surprisingly cordial, considering he was the reason she had been chomped on by a possessed fae lady.

"What gave me away?"

"They say the eyes are the window to the soul." Jewel took a step back to better look at him and to get her bearings.

"Ahh," he said, tilting his head back slightly as he crossed his arms in front of his thin frame. He tapped his lip thoughtfully. *"The eyes, I always forget to change the color. That's what did it isn't it?"*

Jewel didn't want to tell him that she had talked to Dalton about it and that was really how she figured it out. Better to just let him think that she was the only one who knew about his little charade. *"What do you want, Volcan?"* she asked in a voice that sounded much steadier than she felt.

"The same thing you want, Jewel Stone—power."

"I don't want power."

"Ah-ah-ah, no lying. I have seen your thoughts, remember? I have felt your darkest fears and deepest pains. I know exactly what you want, what you crave. You want knowledge, Jewel, because knowledge makes you feel powerful. When your classmates rejected you, refused to invite you to their gatherings, when they made fun of your mother, or teased you about your social status, what did you do? You sought out information in any form you could get it because it made you feel less like the helpless girl that you were."

Jewel gritted her teeth together. She took several deep breaths, attempting to keep herself calm because she didn't want to show the dark fae that he was getting to her. *"And,"* he continued. *"When your test scores started reflecting all of your knowledge, your power, if you will, you began to realize that you didn't have to be accepted by your peers. In fact, you didn't need to be accepted by them because they were beneath you. If they graphed your IQ on a chart with theirs, there wouldn't be enough paper to show the difference from you score down to theirs. By gaining power, you realized that you didn't need approval."*

Jewel's head was shaking of its own accord. That's not how she thought of herself...was it? —Sure she tended to turn to books, to learning, anytime she was once again shunned by peers, or reminded that she was an outcast and always would be. She loved to learn, loved to see how much information she could cram into her mind. And maybe when she realized that the people she went to school with, the ones who had been cruel to her over and over again over the years, couldn't hold a candle to her test scores, she had felt powerful. She had felt in control. But that didn't mean she craved power.

"I am not power hungry just because I want to learn," she informed him.

"No, you are power hungry because you hate the idea of being helpless. Tell me, Jewel." He sidestepped her, moved a few paces away, and sat down on the edge of a large wooden desk that she was pretty sure hadn't been in there the first time she had mentally visited the study. *"What do you think your life as a true mate to a dominant Canis lupis will be like? And what about as a healer to the wolves? Do you honestly believe that it will be different than the life you have known?"* He didn't give her a chance to answer but just kept on bombarding her with questions. *"Have you considered your place in a wolf pack? You are female, and you will be mated to a Beta, the second most dominant male in a pack. He will have expectations of you, just as your pack will have expectations of you as his mate. He will expect your obedience because, as he will tell you, he wants to keep you safe. But perhaps it's just because he thinks you're too weak and unintelligent to be able to take care of yourself? You will always be in his shadow because he sure isn't going to let you walk beside of or in front of him—you are the weaker vessel. And let's not forget your precious role as a gypsy healer,"* Volcan crooned. *"The ultimate servant. I bet no one has told you about that part."*

"Well, I've sort of been in a coma for a couple months, so I can't really blame them," she told him, trying at all costs not to reveal that his words were beginning to truly plant some serious seeds of doubt.

"Well, I will be happy to enlighten you. As you may know, I am, or rather was, a high fae. As such, I knew every gypsy healer that has ever been. I have spent time with them, time with the packs, and seen exactly what it is to be a healer. The wolves will tell you it is an honor and only certain females are chosen within the bloodlines to take on such an important role. What they don't tell you is that you are there to serve, not just a few, but everyone. Your job is to take care of the injured, the pregnant females, the ones that might be struggling with any sort of darkness, or the ones in need of reassurance. You will put pack above yourself because it is expected of you. You will kneel to all and be served by none. I suppose some might find the role of a gypsy healer to be romantic, but truly, what is romantic about a male who is willing to let his mate practically be a slave?"

He was twisting the truth, she knew it, and yet she still heard some solid ring in it regardless of the twist. Would she lose herself under Dalton's dominance and possessiveness? Would she still be at the bottom of her peers as a gypsy healer? There was a part of her that was screaming, *come on get a clue—you are smarter than that.* But then there was another voice—one that she had heard too many times before in the past. The voice that told her she would always be the outcast and always be the one searching for the approval of others but never finding it. The one who ran to the solace of her books to avoid any chance of rejection. She would be stuck beneath a pack of wolves who expect your service and beneath a mate who wants your obedience. She could tell herself until she was blue in the face that she didn't crave power, but if craving power was the same thing as craving knowledge then she was guilty as charged.

She had vowed to herself that as soon as the final grade was set and the diploma was printed, she was going to move on with her life away from the people who had treated her as though she were nothing but an annoying quadratic equation that they must deal with before they move on to something enjoyable. Now she was in a world that she never knew existed—although to be fair, her mother had tried to warn her—and there were so many new possibilities. But she didn't know if those possibilities were any different from the life she had already endured for too long. She felt a deep pang in her chest, and she knew it was the stab of disappointment because she so badly wanted it to be different.

"Maybe you don't know all the facts since you are a fae and not a Canis lupis," she said, grasping at straws.

"I know that I can offer you what you want without expecting you to be my servant."

"That's not totally true, Volcan. You want whatever power it is that a gypsy healer possesses. You want me for my power. How am I any less of a pawn for you?" She knew she shouldn't even be arguing with him. She shouldn't even be attempting to see what he wanted because she shouldn't be interested in what he was offering. That hadn't been the plan, and yet a little voice inside her whispered, *you would never be*

insignificant again. She should tell the little voice to jump off a cliff, but instead she waited to see what the dark fae would say.

"I will not deny that I would like for you to share your magic with me. But I can give you so much in return. I can give you thousands of years of knowledge. I can teach you secrets that books never could. I will not expect you to serve me, but to simply be my companion."

The wheels in Jewel's mind were turning as she desperately tried to keep the walls up in her mind so that Volcan couldn't know her true thoughts. She could not deny for a second that some of what he said resonated deep inside of her. She hated feeling insignificant, hated feeling as though she was helpless to change her situation or the opinions of others. If she stayed with Dalton and became his mate and lived out the whole gypsy healer scenario, would that mean she would always be seen as helpless and weak? But if she agreed to be Volcan's companion, did that make her evil?

"I need some time," she finally said to him.

"I can understand that; it's a big decision. I will allow you three days. When I return I will expect your decision."

"What decision is that?"

"Your life or theirs," he said coolly. *"If you agree to come with me, be my companion, and allow me access to your power, I will in turn give you the knowledge you seek in order to not feel helpless and weak. I will teach you everything and anything you want to know. I will also leave the other healers alone, and I will leave the wolves to themselves."*

And there's the catch, Jewel thought. He wasn't really giving her a choice. She either went with him and did what he asked or he would hurt those she cared about. The real choice was not whether or not she went with him; it was whether or not she went with the intention of simply saving the other healers or to help herself.

"Three days then," she told him and watched as his image faded from her mind. Jewel wished that she wasn't in a coma because it was one of those moments when she desperately needed to throw her body back on her bed with a loud sigh. Not to mention, a nice hot shower was appropriate as well considering how disgusted she was with herself. How on earth could she even consider his words, even if there might be some truth to them? She wasn't guilt free, she definitely had her transgressions, but she had never thought of herself as evil. Did she want to be powerful? Maybe to a certain extent, but she didn't want to exert that power over others; she simply wanted to have the power to change her circumstances. She wanted to have the power to not be hurt by others and to not feel inadequate because of the place in life others had put her. Knowledge gave her that power. But she would never want to use any of her knowledge to hurt others.

Her mind traveled back to the decision at hand. Part of her wanted to laugh at the irony of being in a coma like state and yet having to make the biggest decision of her life. She would go with Volcan because there was no way she would let innocents suffer if she could stop it. But what would she tell Dalton? Would she tell him the real reason, which in turn would make Dalton feel guilty and responsible for not being able to save her, or would she tell him a lie? Could she convince him that she wanted to go with Volcan? That it was her choice because she didn't want to be the weak little mate hiding behind her big bad werewolf husband and kneeling at the feet of those who needed her to clean their cuts? Could she tear his heart out by telling him she didn't want him, just to keep the healers she knew and ones she didn't safe? She let out a mental sigh. *Can I break my own heart,* she thought as her mind wandered to Dalton. *Can I really give up the first good thing that has come my way?* The better question was did she really have a choice. *No, I don't.*

10

"I can feel her. She lives inside the very blood that courses through my veins. She is a part of the marrow deep inside my bones. Her soul melded with my own before I ever gave her permission and all that I am and all that I have is for her. And even though I'm willing to give her everything I still can't save her. I can't save her because she doesn't want saving." ~Dalton

Dalton felt her confusion though she was attempting to block him and doing a rather good job of it. What Jewel didn't know, couldn't possibly know, was there were some emotions so deep that they would be impossible to block fully from a true mate. His first instinct was to run back to her, but he needed some space. He hadn't realized how upset it had made him or his wolf to hear that she was considering trying to get close to Volcan, even if it meant she could help them find the evil fae. Was she right? Maybe. Did that mean he was going to let her get close to a monster that wants all of her blood? Hell no. He knew that he had come off as possessive and controlling, and he didn't want to smother her before she was even conscious and had met him in person, but he'd be damned if he was going to lose her.

He shed his human skin and phased into his wolf in midstride as he took off in the fae forest. He needed to run, to get all the pent up energy out. He'd rather get rid of it in more pleasurable ways, like kissing Jewel, but until she was conscious and no longer attempting to save the world by running headlong into the hands of a twisted psycho, running in his wolf form would have to suffice.

Dalton allowed his wolf to take over as the night enveloped him. As the moon smiled down on him, the cool fall air slid over his muzzle and down his back in a sensual caress. His beast reveled in being part of the shadows of night. He took joy in the hunt, especially when he was frustrated. He ran for what seemed like hours, but he knew wasn't because he wouldn't spend that much time away from his mate. It was as he was running back to her that the images filled his mind. His usually graceful feet stumbled beneath him, nearly causing him to face plant his muzzle into the unrelenting ground beneath him. He phased without thought to his human form as more and more images of his Jewel in the arms of another male assaulted his mind.

They came faster and faster. Jewel kissing a tall thin male with white hair, laughing with him, and doing other things that made Dalton want to puke and to make it very clear who her man was. There were also other images—terrible images of Jewel making sacrifices to something dark and unseen. The final scene that threw him over the edge and had him gagging and dry heaving was the image of Jewel, dressed in a black semi-transparent gauzy dress, with a baby in one hand and a knife in the other. Volcan was mocking him. As the maker of witches he would have known of Gwen and known that she had attempted to become a witch, and obviously he knew that Dalton had killed her before that could happen. He let out a low snarl as he forced himself to his feet only to be shoved by an unseen hand back to the ground.

"There are always consequences for crossing me, Dalton Black," Volcan's voice resonated in his mind and he realized that the dark fae was once again using the mate bond. Jewel definitely hadn't shut hers down like they had discussed. *"even centuries later. You took a potential acolyte from me. She held great promise."*

"Why? Because she was particularly sick and twisted in the head?" Dalton growled.

"Insults don't affect me, wolf. The point is you have something that I want. You took a witch from me, and now I will take a healer from you. She's powerful," his voice was a purr and Dalton felt a level of violence rise up in him that he hadn't thought possible.

"She's mine."

"Are you so sure about that?" Volcan questioned. *"Does her loyalty really lie with you just because you happen to be her true mate? She's a human, not a wolf. Do you really think that whole true mate business really means that much to her?"*

Dalton didn't answer him. He was too busy trying to figure out a way to get the prick out of his head.

"Don't bother," Volcan told him. *"As long as her end is open, I'm here to stay."*

"What do you want with me?" Dalton finally asked.

"I don't want anything with you. I simply need you to be occupied for a few days so that you can't be near our little dove while she is making a very important decision. I wouldn't want you swaying her choice."

"What are you talking about?"

"All you need to know is that whatever wonderful future you envisioned with your mate will now be mine. You, who have lived by choice alone all of these centuries, will endure loneliness by the choice of your true mate when she comes to me, willingly, of her own free will. Take a few days out here in nature and think about all that you wish you could have but can't. And while you're at it, because I'm such a generous man, any time you think of your little dove, I'll continue to give you little previews of the plans I have for my Jewel. I know I'm not all that much to look at right now, but it's nothing that a little magic can't help. Soon she will be awake, out of that bed, and into mine."

Dalton tried to roar at the declaration; he tried to lunge, at what he didn't know since Volcan's physical form was nowhere near him. All he knew was that he needed to kill something. He needed to rip the dark fae from limb to limb, tearing through muscle, tendon, and bone until all that was left was a pile of unrecognizable mush. He couldn't move. The more he struggled, the more restricted his muscles became until all he could do was breathe and move his eyes. He stared up into the night sky as the stars looked down at him. He imagined them laughing at him, gawking at his audacity to think that he could really have a mate, especially one such as Jewel. Perhaps this was his punishment to have the one thing a male Canis lupis longed for dangled in front of him only to be ripped from him by an evil that he and his kind once tried to destroy.

"Jewel?" He reached through their bond but there was nothing on the other end. He was once again bombarded by an image of Volcan and Jewel, and if he could scream he would have, but it seemed the dark fae had taken care of that as well. Dalton was helpless. His wolf attempted to force their phase, perhaps the transformation magic would break whatever dark magic Volcan was using, but this too proved fruitless. No matter how badly he wanted to run back to her, he was stuck, naked, in a field in Farie with images of his mate and a dark fae dancing through his head.

He had thought centuries ago he had reached the darkest place he could ever fall inside of himself. But as he heard Jewel sigh Volcan's name in his mind, he knew that there was a new depth in hell reserved especially for him.

—

Jewel had no concept of time as she lie there lost inside of herself. Sally came in and checked on her periodically, caring for her daily, but other than that she had no way to keep track of the passage of time. She had no idea how long it had been since Dalton left her after having shown her how to build the wall in her mind. She knew he was frustrated when he left. He had pressed a kiss to her forehead and told her to keep fighting and then he was gone, taking all the warmth and security she felt when he was near him. She wondered if maybe he had been able to sense that she planned to try and help despite his warnings. Had she angered him to the point that he didn't want to speak with her? She had attempted to reach out to him, following the chorded thread that seemed to link them together, and yet there was only emptiness on the other end. Part of her thought that maybe it was best that he had kept his distance, considering she was trying to decide how to tell him that she planned to go along with Volcan's plans. She didn't want him trying to dissuade her. But at the same time, if she was giving up her chance at something better with Dalton in order to appease the evil fae and keep her new friends safe, then she wanted all the time she could get with the male that was created just for her.

Jewel hadn't realized that the last time they had talked, argued really was more like it, might have been their last. She wished now that she had told him how much it meant to her that he had stayed and cared for her, a stranger to him. She wished that she had shared more about herself with him, considering he had poured out all of his past to her, and yet she had given him nothing in return, not really. She thought there would be more time. Jewel hadn't considered that there wouldn't be a future with Dalton. He had always made her feel like she and he were pretty much a done deal, and she hadn't realized just how much security she had found in that until now.

As she lay there wondering if he would return before Volcan, she thought back to all of the times Dalton had said her name, touched her hand, or kissed her forehead. She had yet to lay eyes on his physical form and yet she craved his touch. She wanted to hear him call her Little Dove just one more time before she faced forever without him. Jewel didn't think that she could hurt any more, not after all that she had been through, but lying there knowing she was going to walk away from her destiny created an ache in her that she knew would never be dulled.

"Please come back," she whispered into the bond hoping he would hear her. *"There's so much I need to tell you. So much I've never told anyone and I finally have someone besides my mom who wants to listen."* She waited, hoping he would answer, hoping his deep voice would send a warm shiver down her spine. But she was answered with the loudest silence she had ever heard.

—

"Where in the world has he gone?" Sally asked throwing her hands up in the air as she paced the yard with the others watching her. "It's not like he could possibly have somewhere more important to be."

It had been over two days since Dalton stormed out of the house with the other males and Sally staring after him. She had thought that he was finally on board, that he had accepted his fate, and that he was actually happy about it.

"He wouldn't leave her," Dillon spoke up as he stood with his arms crossed over his chest staring out into the forest beyond Peri's home. "He loves her."

"No male would stay away from their female for nearly three days, especially not if she was injured," Sally pointed out. "So either he had another one of his I'm not worthy, my past sucks blah, blah, blah moments, or he ate a rancid rabbit and has gone to meet his maker. Why else would he leave her lying there, alone for three damn days?" *"Sally,"* Costin's soothing voice brushed over her mind as he attempted to calm her. She didn't want to be calmed. She wanted that stubborn, massive moving mountain to be there with Jewel.

"I'm fine, Costin. I just hate that she's going through this alone."

"You don't know that she is. Their bond has opened remember; she might know exactly where he is."

Sally turned on her mate, her hands plastered on her hips as her eyes bore into his. "Surely you haven't forgotten that I am a gypsy healer and that must mean that you know that I would know if she knew where he was."

Costin took a step back with his hands raised. "Okay, first of all, what?"

Sally growled as she stomped her foot. "I can see inside of her to an extent; I can feel her. She doesn't know where he is. She's confused and she misses him. I'm telling you he did not inform her that he was going on a vacation."

"We will give it until the morning," Peri spoke up, her voice unusually flat. "If he hasn't shown by then his Alpha can hunt him down." She glanced at Dillon from the corner of her eye who gave her a slight nod.

The group dispersed leaving a still upset Sally and gun shy Costin standing in front of Peri's home. She continued to pace back and forth, her hands resting on her sides as she considered all the emotions that she had felt running through Jewel the last time she had taken a look inside the healer.

"What's going on, Sally mine?" Costin asked gently. He didn't approach her but gave her some space as he waited for her to open up.

Sally didn't know how to answer him because she honestly didn't know what was up. All she knew was that Jewel was hiding something, something big. Part of her felt like she should speak up because it might have something to do with Dalton's sudden disappearance, but another part of her felt like if she did say something she would be betraying her fellow healer. So instead she kept it all bottled up, and the more she paced, the more she felt like a carbonated beverage being shook. The pressure was building and she knew that all it would take was small twist and everything would come spewing out.

"Sally."

"I DON'T KNOW!" she yelled. Her frustration was at an all-time high. She felt totally useless and the waiting was beginning to drive everyone, herself included, a little mad. "I just, something doesn't, I…," she stumbled still unsure of whether or not to tell her mate her suspicions.

"Do you want me to just take a look and then you can blame me if I know something I shouldn't?" Costin asked her.

She narrowed her eyes at him. "You taking the information from my mind is just as bad as me telling you." They had had this argument before—patient confidentiality as she called it. She knew that there would be things that she wouldn't be able to help seeing when she healed others, but that didn't mean that she had the right to tell anyone about the private things she saw, her mate included. Costin didn't see it that way. He felt as her mate, and basically the other half of her soul, he had a right to anything and everything in her mind. *Dang stubborn, nosy wolf,* she thought, not for the first nor last time.

"I can wait until you're asleep so you won't know that I'm taking a peak," he said as he waggled his eyebrows at her.

Sally laughed. "Well now, that won't work because you just told me what you were going to do, dork. And man that sounded sort of creepy."

"Ahh, maybe so, but I also got a laugh out of my beautiful, stressed out mate." He reached out his arms to her and she went into them willingly. They both let out relieved sighs as if being apart was physically difficult and unnatural, which Sally knew was actually very true at times. She pressed her cheek to his chest and took a deep breath of his masculine scent and felt her nerves relax as his scent enveloped her. His wolf rumbled at her appreciatively and she grinned.

"I love you," he told her seriously. Sally could hear the worry he felt for her in his thick words. She hated that she was causing him apprehension, but was also thankful that he wasn't one to continually push her. He knew she would tell him when she felt she could.

"I know you do," she whispered against him. "I love you more."

He chuckled and tugged playfully at her pony-tail. "In a world so full of possibilities, you pick the one thing that is an impossibility."

"What can I say, I like a challenge."

"I'll remember that when you're being all handsy with me."

Sally's head rose to look up at him and wasn't surprised to see the flirty, dimpled grin plastered on his too handsome face. "Handsy? I do not get handsy."

"So what would you call what you were doing the other night under the covers?"

Sally slapped a hand over his mouth as her own mouth dropped open. Her head swung from side to side as she checked to see if any of the others were close enough to hear her mate spouting off his out-rageous claims—even if they were true.

"I was looking for something," she said before she realized how it would sound.

"Oh, I'm sure you were," Costin laughed and tried to jump back away from her swinging hand. "What audiences everywhere want to know is did you find what you were looking for?"

Sally was pretty sure her face couldn't get any redder.

Costin's eyes closed and a low growl emitted from his chest. "If my memory serves me correctly, I'd have to ease the public's mind by saying yes; yes, you definitely found what you were looking for."

She was wrong, her face could *definitely* get redder.

"That's it," she said turning on her heels. "I'm going inside now, you coming?"

"That depends, are you going to be looking for something under the covers again?"

"UGH! Costin, seriously?"

"It's a valid question to ask when your mate asks you if your co—,"

"Don't," she said and turned to face him but con-tinued walking backwards towards the house. "We've got Jewel in a coma, Dalton MIA, the other healers dealing with pixies, and Volcan planning who knows what; there is no time for you to be trying to, as you call it, get a little practice in."

Costin laughed out loud and as usual his care-free, playful attitude had her heartbeat increasing. "If now is not the time to get a little practice in, female, then when is? No time like the present, love."

"Sure there is," she argued. "It's called at night, when the lights are off, some mood music is playing, and the end of the world is not happening!"

"Awe, babe," Costin whined as he reached for her. "If we wait for that we will never get practice."

"Okay, I'll compromise."

"Really?" he asked eagerly and she couldn't help but laugh.

She nodded. "The world can be ending, but someone I care about can't be in a coma."

Costin's smile dropped. "Well crap, every time we turn around someone you care about is unconscious."

Sally patted his head and puckered her lips. "Awe, hang in there, big guy. I'm sure Jewel will wake up soon."

He took her hand and pulled her toward the house. "If this trend continues you do realize that we won't be able to have pups because I won't know how."

This drew a snicker from Sally.

"What?" He looked at her incredulously. "Haven't you heard practice makes perfect."

"Psht, please, mate. You can hardly say that you haven't perfected your practice." Sally felt her cheeks warm again.

Costin's dimples deepened. "Oh hell, woman, I love it when you talk about my practice."

"Get in the house," she huffed as she pushed him through the door he had just opened. "And quit talking about practicing."

He leaned forward as she walked past him and pressed his lips next to her ear. "I'll compromise; I'll stop talking about practicing if you will give me a game."

Sally choked as all eyes in the living room landed on them. *Damn wolf hearing,* she grumbled inwardly.

"Chess," Sally blurted out. "He's talking about chess."

"Did you say *chest?*" Peri asked, drawing out the "T" at the end of the word.

"Good one P," Costin laughed.

Sally threw her hands up in the air. "I'm going to check on Jewel."

"What about our game?" Costin called to her as he attempted to hold back his laughter.

"Yeah, don't go Sally; we want to hear about this new game called chest," Peri teased.

"Kara," Sally hollered. "Come help me with Jewel. Dalton's crap about me being the only one near her is moot now that he's decided to up and disappear. Costin, get your furry butt out here. If you get desperate for a game of chest, I'm sure one of these other males who aren't getting any practice would be happy to accommodate you."

The door closed behind Sally and she let out a deep breath. She wasn't about to admit to Costin that she needed him in more ways than one, not when Jewel needed her. She needed some space from him or else everyone was going to see the longing she had in her eyes for her mate. She was pretty sure that she would invent a new shade of red if that happened.

"Everything okay?" Kara asked as she walked over to Jewel's bedside.

"Kara," Sally's voice was clipped as she gathered the items for Jewel's nightly bath. Kara watched her quietly as she continued to talk. "My advice to you is live it up for the next two years."

"Why?" she asked truly curious as to what Sally would say.

"Because once your true mate finds you, you will spend so much time fending off his advances that living suddenly turns into *just trying to not be pawed to death.*"

Kara snorted. "And tell me again why having someone that looks like Costin pawing at you is such a hardship?"

Sally's eyes snapped up to the young healer and a smile spread across her previously frustrated face. "He is pretty hot, isn't he?"

Kara rolled her eyes. Sally wasn't fooling her for a second. It was more than obvious that the brown eyed beauty was head over heels for her bartender, but Kara thought it was cute that Sally tried to act otherwise. "Oh brother, so it's all a front isn't it. The truth is you would much rather be playing chess, or what that implies, than be in here acting all mad at your man."

"Of course," Sally shrugged. "But as soon as he realizes that you want him, as bad as if not worse than he wants you, you lose the upper hand. And Kara, with these male dominants you have got to keep the upper hand at all costs."

Kara nodded as she took the towels Sally held out for her. "Okay, noted. Keep the upper hand. What else do you got for me?"

"Never admit to liking any of their dominant, possessive, bossy ways."

She grinned as she looked at Sally with what she knew was her innocent wide eyed look. "But what if I like that?"

"SHHHH!" Sally interrupted her quickly, batting her hands at her and glancing back at the door as if the males would bust in at any moment. "Holy crap, girl, I'm glad we've got two years to get you ready to put on a game face because as soon as I listed those three qualities your eyes went into bedroom mode. Chick, you are sixteen; there should be no bedroom eyes mode for you yet."

Kara was laughing. "Wait, did you have bedroom eyes mode at seventeen, when you met Costin."

Sally paused then shook her head. "Not the point."

"She totally did!" Costin yelled through the door. "She had bedroom eyes, bedroom lips, bedroom—,"

"NOBODY ASKED YOU!" Sally growled as she bit back a grin.

Kara shook her head at the couple as she began to help Sally care for Jewel. It broke her heart to see the redhead so still. She wanted Jewel to have what Sally did. She wanted Dalton to put the kind of light in Jewel's eyes that Costin did in Sally's. If she was being honest with herself, she wanted a mate of her own to give her the same thing.

"Did I mention to live it up while you can?" Sally asked her as she washed Jewel's feet.

Kara chuckled. "Honestly, Sally, everything I've been doing up until this point hasn't been living. I don't think that I'll start living until I have one of those," she motioned to the door where Costin stood on the other side, "looking at me the way Costin looks at you and the way I've seen Dalton staring after Jewel when I've caught him at her window. The way Lucian looks at Peri and Adam looks at Crina; those are things worth living for."

Sally paused and looked at her, head tilted slightly to the side with her brow raised. "Your future mate is a lucky wolf," she finally said after several heartbeats.

Kara's mind immediately jumped to Nick but she squelched it before the fantasy could take root. "So is yours," Kara whispered.

"YES, YES I AM," Costin yelled through the door having heard even Kara's whisper.

"Stupid wolf hearing," Sally muttered and winked at Kara.

—

Volcan stood just outside the veil of Farie. The strain of cloaking his presence was wearing on him, but he knew he wouldn't be able to flash from the draheim realm to Peri's home and back again with Jewel in tow. His power was growing, especially with the connection he had to Jewel, but he wasn't back to full strength yet. He found that he was restless and jittery with excitement. It had been a long time since he had wanted anything other than power, but after having spent time in Jewel's brilliant mind, he realized that he wanted something else. He wanted someone to share his success and power with. He wanted to have someone see all that he would accomplish and experience it with him. But it couldn't be just anyone. It had to be someone powerful in their own right and someone as intelligent as him, or at least close; he was done contending with imbeciles. And now Jewel had practically fallen in his lap, with Lorelle's help he added begrudgingly.

He had told her that he would give her three days to decide. He didn't bother to tell her that he would be taking her with him no matter what or that the other healers would still die even if she did choose him. There was no sense in having her hate him. He would tell her what she wanted to hear, and she would fall in love with him because of his power. Once she realized all that he could do for her and give her, she would forgive him and probably understand why he had to do it in the first place.

Someone of Jewel's intelligence wouldn't grieve needlessly over loss of life if it meant knowledge could be obtained. It was obvious to him that she was his perfect counterpart. There was no way that she hadn't been created to rule with him. And together they would bring a new era to the world not just the human realm but all of the realms.

—

Dalton felt whatever invisible weight had been holding him down suddenly lift and his limbs were his own again. His body felt stiff and heavy after having been unable to move for three days. He clamored to his feet feeling as clumsy as a new born pup and shook off the effects of Volcan's magic. His only thought was of her. He had to get back to her. He phased without thought and took off, extending his stride as long as he could to cover as much ground as possible. The run seemed impossibly long and he felt sure that he had not wandered so far. It had to be another one of Volcan's tricks.

He attempted reaching her through their bond as he ran and, to his surprise, he felt her. His heart leapt and his wolf called out to her both vocally, through a soul piercing howl, and mentally.

"JEWEL!" His soul longed for her in a way he had yet to experience. The separation that Volcan had somehow accomplished between them had become painful, and he hadn't even realized it because of his anger at being unable to get back to her.

"Dalton?" Her weary voice nearly crushed him as he realized that without him she had grown weaker.

"I'm on my way. I'm so sorry, Little Dove. I didn't stay away on purpose." He felt her confusion and tried to push his love and reassurance through their bond so that she would know he hadn't left her. He hadn't abandoned her and never would.

"I thought you were angry with me."

"Frustrated, yes. But not angry," he admitted.

"You will be." The regret in her voice had him pushing himself harder. Something wasn't right and his wolf felt frantic to get to her, to hold her, and to see for himself that she was alright. He finally saw Peri's home come into view and it only served to make him run faster. He reached the door and ripped it open stopping only long enough to grab a pair of sweats and ungracefully jerk them on as he tried to keep moving, needing to get to her as quickly as possible.

The sight before him when he pulled the door open had him so weak in the knees that his huge form nearly crumbled to the ground. He braced himself on the frame of the door as he stared at his mate, who was standing at the foot of the bed she had laid in for months, staring back at him. Awake. She was awake and she was beautiful and she was crying.

"Where have you been?" she asked him. Hearing her voice out loud for the first time was music to his ears and balm to his soul. The tears in her eyes quickly removed him from his stupor as he closed the door and moved towards her in an instant. He didn't hesitate as he wrapped his arms around her and pulled her into the shelter of his much larger body. He buried his face in her hair until his nose was against her neck and instinct took over as he pulled her tender flesh between his teeth giving her a quick nip without breaking the skin—a dominate mate establishing his possession of her. She immediately molded to him, her arms coming around his waist and her head tucking into his chest.

"I had some trouble while I was hunting. I had no intention of leaving you for so long." Dalton didn't want to bring up Volcan just yet; he knew the evil fae must have been the reason she was so upset.

Dalton struggled with his need to touch her and his need to keep her pure, untainted from his past. He felt dirty and unworthy to hold something so clean, so precious, and for a fleeting moment wondered if all the past women he touched could somehow tarnish her. He knew she was completely innocent. His lips had caressed many a lover but should have only been reserved for her, his one and only. Her arms had never embraced another male, and yet his arms had been like a revolving door for females. It sickened him and he hated the day that she might run across those memories—memories he wished could be scrubbed from his mind and kept far from her innocence. No, he truly wasn't worthy of the gift of her flesh, especially when he had nothing to offer her. But he was not foolish enough to think it would keep him from partaking of her when she one day offered herself to him as his bonded true mate.

He felt her body tremble as her crying intensified, and Dalton felt completely inadequate to help her. He didn't know why she was crying. He knew they weren't tears of joy because she was finally conscious. The emotions coming off of her were too dark and full of despair to warrant that. She felt defeated. He leaned back so he could look down at her. His hands moved of their own accord as the need to touch her overcame him. Dalton ran his right hand down her hair and pushed the strands behind her ear so he could better see her. His fingers trailed along her jaw, over her lips, and down her neck. He had longed to touch her, longed to show her his reverence by the care he would take with her. Her tears didn't slow as his hand wrapped around the back of her neck in a possessive gesture and tilted her head back just a tad so that she had to look at him. Blessed be she was beautiful. She felt perfect in his arms, as if she had been there all along. He felt the darkness in him recede just a little as the light from her soul reached out for him. He felt his canines begin to elongate in response; the need to claim her and to tie her to him for eternity was nearly overwhelming. Her hiccups in-between sobs finally drew him out of his thoughts.

"What is it, Jewel? What has happened?" He hoped that his voice was gentle and didn't convey the carefully controlled rage that was simmering just beneath the surface. She shook her head at him and tightened her hold. Everything tumbling out of her through the bond called to his protective nature—his instinct and drive to keep her safe and happy. Yet he was at a loss as to how to do that. "Please, talk to me."

She pulled back and looked up at him. Her face was swollen and red. Tears stained the porcelain skin of her cheeks, and the ache in her eyes was enough to cause him physical pain.

"Did you know that when wolves mate in the wild, during courtship the male wolf will bow to the female, nuzzle her, and swing his head in a strutting fashion? He's actually flirting with her, showing her his physical attributes and also caring for her by grooming her. And after an Alpha female has had a litter of puppies, she often retains control of the pack. The other pack members, including the Alpha male, serve her. In fact, there are instances where the lower ranking females are so afraid of the Alpha female that they won't even go into heat."

Dalton was taken off guard by her comments, and if the situation had been different he would have definitely been intrigued and would want to hear more. But in that moment he wanted to know what had her falling apart and what finally awoke her from her unconscious state.

She smiled, ducking her head with a warm blush. "Sorry, when I get nervous I tend to spew facts out like a full baby that's just been thoroughly shaken."

"You spew whatever you need to, Little Dove, I'll listen."

Jewel started to take a step back but he wasn't ready to release her. His grip tightened just enough to let her know that she wasn't going anywhere. He liked that she gave up without a fight. She was where she belonged and he wanted her to know it.

"I'm pretty sure that you aren't going to want me anymore when you find out what I've done." She looked up into his eyes as she spoke, and he was surprised that she didn't attempt to avoid his stare. She wasn't intimidated by him and that was something that made him feel many things— desire, pride, respect, and admiration being among them.

"There is nothing you could do that would ever make me not want you," he told her as his wolf pushed forward, desiring to convey the message even more strongly by marking her. "Does it have to do with Volcan and his delusional idea that you are going to be going with him?" Her eyes widened at his questions and he felt shame rolling off of her in waves. He was surprised to feel his wolf fighting him so adamantly for control; he did not like seeing their mate so upset.

"I didn't build the wall."

"I never thought you would."

"He came back." She paused. "At first I thought I'd be able to keep up the ruse of pretending that I believed him to be you. But when he called me Little Dove…,"

Dalton's jaw clenched and a wave of jealousy flooded him. He knew then that he wouldn't handle anyone else giving Jewel pet names. Silly, maybe, reality, definitely.

"It made me sick. Then the thought of him touching me again, kissing me even though it was just a mental projection of us, made me feel as though I would be cheating on you. So I told him I knew that he wasn't my mate. I asked him to stop looking like you and then he revealed himself." Her body trembled beneath his hands and he found himself unconsciously rubbing her back in small, reassuring circles.

"We talked. I basically asked what he wanted and his answer was blunt. He wants me." The low growl from his chest didn't even give her pause as she continued to talk. "He said some things, and I couldn't deny most of them, and then he gave me an ultimatum, an offer that I had to accept. In every conflict in history there have always been sacrifices to be made…,"

"No." Dalton cut her off not wanting to hear what she had to say because there was no way in hell he was going to let her do what he realized she was planning.

"One person as opposed to five, or more, Dalton. One person who has the potential to bring him down. I've lived in my books my whole life. I've read stories of great evil and how good overcomes it and never thought I'd ever have to make the choices that those characters make. I always wondered if I would be able to be that selfless, and the truth is, I don't want to be. I want you. But after the things Volcan said, I'm pretty sure I don't deserve you. If I go with him, he will leave the other healers alone."

"Is that what he told you?" Dalton asked. "And you believe a psychopath who has killed thousands?"

"Statistically speaking psychopaths are actually very honest because they have no moral compass so lying doesn't necessarily benefit them."

"Don't really care at the moment, female." Dalton knew that his voice was even and calm, something he had perfected over the centuries. "So you're telling me that you've struck a bargain with the devil and expect the devil to keep his end of the deal?"

She nodded; her eyes were wide as she studied his face. He could tell she was memorizing him, taking in every aspect of him because she thought she was leaving him. He felt her attraction to him as her gaze ran over his rugged jaw and full lips. She wasn't attempting to hide her feelings from him, and he ached for the touch she longed to give him. *Don't do it, Jewel, don't touch him.* He heard the thoughts though they weren't directed at him. She was bolstering herself, attempting to make herself strong for what she was about to tell him. He wouldn't make it easy on her. Dalton held her stare with a daring one of his own, challenging her to tell him.

"I have to go. Knowing what he will do if I don't is not something I could live with."

"But you can live without me?" It was harsh and perhaps not a fair question, but he wasn't playing fair; he was playing for keeps.

"I can live knowing you are safe, knowing all of your race is safe, and the gypsy healers aren't in his clutches where he can use them."

He released her and stepped back afraid that if he held her while his wolf was growing more and more volatile he might hurt her inadvertently. Foolish female, that's what he wanted to say but his wolf bit his tongue. He wouldn't allow the man to say hurtful things just because he was hurting. But he would allow him to speak the truth.

"But I won't be safe. They will have to kill me, Jewel. If you walk away from me my wolf will take over; there will be nothing left and no reason for me not to give into the darkness. No one will be safe." His voice shook with the need his body felt to grab her and run, to take her far from this place and hide her away to keep her safe.

"I don't believe that. I've seen inside of you. I know your wolf; there is still good in you." Her voice was raw from the tears she had been shedding, her face was red and swollen, and yet to him she was still the most beautiful creature he'd ever seen.

"You!" he snarled taking another step back. "You are all that is good in me!" He turned from her; his shoulders were rigid as he attempted to get his emotions under control. Until Jewel he had not had problems with his control in a very long time, and in a couple of months she had managed to turn him inside out. He didn't know how to make her understand that she was his light. She held the other half of his soul and without her he would be lost. He wanted to kill something, to feel flesh between his teeth, because if he lost her he would be reduced to a beast hell bent on killing everything in its path.

"If I was all that was good in you then you wouldn't have spent all these years in your pack, helping them, being the wolf Dillon needed you to be. *You* did that Dalton, without my help you did that."

"Dammit, Jewel." His head tilted back as he stared up at the ceiling, fighting to remain calm, but failing. "I was barely holding on! I wasn't living; I was surviving and had I not found you when I did I was ready to ask my Alpha to end my misery. Every day is a struggle not to give in to the darkness, to just let my wolf take over. It would be easier because then I wouldn't have to deal with the guilt and memories of my past. The only thing that has stopped me is the desire to not sink as low as those who harmed my family. I will not kill innocents, and the only way for me to keep that promise is to leave this life." His heart nearly shattered when he heard a sob pour out of his mate. He had been avoiding looking at her because it was too painful. She was standing right there within his reach and only moments ago he held her. Yet now he felt as though she didn't want him to touch her. It was too much. But now he looked down to see her kneeling; her shoulders shaking violently as his usually composed little dove fell apart once again. He wanted to go to her, to hold her, and tell her it would be alright, but he couldn't bring himself to move. She had pushed him away by being willing to walk away from him and hearing her say that had broken something inside of him. He had thought nothing could hurt him the way losing his parents, being tortured and molested, and then lost for centuries had hurt. He was wrong. To be rejected by his mate was worse, and he would take torture over that any day. Dalton couldn't reach out for her, because he wouldn't be responsible for his actions if she turned away from him again.

So instead he just stood there watching the one person he never wanted to hurt shaking with the pain of all that she was feeling. She was confused; he could feel it through their bond. Her mind was chaotic and he couldn't pick up on a single thought because there was just so much. Dalton didn't know what to say. He'd never been good with words; hell, he wasn't good with people and up until Jewel he'd never given it a second thought. Now he would give anything to be eloquent and convincing.

"Jewel." He found himself kneeling where he stood, mimicking her position though he didn't move any closer to her. She was at least ten feet away. It was the longest ten feet he had ever seen in his life. "Talk to me, Dove. Please just talk to me. Tell me what your logic is. Help me understand how you could possibly come to this conclusion." He decided that if he couldn't appeal to her emotions, maybe he could reason with her knowledge or lack thereof.

She finally looked up. Her cheeks were red and streaked with tears. Her eyes were deep pools of sorrow that he found himself drowning in. Sucking in breaths between the small sobs still forcing their way out of her, she met his gaze.

"Why would you think you should be with him, that you deserve him but not me?" Dalton nearly choked on the words. His wolf was ramming at the boundaries he'd forced around him to keep him from taking over. He didn't want to hear anything about Jewel going with another. The wolf didn't want Dalton discussing it with her because it wasn't an option, not to them anyway.

"I'm a gypsy healer," she said and her voice wavered slightly. "I was created to serve the Canis lupis—a servant, Dalton," her voice grew stronger as she spoke. "The lowest of the low, that is my lot in life; it has always been my lot in life and just when I think that will change, just when this magical world dropped in my lap, I find out that nothing will change. I will still be the one on the bottom. I know that compared to what you have endured my grievances are miniscule, but to me they are painful. For once I want to not feel helpless. If I stay with you, I will serve the wolves and I will serve you; I will feel as though all the protection you feel is so necessary simply means that you don't think I am capable of taking care of myself. I will live in your shadow, submitting to your every command because you're my Alpha, right? You might be Dillon's Beta, but as my mate *you* are my Alpha, and I will never be your equal. I don't want to be the one hiding in the shadows anymore. I can't be."

Dalton took several deep breaths before he spoke. The air felt heavy and stifling in his lungs, but he knew if he didn't take a moment to compose himself, all that would come out were growls. Every word that came out of her mouth was a thought planted there by Volcan. Jewel knew how precious his species considered the gypsy healers. She knew that she was everything to him, and he would never consider her lower than himself. Once he had decided to take her as his true mate, to not walk away, he had never hidden any of his emotions or feelings for her. She could not possibly truly believe that he would expect her to simply obey him like a mindless slave. "Do you really believe what you are saying? Do you really think I could ever treat you as though you were beneath me, like a servant?"

He watched her carefully, searching for any sign that his Jewel was still there—the Jewel who had endured hell at the hands of Lorelle, holding on just five minutes longer, over and over again. He saw her lips tremble as she fought some silent emotion and finally nodded.

"Now you're just lying to me." His eyes narrowed on his prey, because that is what she was becoming to him. She was running from him and it was stirring up his wolf's desire to hunt. He would be victorious in this hunt, any other outcome would destroy him.

"I," she began but he shook his head slightly cutting her off.

"No more lies, Jewel Stone. I have a pretty good idea of the poison that Volcan filled your mind with;

although I don't understand how he got you to so thoroughly believe him. As much as I hate to state the obvious, let alone repeat myself, I will go ahead and say this again and I'll say it until you believe it. You. Are. Mine. My mate, created for me and I was created for you. There isn't a male Canis lupis alive that would allow another to take his mate from him and I am not the exception. I will not let you leave me and if you think that means I consider you less than me, then you haven't been listening to me very well."

"Dalt—,"

"Let. Me. Finish." he bit out each word. He was angry, no that wasn't strong enough for what he was feeling. He was completely enraged. He didn't want to scare her, or intimidate her, but she needed to understand that there was no way in seven hells he would give her up. He would not condemn either of them to an existence without the other; it would be agony. "From the moment I realized that you really could be my mate, I prayed that it wouldn't be true. Not because I didn't want you, but because I didn't think that I deserved you. I was a fool to think that my will could compete with the Great Luna's ordained plan. I realized that there was no walking away from you, and then I realized that I didn't want to walk away. I wanted you. The revelation hit me like a two ton battering ram, and I knew that I would tear down any obstacle, kill any opponent, destroy any species, level any kingdom, and sacrifice all that I am to keep you. I've envisioned the life we could have, and I want to grab onto it with both hands and never let go. I've seen you in my minds' eye in my bed, lost in my arms. I've seen you swollen and glowing with my child, holding our baby as I held you. Every possible dream I never thought I would get, I have seen with you. And if you think your inferiority complex is going to keep us from having that, then you need to check your facts."

Her eyes were wide and her mouth had dropped open slightly as she listened to him. He had not meant to be so blunt, but then he was literally fighting for his life. He would stoop to any level necessary.

"We, I," she stammered. Finally taking a slow breath and squaring her shoulders she tried again. "We are two broken people, Dalton. It's a case of the blind leading the blind; how can two broken people be good for each other? How can I be what you need when I'm constantly analyzing your intentions and wondering if all of this sweetness is just a ploy to make me yours? Because let's face it, Dalton, you are not the type of guy that ever takes a second look at a girl like me. And what about you? You can barely touch me for fear that you are going to contaminate me from your tainted past. Yes," she nodded. "I heard those thoughts. You might have thought I wasn't listening but I heard how hard it is for you to put your arms around me, how you have to force yourself to touch me because your wolf demands it. How is that supposed to make me feel? The man who is supposed to be mine doesn't even want to touch me! How can we possibly be good for each other?"

"WE LEARN!" he roared finally giving into the wolf just a little. His wolf hurt over the fact that he, the man, struggled with touching their mate. But Jewel had it wrong, it wasn't because he didn't want to touch her. "How did you come to know all that you know? Were you just born full of knowledge? No, you studied, you read, and you learned the things you know. We will choose to learn how to be mates." The distance between them was beginning to tear a hole inside of him so he stood and walked towards her. His, no doubt glowing, eyes held hers as he stalked her, and once he was standing in front of her, he reached down and grasped her arms pulling her to her feet. Even standing she still had to tilt her head to look up at him. "I can promise you that I will be the most diligent student you have ever seen. I will make it my life's mission to study every aspect of you, to learn you inside and out, so that I can meet your every need, your every desire, and your every want. I will spend the rest of our lives showing you that there is nothing that will stand between me and you. Not your past, not my past, and sure as hell not an evil fae who wants to convince you that he is better for you than your true mate." She was shaking in his hands but he didn't let her go. He wasn't about to break the connection he finally had with her.

"And for the record I *want* to touch you. In fact, if you knew how desperately I crave to touch you it would terrify you. The reason I am afraid to touch you is because I know that once I have a taste of you, once your skin is burned into my hands and my memory, I will never be sated. I will need more and more of you, like a drug you will ensnare me and hold me captive to your will." He leaned down closer to her until his face was less than an inch from hers. "The few times that I have allowed myself the luxury of touching you nearly drove me mad. I want to wait until we are bonded and the Blood Rites are complete before I give into my need of you. If I had known that you took my struggle with touch as rejection, I would have explained it the moment the thoughts entered my mind. It seems one of the things we are going to have to learn is communication. I will consider this my first lesson. Now I will give you your first lesson."

He saw that she was going to argue with him, but he pressed a finger to her lips. "Listen, learn." Dalton took her face in his hands cradling her as if she was the most priceless treasure because that's what she was to him. "Close your eyes." He waited until she complied and then continued. "Open yourself completely to our bond. Reach into my mind and learn something about your mate."

Jewel closed her eyes as the fight slipped out of her. She knew everything he had said was sincere and true. But everything Volcan had said had been true as well, hadn't it? Dalton's voice drew her back to the moment and she found herself doing as he instructed. She released the tight hold she had kept on their bond, and the emotions that rushed into her would have knocked her back to her knees had Dalton not been holding her. She reached up and put a hand on his chest, centering her mind and pushing her magic into him. He wanted her to learn something about him. After what she had put him through, she owed him.

She was hit immediately with a need so strong that she felt as though it was her own. As she pushed further she finally caught the source of the need. *"Touch, mine, mate,"* his voice rumbled in her mind but she realized that it wasn't him talking to her; it was like his thoughts were on a loop. Over and over they repeated. *"Taste, hold, mine, hers, want."* What surprised her more was that they weren't just thoughts, they were feelings. Dalton hadn't been exaggerating when he had told her that his need to touch her was like a drug. Jewel felt his hands on her face slide down to her neck; the heat of his skin warmed her own and had her leaning into him. She saw his memories then, memories of her. She watched as he sat on the edge of the bed where she had lay unconscious for months and stared at her longingly. He turned to look at the door as Sally stepped into the room and the change in his face was remarkable. As if transformed by cinematic computer graphics, he instantly went from an adoring mate to a stoic male, his face betraying no emotion. Sally froze in her tracks. Realizing her intrusion might spark the already volatile wolf, she backed out slowly. As soon as Sally left the room and Dalton turned back to look at her, his face morphed, returning to the affectionate male he had been moments before. The tight line of his lips loosened, his eyes softened dramatically, and every muscle seemed to relax.

To her surprise he reached out, his hand shaking like a druggie, and touched her face. It was a tender caress, and by the look on his face it brought him peace. As that memory faded, another emerged in its place. She stood before him, finally awake, though not of her own doing. She knew, though she had yet to mention it to Dalton, that Volcan had released her enough so that she slipped back into consciousness. Dalton had just walked into the room to find her standing, and she watched as he nearly fell to his knees. When he was finally close enough, he reached out and pulled her into the shelter of his strong arms. He buried his face in her hair and she could feel the sensation as if it were happening all over again. A tremor ran through her as she watched him nip her neck, remembering the sensation and utter joy at having him so near and her knees buckled. All the while as she watched his memories, she could feel the control that it took for him not to mark her, not to claim her, seduce her, and make her his in every way. No man should be able to have that much control over needs so powerful. It seemed impossible and she didn't know how he had kept himself from giving in because he would have been successful. Jewel would have been a puddle at his feet if he ever turned that charm of his on her.

"Do you see?" Dalton's voice filled her mind. *"Do you feel what I feel for you?"*

She nodded and was unable to speak for all the emotions, hers and his, flooding her senses.

"Do you feel my touch now, Jewel? Do you feel my skin on yours?"

Jewel sucked in a breath as she felt his hands slip under her shirt and up her back. She was surprised to feel a slight tremor in his large, warm, powerful hands spread across the expanse of her back. She could hear his wolf growling, and then she heard him speak to her. *"Mate, ours, we won't let you go. We are yours and you are ours. Feel, know, and learn us. We will learn you."* Other than the tremble, Dalton's hands didn't move on her back. He didn't stroke her or caress her, just simply held her and yet it was more desirable than if he had been exploring her.

"Ask me," he rumbled in her mind. *"Communicate with me, Little Dove."*

"Why are you so still? If I had my hands on your bare skin I wouldn't be able to keep them still for want of needing to know how you felt."

"I know my limits. If I allow myself more than this, I won't be able to stop and you won't want me to."

"I'm confused," she admitted quietly after several minutes of them simply holding onto one another. She hadn't meant to say it, but she couldn't hold it inside any longer.

"Finally," he muttered as she opened her eyes and met his pale blue ones. She could see his burning need for her to talk to him and be open with him as he waited for her to continue.

"I believe you both. The things he said were true; they felt true. But then the things you said are as well. Am I evil, Dalton?"

"No," he said firmly. "You have the capacity to do wrong, because you're fallible. But you aren't without compassion or empathy. You do not act without remorse or regret." His eyes softened as he pulled her tighter against him. "No, Little Dove, you are definitely not evil."

"Then why does some part of me still feel like choosing what Volcan offered is the right decision? I mean, I know he is evil."

"Why does anyone choose to do the wrong thing? Is it because the wrong decision is ugly, without allure or appeal? No, it's because it has such great magnetism and it calls to us. Evil portrays itself as something good and right, twisting its purpose until it feels as though to not choose it would be foolish. Power is a very seductive enticing lover." She felt as though he was trying to memorize every detail of her face. "When a person has spent their life feeling helpless, or stuck the way you did, that power becomes even more alluring. I can understand not wanting to be helpless to the judgment and whims of others. If you remember, I was held captive and tortured and molested. I know exactly what it is to feel powerless."

She let out an un-ladylike snort. "Yeah, but I don't see you jumping on the evil bandwagon as it drives by."

A single brow rose on his handsome face. "No, I just went on a century long killing spree and sexual binge. Nothing to worry about at all."

"You only killed people who were bad," Jewel pointed out.

"I had no right to be their judge and executioner. I was angry; I wanted to vengeance." He paused and his head tilted slightly as his eyes narrowed. "What do you want, Jewel?"

Jewel tried to shut the bond before he could see her thoughts. She wasn't ready for him to know that even after everything he had said, after all declarations and though she wanted to choose him, she still *had* to go with Volcan. If she didn't he would kill everyone she cared about. She wouldn't be responsible for their deaths when she could prevent it. She watched as his face hardened as he realized she was once again shutting him out.

"My precious dove, for someone with the IQ of a genius, you are incredibly thick sometimes," he growled at her.

"Why do you call me Little Dove?" It probably wasn't the right time to ask such a question, but Jewel didn't know if she would ever see him again and she wanted to know.

Dalton shook his head at her. "The night that we are bonded and I take you as my mate I will tell you."

Jewel's heart plummeted to her feet. She wanted that night more than she had wanted anything and yet it just wasn't meant to be. As she had said to him, sacrifices were a casualty of conflict, and she had found herself smack dab in the middle of a feud that had been going on for centuries.

"Am I to guess that by the way your face just fell and your soul just cried out for mine, you aren't expecting to ever have that night with me?"

As she stared at him, unable to answer him for fear that she would simply fall at his feet and beg him to make it alright—to keep her safe—she saw realization dawn on him.

"He's coming for you isn't he?" The darkness that seemed to envelop Dalton as his face morphed into the stone mask that he kept in place with everyone but her made his deep voice sound even more sinister. His pale blue eyes began to glow and she watched in awe as his teeth grew in size. "That's why he said you would go with him willingly. He's coming for you and you agreed to go."

She stepped back from him, all the while going over the facts in her mind about prey not running from a predator. But from the look in his eyes she totally understood why they forgot that rule and bolted for the hills. He took another step forward and she matched it by taking another back.

"Is he coming for you, Jewel?" he asked her again, slower this time as if she hadn't understood him the first time. "He thinks to take you from me and you think to go."

Jewel wanted to shrink back at the accusation in his voice, but he was right and had every right to throw it at her. She was hurting him. It was the last thing she wanted, and yet the only choice she could see that she had.

Dalton couldn't hold back his beast any longer. Now that he understood why his mate was so upset, he lost control of the beast. She was going to leave him. He could see the set determination in her jaw, though in her eyes she was begging him to stop her. Dalton didn't think she even realized that her soul was crying out to its mate. Had she been a Canis lupus, her wolf would have been thrashing inside of her attempting to get to him. And though he wanted to answer her, he was at a loss as to what to do. Volcan was not physically stronger than Dalton, but he wielded dark magic that Dalton didn't understand. The fae was powerful and Dalton wasn't too proud to admit that he had no idea how to defeat him.

He took another step towards her and when her back hit the wall, her eyes widened as she realized that she was trapped. His wolf wanted to howl victoriously at his caught prey. Dalton stepped forward until his body was inches from her own and looked down at her. Jewel tilted her head back against the wall to look at him, and her chest rose and fell rapidly as her heart rate increased at his close proximity. Her scent was intoxicating to him as it swirled in the air around him, calling to him. Seducing him, it drew him closer. His left hand gripped the back of her neck and tilted her head to the side, exposing her neck. With his right hand he tugged on her shirt until she was bare from shoulder to throat. Her scarred flesh taunted him, dared him to take what was his, to add his bite and place the only mark that had the right to be there on her, and he knew he was fighting a losing battle.

"Dalton," her whimper only stirred the wolf more.

Claim, protect, mine, he growled inside his mind. If she was hell bent on leaving him, on giving her life up for the good of others, then he would make damn sure that he would be going with her. His lips pulled back from his sharp teeth and he struck without hesitation sinking his teeth deep into the place between her neck and shoulder. He heard her sharp intake of air and then felt her relax into him as the pleasure of the mate bite consumed her.

Dalton felt the rush of her warm, sweet blood gush into his mouth from the pulsing artery. She was perfect, everything he knew she would be, and yet better than he could have ever imagined. She'd already had his blood multiple times and even once sunk her teeth into him, but he wanted it again. Without releasing her he guided her mouth to his own neck and felt the magic of the mate bond take over as her instincts kicked in. She bit him without a second thought and Dalton's hand tightened on her neck while the other landed on her hip and pulled her against him. He had been right to think she would become his addiction. As they marked one another, taking in the very essence of the other, he felt their bond strengthen as if the chord between was getting thicker. He wanted to keep drinking, her taste and the intimacy of knowing only he would ever have this right was heady, but his first instinct was to protect her, and he didn't want to take too much from her.

Dalton began to pull back and Jewel whimpered in protest. He wanted to give her what she wanted but it was not the time or place. Usually after the Blood Rites were complete true mates would be lost to one another, needing to complete the physical union as well, but Dalton would have to settle for just holding her.

"Jewel, it's enough," he told her as he pulled her from his neck. She looked up at him, drunk on the taste of him, lost in the passion of the Blood Rites and he wanted her. She licked her lips, cleaning off the remnant of his blood, and he groaned as his eyes followed the movement. He knew he had to taste her lips; he couldn't wait any longer. As his head lowered to hers and she tilted her mouth up to him, clearly needing the same thing, he was suddenly thrown back across the room with such force that when he hit the opposite wall his body went through it.

His eyes snapped up as he jumped to his feet. Volcan had his arm around Jewel's waist with his hand dangerously close to an area of her body that no man, save him, had a right to touch. Dalton knew he wouldn't make it to her in time. He was fast, but not faster than the flash of the fae. He heard Peri's shouts and the furious pounding on the door as the others tried to get into him. His eyes never left Volcan.

"You will never touch her again. I hope you enjoyed your little rendezvous, but don't get too used to the Blood bond; it won't last long."

Dalton lunged for the sorcerer just as Jewel reached out a hand to him. Her eyes pleaded with him and the last thing he heard before Volcan flashed his mate from him was her voice in his mind. *"I love you."*

11

"There comes a time in everyone's life when they need a hero. At some point, everyone needs someone to be stronger than they are, for just a little while, to help them bear the load of whatever devastation has befallen them. They will need someone to cry for them when there are no tears left. They will need someone to reach through the fires of hell and pull them out because they have no strength left to climb out on their own. We will all need a hero at some point, and my time is now. I need a hero. I need you." ~Jewel

The door suddenly crashed open behind him as bodies came tumbling through when Volcan's magic dissipated with his parting.

"Where is he?" Peri snapped as her head whipped around the room.

"Where is Jewel?" Sally's desperate voice echoed what Dalton felt, only it didn't even come close to the magnitude with which he felt her absence.

"Gone," Dalton answered in a suddenly very calm voice. The other males were in the hall but wisely didn't enter what he had come to consider as his territory. He didn't want to be there crammed in that room where all of their scents were overwhelming what was left of Jewel's. He needed air, needed space so he could think. "I'll return," he growled as he phased and ran for the window. He hadn't bothered to open it but knew as it flew open just before he expected to smash through it, Peri was the reason he didn't.

His feet hit the ground just as he heard his Alpha's call. It rolled off of Dalton like oil. There was only one thing stronger than the pull an Alpha had on his pack and that was the pull of a true mate. Dalton's true mate was gone. Taken from him by the most evil being their kind had ever seen. He couldn't even begin to think of what Volcan would want from Jewel. If he did, it would drive him mad, and he wouldn't be able to plan her rescue.

He would get her back. He had marked her and could find her anywhere, but he knew better than to go rushing in. He needed a plan, a strategy in order to be successful. Dalton reached the edge of the creek that ran near Peri's home, and he sat down and looked up at the moon. In his mind he could still see her, still smell her, and still taste her, and he was ravenous for more. The mournful howl that ripped from him was full of that longing, and until he had her back in his arms, he knew the ache for her would only grow.

"We must remain calm," Dalton told his wolf. The beast didn't want to obey. It kept reaching for the

bond, whining each time it hit a blocked wall where its mate should be. He couldn't hear her, could only feel that she was alive but nothing more.

"I am loyal to none but her," his wolf informed him. *"She alone is my concern. I will concede to your human knowledge, but I will kill anyone who gets in our way."* Dalton had only heard his wolf talk in complete sentences like that a handful of times, and it always was unnerving to hear the animal think like a human. *"Then we are on the same page,"* Dalton told him.

"The sorcerer will suffer for touching her, taking her," Dalton agreed wholeheartedly with his wolf. Volcan would burn for taking his mate. A quick death was too good for that scum, but as long as Volcan was alive, even if it was to be tortured, he would be a threat to his mate.

"Dalton," her voice suddenly broke through the block.

"Jewel!" He phased to his human form as if he would be able to snatch her with his arms through the bond back to his side.

"Can he break the bond?" The fear in her voice ripped through him.

"I'm not sure. He is powerful. Do you know where you are?"

She ignored his question and asked another of her own. *"Scientists have proven that the will is often times stronger than the body, even stronger than diseases. I won't let him break it. You told me to keep fighting, that you would be back, is that still true?"*

264

"I will always come for you. I won't give up. I will always fight with you, by your side, as your equal." He could feel her slipping away again and he was desperate to hold onto her. *"Keep fighting, Little Dove. I will be there soon, very soon."*

"Just five minutes longer," she told him and he felt her hand on his face and her breath on his lips and then she was gone.

The silence left in her absence was absolute. Her light was gone and he was suddenly plunged into a darkness he had never experienced. When his parents had died, when his will had been taken, when his dignity had been stripped from him and his moral compass derailed, he hadn't felt as utterly consumed by the darkness as he did in that moment. He was so focused on trying to breathe, trying to not suffocate by the sudden weight that seemed to have descended on him, that he didn't hear anyone approaching him.

"Talk to me, Dalton," Dillon commanded his Beta as he threw a pair of shorts to him. It had been several hours since Jewel's disappearance, and other than Dalton's initial reaction, there had been nothing. He had watched him from a distance once Dalton left Peri's home, worried that they would have to step in when Dalton lost control. But so far the only pain that Dillon had seen was the one lone howl and the anguish in Dalton's eyes. His face was as blank and stoic as ever. There was no pacing, no yelling or throwing things, and no out of control behavior that would normally be seen in a male whose mate had been taken from him. If Dillon was honest with himself, Dalton's lack of reaction made him more concerned than if the giant man was losing his cool.

"What did she say before she was flashed away?" Still his Beta said nothing. Dalton slipped on the shorts and then stood staring at the creek that ran through Farie. The scene was so picture perfect that it was hard to believe that something so horrific had just happened.

"Dammit Beta! Answer me!" Dillon snarled. As Alpha his need to protect his pack was on a whole other level and now one of his own had lost his mate and all Dillon could think was that he needed to fix it.

"How long have we known each other?" Dillon continued when Dalton still didn't answer. "How many times have you been there for me? When I left to be with Lilly, who took care of things for me? Even though you weren't my Beta then, you defended me to those who questioned my whereabouts. Who was I able to talk to about that time in my life which was in complete contradiction to what we teach our males? YOU! You have been there for me in your silent, brooding, grumpy ass way, but you were always there. Let me be there for you. Let me help. It's my right as your Alpha. Please don't make me use the Alpha command on you. You know that I will if I have to. I will do whatever it takes to protect my own. And if I can't control you, I'll go to one who can. I'll seek out Vasile if need be." Dillon's arms were crossed in front of his chest, and his jaw was clenched tight as he glared at the wolf he had called friend for so long. A male who had already been through so much was now going to endure something even worse—the loss of his mate.

"I bit her." Dalton's deep voice rumbled. It was not the words Dillon expected to hear from him.

"She bears your mark? You're blood bonded?"

"Yes," Dalton growled.

"So we can find her."

"And when I do I will kill him and tan her hide for ever thinking she had the right to sacrifice her life."

Dillon tried not to smile because it was such an uncharacteristic thing for Dalton to say, but then he supposed that once a male found his true mate he did a lot of things that were out of character. Adapt or die, his mate always told him. It seems it's true in more instances than just living for centuries.

"Is there a particular reason Dalton is standing so calmly while his mate is in the clutches of a witch maker?" Peri suddenly appeared next to Dillon.

"Not helping, Peri," he growled.

"Don't give a damn, Alpha," she snapped back. "*He* has her, which means he has her blood and her power, and now he can and will be turning any willing, wicked woman into a witch until he rebuilds the covens that we destroyed. He will make Desdemona look like a freaking fairy godmother. We cannot let him rebuild the covens."

Dalton turned and faced his Alpha and the high fae. They stood, both appearing battle ready simply staring at him. He knew that the mask he had so diligently perfected over the centuries was firmly in place, and they would not be able to see any of the burning inferno of rage building inside of him. They wouldn't know that he was barely holding on to his control as everything inside of him shattered. She hadn't wanted to leave him and that gave him some small measure of peace. She had reached for him before Volcan had taken her. Though she spoke of sacrifice and keeping others safe, she wanted to be with him. She loved him; he could see it in her eyes before she ever said it. He had heard it in her voice when she finally told him what she had promised Volcan. He could feel it in her soul as she broke not only his heart but her own by telling him she was going with the evil sorcerer. Dalton knew that Jewel truly believed that she didn't have a choice. She believed that in order to keep the others safe and him safe that she had to do what Volcan wanted. He knew it was just part of her ignorance of their species; she couldn't possibly know that there wasn't a wolf alive that would allow a healer to be in the clutches of one so evil as Volcan. Even if he died and they weren't blood bonded, the Canis lupis would pursue her until she was back in their care, where she belonged. "Can you find her?" Peri asked him drawing him from his thoughts. She apparently hadn't been eavesdropping when Dalton had told Dillon he'd completed the Blood Rites with his mate.

"We completed the Blood Rites before he took her. She is mine; the bond is complete."

"So not only can you find her, but she will begin to feel the discomfort of being separated from you and, by the way, where in the world have you been for the past three days? Did Volcan have something to do with you being AWOL?" Sally suddenly materialized out of the trees with her mate beside her. Dalton was beginning to feel like it was some sort of twisted intervention. But the compassion in her eyes, despite her obvious irritation at him having been gone, was humbling considering he had not been one of her favorites for some time now. Dalton had known when he marked Jewel that he would only be increasing the pain she would endure at being away from him, but that wasn't enough reason for him to leave her unbound to him. He needed to know that if she left this world, he would be joining her—as was his right as her mate.

"She will," he agreed as his eyes met Sally's. "And yes, my absence was Volcan's doing." He left it at that. There was no need for them to know that he had laid naked, frozen against his will, unable to aid his mate in a fairy field.

"She's strong, Dalton," Sally said her lips attempting a small smile.

Dalton nodded once. "She's stronger than she knows."

"So are we just going to stand here complementing her and hoping that her awesome strength will rescue her own ass, or are we going to do something?"

Peri's hands were on her hips as she tapped her foot restlessly.

"I'm leaving within the hour, but I have a stop to make before I begin to hunt my mate." He had been contemplating his next move and one thing he felt with absolute certainty was that there was one person who might be able to help him.

His Alpha's eyes narrowed on him. "Where are we stopping?" Dalton didn't miss the fact that Dillon had just subtly told him that he would be going with him whether Dalton wanted him to or not.

"Yes, do tell. What could be as important as going after your female?" Peri asked.

"I need to speak with her mother."

Their eyes widened at his words and Sally took a step forward. "Do you think now is the time to be meeting your future mother-in-law?"

"She knows things. That was the only explanation he offered. He didn't want to explain that he knew a little about the power of names related to the elements. Jewel's mother had obviously known as well because she gave Jewel a powerful name. The woman had obviously foreseen that her daughter would need it. "She might be able to help," he added, in case they didn't catch on to that fact. Dalton felt edgy as he stood there with the group watching him, as though they expected him to suddenly break into hysterics. If they were expecting him to express how he felt about losing Jewel, then they would be disappointed. He didn't want to talk; he wanted to move. But he knew the worst thing he could do for his mate was to run headlong into the fight without a plan.

"She's yours," Dillon said. "So I'll let you take the lead on this hunt."

Dalton nodded his thanks at his Alpha, but didn't bother to mention that there was no one who could stop him from taking the lead. Jewel was his. He had been through hell and back and endured centuries of loneliness and finally found her. He couldn't lose her and he wouldn't entrust her rescue to anyone but himself.

Peri let out an irritated huff as she turned to leave. "Fine, we go in an hour; Dalton leads the hunt and, Sally, please be a dear and write this down for future reference. If we needed the damn gypsy healers to sacrifice themselves in order to protect the rest of us, I would be the first to start passing them out like Halloween candy."

Dalton watched Peri flash and then turned to Sally his brow slightly furrowed.

Sally shrugged sheepishly. "She's a little bitter over the fact that I died to save her."

Costin growled as he looked at his mate but spoke to Dalton. "It seems our healers have a tendency to want to help."

Sally rolled her eyes. "Imagine that, a gypsy healer wanting to help, oh the horror," she said dryly.

Dalton let out a huff of laughter that was anything but humorous. "Perhaps, you should warn the other potential mates to the healers." He looked at

Dillon and then back at Sally. His voice was unyielding as he spoke. "The females of our packs are the heart and soul. It is never your place to sacrifice yourself. You are to be protected, cherished, and loved. Never put your mate through that again." As he turned to go he met Dillon's gaze. "One hour." Then he took off in a jog back towards Peri's home.

He jumped through the window as he had done so many times before, but this time there was no one for him to see. There was no beautiful redhead lost inside of herself in need of his company. The room felt lifeless and void of all of the light that she brought to it simply by being there. He crossed over to the bed and picked up the pillow that her head had laid on. Her scent hit him before he even pressed it to his face. He breathed deep, treasuring the precious scent of his mate. It amazed him that her scent alone stirred his wolf. In all of his long life no other smell had ever created such strong and numerous emotions.

"Can I just be really honest and say if I didn't know about this whole true mate thing, that would be really creepy," Kara's voice drifted in from the hall, and she wasn't alone; he could smell Nick nearby as well. That was a thought that would have been interesting to him had he not just lost his mate. Dalton didn't turn to face her. He knew his eyes would be glowing with the wolf so close to the surface, and he didn't want to scare the young female.

"Is there something you need?" he asked as gently as he could. He knew that the only reason he was even taking time to speak with her was because Jewel cared about Kara. They had gone through something traumatic together, and it had created a bond between them. Dalton would never want to hurt someone Jewel loved, because it would in turn hurt his mate.

"I just wanted to tell you that I have faith in you. I know you will get Jewel back." Her voice didn't shake nor did he hear any tears in it. But he didn't doubt that Kara was hurting. She was simply hardened by already having lived a life wrought with pain and fear. He didn't know her story, but he could see that Kara's eyes were much older than they should be at the tender age of sixteen. She had seen too much, been through too much, and though she seemed okay, there was no way she had emerged unscathed by her past.

Dalton was surprised by her words. He couldn't remember the last time a female, other than Jewel, had seen something good in him or bothered to tell him. He didn't say anything in return; he simply nodded as he placed the pillow back on the bed. He heard her footsteps begin to walk away and then she paused. "Are you alright?" He heard Nick ask her and the gentleness in his voice surprised Dalton. "I just wanted him to know that he is capable and that I have faith in him," Kara explained. "Did you need something?" Because their connection was obvious to the big wolf, Dalton waited for the male to say something like, *yes I need you*. Dalton understood the other wolf's hesitancy, perhaps because he had tried to deny his own bond. "I just wanted to make sure you were safe. Male Canis lupus can be a little volatile when their mates are in danger," he answered. A shy thank you was the end of their conversation and they finally walked away and Dalton was thankful to be alone again.

As he glanced around the room his mind sifted through the memories of the nights that he had spent there reading and talking to her. He thought of all the times he had held her hand, kissed her forehead, or ran his fingers through her hair, and he vowed that they would not be his last.

With one last look at the bed he turned and left heading for the living room where he could hear the others gathering.

Peri stood on the first step of the stairs so that she could be a little close to eye level with all of the males. Her eyes met Dalton's as he entered, and he gave a nod to her as he stopped in the center of the room and folded his large arms across his chest.

"Listen up, wolves," Peri called them to attention and the rumbling voices grew silent as all eyes turned to her. "Dalton is in charge of this rescue mission. You will set aside your dominance issues and get on board, or I will bind you to this house, put an apron on you that reads *this is what stupid looks like,* and you will stay here cleaning toilets and washing windows. Get me?" She waited until every head had nodded. "Good. Now, listen up to what Goliath has to say because I have a feeling he will only say it once."

Dalton cleared his throat before he began. "For the time being I will defer most of your tasks to Peri. I prefer to work alone. Since I know that is not going to happen, I will agree to three of you. Take no offense," he said as he glanced at each male from the other packs, "but my control is not what it needs to be and I feel it would be easier for me if I wasn't around unmated males. Dillon, Peri, and Lucian will accompany me." He turned his gaze on Sally and Costin who looked like they wanted to argue. "You two need to stay here with Kara; it would not be right for her to be here alone with all the unmated males. Once we know more we will come up with a plan that will utilize as many people as necessary to get my mate back. Are there any questions?"

"Do you have a plan right now?" Drayden asked.

Dalton clenched his teeth as he attempted to remain patient. He didn't want to be answering questions; he wanted to be moving, needed to be working towards the ultimate goal of getting Jewel back. "Not fully. As soon as we are done here I'm going to find Jewel's mother to speak with her." He turned back to Peri. "Are we ready?

Peri shrugged. "You're the one in charge; we're ready when you say we are."

Dalton nodded once. "In that case I will no longer spend time explaining myself. You can follow without question or stay behind." There was no anger in his voice, no irritation. He was simply being honest. It was best that they knew what to expect if they were going to work with him, because when they did start asking questions, which they would, he would remind them of this very conversation.

Peri headed toward him with Lucian and Dillon flanking her as she gave a sardonic laugh. "I have a feeling you've used up all your words for the next month so it's not like you're going to say anything more. Might as well be on our way." She glanced at Costin. "Don't let your mate, or Kara for that matter, do anything that they might think is heroic and/or sacrificial for the pack." Then to Sally and Kara. "And if either of you feels the need to save someone, for the love of werewolf sanity everywhere, please just plant a tree, drive a hybrid, turn off a light, and save the earth like the rest of the humans." She held out her arms on either side of her for Dalton, Dillon, and Lucian to touch. "Let's go boys, we've got a Gem to find."

Dalton grabbed the smallest piece of Peri's shirt that he could on her sleeve and then he was swallowed by the darkness as the fae flashed them from her home. They reappeared on a crumbled sidewalk, tall thin weeds bursting forth from its vein-like cracks. As Dalton looked around he saw that the neighborhood was long past its picket fence days.

"This is it." Peri's voice pulled his attention to the small shack of a house in front of them. His eyes narrowed on the rundown structure and his lips thinned into a straight line. "This is where she grew up?" He turned to look at his Alpha. "I could have prevented this."

Dillon shook his head. "She is who she needs to be because of where she's from. There is a reason she's lived the life she lived."

Dalton knew he was right, but that didn't mean he had to like the fact that his mate had lived in a shack in an unsafe neighborhood with no protection from a loving male.

Suddenly the door opened and out stepped a woman. For a split second Dalton's breath caught because he could have sworn it was Jewel standing there. But then she stepped into the daylight and he saw that though she did look very much like her daughter, and was still very beautiful, life had taken its toll on Gem Stone.

"I have dreamt of you," she said without introduction. Her voice was strong as her eyes met his and held. "If you are here, then it means that he has her."

"How do you know who I am and why I have come?" he asked her, needing confirmation that Gem truly was a seer as Jewel had told him. There were hundreds or more humans that played at being seers, or fortune tellers as they called them, but there were few that truly had the ability. He did not want to get his hopes up if Gem was one of the posers. Her eyes seemed to cloud over and the wind around them picked up. "Dalton Black, only surviving son, once a tortured soul, avenger, executioner, lone wolf but now...." Her eyes snapped open. "You are mate, friend, lover, savior to my daughter. I have seen you, I have named you, and now I so call you to be her champion. If you fail, our world will come to an end and a new era will begin. An era of darkness, blood, and death ruled by a merciless king, and if you fail, Jewel will be his queen."

Peri turned to look at Dalton, a single brow raised. "I suppose it would behoove you not to screw this up, just the fate of all mankind and the soul of your female at stake."

Dalton ignored the fae and looked back up at Gem. "Do I succeed?"

The strange power that swirled around her was now gone and the air had died down. Her eyes were clear and bright again as she shrugged. "I don't know. I cannot see what happens."

"Why not?" Dalton asked.

"Because I die before it is made known."

"Man, that's a bummer," Peri muttered under her breath.

Gem looked the fae and added not unkindly. "Many will die before the end."

Peri let out an exaggerated sigh. "A-a-a-a-nd it just keeps getting better and better."

"You have much to do," Gem told them. "But before you begin your journey there are things you need to know." She motioned for them to follow her as she turned and headed back into her house.

Once they were inside Gem motioned for them to take a seat at a small, circular dining table. They crowded around it and though Dalton knew that it would be more polite to wait for her to begin, he found that with his mate in the clutches of another he was running very thin on courtesy.

"Will what you tell us help us defeat Volcan?

Gem looked at him with wide eyes and a creased forehead. "Volcan cannot be defeated."

Dalton felt his heart drop. He had no idea what to say to that. Peri wasn't quite so tongue tied.

"What the hell do you mean he can't be defeated?" she barked as Lucian put a hand on her shoulder attempting to soothe his prickly mate.

"Volcan's downfall must be of his own making. His demise must come from the decisions he makes. You're only chance at victory is to force him to move in the direction that will lead him down that path."

"So this is more like a battle of strategy, not magic and fur?" Peri asked.

"He must believe he is outsmarting you."

Dalton's muscles tightened as he processed the information and as he considered the possibility that they might not be able to beat him. He then remembered what Gem had said outside. "You said that if we do not get Jewel back that she would become his queen. What do you mean by that?" Dalton's eyes narrowed as Gem's face grew pale. Whatever she was about to tell him brought her pain, and he could tell she didn't like having to be the one to tell him.

"Dark magic is a seductive force, Dalton Black. Like radiation soaks into everything that stays in its proximity, so dark magic does as well. It calls to the part in us that desires to serve self and nothing else. It whispers to us that we deserve power, that we are entitled to anything and everything, and we begin to believe it. The effect that darkness has on an individual is based on the length of exposure, the depth of the depravity of the exposed individual, and the ability for the victim to resist the pull. I know my daughter. She has much goodness in her, but she has not emerged unscathed from her childhood and adolescence. She bears not only the physical scars from her encounter with the sorcerer, but scars on her soul as well. She has endured painful things that have created crevices for bitterness to take root, which gives darkness and evil a foothold. She isn't evil, but the longer she is surrounded by the evil that has so completely engulfed Volcan, the greater the chance that she will not remain unaffected."

Dalton wasn't surprised that Gem knew of Jewel's injuries; she had proven herself true.

"You're saying she will choose to be his queen. She isn't forced."

"Sometimes, only the goodness of another steering us in the right direction can keep us from falling. You are her goodness, Dalton, just as she is yours. She brings out the best in you and you do the same for her. You can help her heal those cracks that have opened and let the darkness in. You can love her as no one else can, and love covers a multitude of sins. Love gives hope and hope leads to belief and belief leads to action." She paused and took in a deep breath. "There's more."

Dalton nodded his head for her to continue though he was pretty sure he didn't want to hear what she was about to say.

"If you do not get to her in time, even before she is queen, she will become with child."

"If that's not a kick to the balls, I don't know what is," Peri said as she pinched the bridge of her nose.

Dalton was pretty sure that he wasn't going to be able to take in another breath. He was going to suffocate right there in the home of his mate's mother.

"Volcan will be the father?" Dalton asked nearly choking on the words.

"It is unclear who the father will be."

Peri's face was taking on a sickly shade of green. "I'm pretty sure I just met my quota of sick, twisted, and utterly disgusting news for the year."

Dalton pushed away from the table taking deep breaths, attempting to prepare himself for the answer to his next question. "Why not?"

"Because he intends for her to be *the mother.* The beginning of a new class of witches. Every child she bears will have not only witch blood, but gypsy healer blood as well. Though he does desire her, he will always desire power more. If that means Jewel must have other bed partners, he will allow it."

"Okay I was wrong, *now* I have reached my quota." Peri's lips were tight and her face more severe looking than Dalton had ever seen it.

Lucian turned and looked at Dillon before speaking to Dalton. "You realize what this means?"

Dalton nodded. "If she becomes with child, my life must be forfeited so that the bond will take her life as well." There was no inflection in his voice, no emotion on his face to give away the soul wrenching anguish that was threatening to drag him to his knees. "You will grant me this request?" he asked his Alpha.

"I will; you have my word."

Dalton looked at Lucian and Peri. "I would ask something of you as well. Retrieve her body. Don't leave her with him."

Lucian nodded. "We will not abandon her, whether it be in life or death that we search for her."

"Okay, that is enough!" Peri said as she stood from her chair. "Gem Stone, while I appreciate your gift and the information, I'm done with the gloom and doom. Dalton will not have to be put down like a mangy dog, Lucian and I will not have to retrieve Jewel's body, and Jewel—sure as hell—isn't going to be bearing a bunch of little snot nose witch kids. I don't know how many times I have to tell you thick skulled people this; *I. Don't. Lose.* Now if you all are done bellyaching over a future that will not come to pass, could we please get on with the plan to save our girl and once again a world that is completely oblivious to our awesomeness?

———

"We haven't heard from Peri in quite a few days," Stella said as the group sat around the crackling fire.

The flames danced around them, casting an eerie glow on their faces. This had become their nightly routine. They gathered around the warmth of the flames and talked, sometimes in hushed tones, discussing what might be happening in the world beyond the pixie realm, and sometimes in boisterous laughter, they shared stories with one another. Stella preferred the boisterous laughter because it helped keep her mind off of the growing need to go to him, whoever he was. She could tell that while Anna and Heather were truly enjoying their time bonding, they were growing more and more restless by the day. And they were rubbing their chests a lot more often. Every now and then Anna would meet her eyes and the understanding that ran between the two of them helped Stella remain calm when she began to feel all weepy.

"Speak of the devil," Anna chimed just after Peri appeared before them.

Peri looked at her and smiled with a wicked gleam in her eyes. "And he will arrive to drag you down to the bowels of hell with him. Which is ironically close to what I will be soon doing to you lot."

"What's happened," Elle asked as she stood from her spot on the ground.

"Cliff notes version goes something like this," Peri began. "The bond between Dalton and Jewel opened. Volcan used the bond to get into Jewel's mind and blackmailed her into agreeing to going with him. He came and got her, but not before Dalton completed the Blood Rites just after Jewel finally woke up. Dalton is scarily calm. We've been to see Jewel's mother, who turned out to be some kind of legitimate seer, and she basically informed us that the world is coming to an end. Jewel will become a witch breeding machine, and Dalton will have to die in order to keep Jewel from spitting out mega witches from her lady parts. The whole scenario of course is based on us failing to retrieve Jewel." She clapped her hands and let out a breath. "So everyone caught up, yeah? Good, now Dalton should be able to locate Jewel since they completed the Blood Rites. We have no idea what we will be walking into. That said, I have a job for you. Gem also said that Volcan cannot be defeated."

"For some reason that seems not to bode well for us," Heather interrupted.

"For a blind chick you are quite astute," Peri quipped.

"Points for effort, but that one was sort of lame," Heather said dryly.

"Cut me some slack, Helen, I'm sort of trying to prevent Armageddon. - Peri closed her eyes briefly gathering her thoughts. "Now, as I was saying, Volcan can't be defeated. She said that his demise would be of his own making and that our attack strategy would need to be forcing him to move in the direction that will ensure he makes the choices necessary to destroy himself."

"Like a game of chess," Anna spoke up.

"Exactly," Peri agreed. "Since you all are just sitting here coming up with ways to annoy Ainsel, you might as well be useful. I need strategies. I need you to give me *what ifs* and what to do in case of those *what ifs,* and I need you to have multiple options in play so that we can adjust to his moves. As soon as I have information on what he is up to, where he is, etc., I will get the information to you so you all can get to work on setting up the plans."

"So we're the war planning party?" Stella asked.

"Yes, you will be responsible for mounting probably the most strategic war in history, but I do apologize that no one will ever know of your mad skills."

"I suppose saving the world will have to be reward enough," Stella huffed dramatically.

Peri turned to the three healers and opened her hand. Three stones appeared out of nowhere. "You all need to continue to practice the things Sally had begun to teach you. The fae stones will magnify your power. You need to learn to bend your power to your own will so that it will answer you when you call for it." She paused and looked around at the group as they listened so intently. In that moment she realized that if she could pick anyone wolf, fae, warlock, human, gypsy healer, or elf, to go into battle with her to fight to save the world, these individuals would be at the top of that list.

"How is Dalton truly holding up?" Sorin asked her.

Peri was not fooled by the façade that Dalton Black held in place. He was a ticking time bomb and she wasn't sure if she wanted to be in the vicinity when he finally went off. "He's coping, for now."

"Can Dillon control him?"

"If it were Elle in Jewel's place, could anyone control you?"

Sorin bowed his head to her. "Good point."

"Stay vigilant," Peri encouraged. "And healers," she said as she turned her gaze on them. "I am going to tell you what I have had to tell the other gypsies. If any of you suddenly gets this intense urge to be a hero. Don't."

She flashed and was gone before they could respond.

Heather snorted. "She has way too much faith in me if she thinks I'm going to be charging out like some fierce warrior goddess. I'd run smack dab into a tree before I ever got close to the battle."

"You have to admit that would be pretty freaking hilarious," Crina offered, smiling at the girls.

"Well if I can't live to help others, at least I can give them something to laugh at," Heather sighed.

"And we truly appreciate that," Elle added.

Heather laughed. "You're welcome."

The group once again resumed their places around the fire. They were quiet for a time and Stella imagined the other two were thinking the same thing that she was. "At least this will get our minds off of this bond that seems hell bent on dragging us through a forest back into another realm toward male werewolves that we don't know."

"When you put it like that it really doesn't sound very romantic," Heather told her.

"Well it bloody well doesn't feel romantic," Anna huffed. "It feels like my heart is trying to carve an opening out of my chest so it can go crawling off on its own since I'm not doing what it wants."

Heather threw her hands in the air with a groan. "Okay, now that too is quite disturbing. How about we don't hear from the voodoo lady or stripper for a while? Let's not talk about being drug through a forest or our hearts suddenly growing arms and carving themselves from our chests."

"Fine," Stella mumbled. "Let's talk about planning a war instead. Dead bodies, bloodshed, witches, and sorcerers all seem like much better topics."

"Exactly," Heather said smiling.

"I think the mate bonds are making them a tad testy," Crina whispered to Elle.

Stella's head whipped around and her eyes narrowed.

Elle nodded. "I can see how you might get that."

"War people," Stella growled. "Let's talk war."

"Oh dear," Elle muttered

"I don't think this is going to end well," Adam added.

"What gave you that clue? Stella looking like she's ready to kill something, or Anna nodding way too eagerly at Stella's ranting?"

Just then Heather called out. "War, war, it's good for the heart; the more you kill the less you think about the wolf you are supposedly going to mate with."

"Yep, totally not going to end well," Elle agreed.

—

Sally finished making the bed in the room Jewel had occupied. She felt the need to keep herself busy so that her mind couldn't contemplate all the horrible outcomes that might befall her and her friends. She was beginning to wonder if they would ever fully defeat the darkness that seemed to continually rise back from the depths they chased it into. Could evil be fully eradicated? And if they were here to defeat it, if there would come a day when peace reigned, why was the Great Luna rebuilding the Canis lupis and gypsy healers now? Additional wolves and healers weren't necessary unless something bigger was coming or unless she knew that they would never be able to completely defeat their foes. Perhaps, she knew that as one evil is put down, another will continue to rise in its place, like a multi-headed hydra hell bent on destruction. Perhaps, she intended them to be some sort of guardians for the human world and other realms against such evil. Whatever the reason, Sally hoped with everything in her that they were up to the task.

"Are you going to come to bed any time this year, Sally?" Costin's voice rumbled from behind her.

"I have too much on my mind for sleep," she told him as she continued to straighten the room.

Suddenly his hands were on her hips holding her still and pulling her back against his chest. His lips brushed her ear as he spoke. "I would be happy to distract you until you are too tired to think."

Sally felt the intent of his words down to her toes and her stomach did its usual flip at Costin's close proximity.

"Costin."

"Hmm," he responded distractedly as his lips ran down her neck.

"Do you think we will be enough?"

He paused. "What do you mean?"

"What if there comes a day that we can't defeat whatever evil it is that we are facing? What will happen to the world and the other supernatural beings?"

Costin turned her to face him and took her face in his hands. She felt small and protected in the shadow of his body and wanted so badly for all the strife in the world to fade away so that they could just be.

"I don't know what would happen, Sally mine. All I know is that because of what we are, what we are capable of, we must always answer the call to defend the innocent. If we fail, it won't be because we didn't give it everything we had."

She wished his answer gave her a measure of peace, but as he pulled her into his arms and kissed her forehead, she felt as if the clock was ticking for them. With each minute that passed they were getting closer and closer to something they couldn't defeat—and with it would come great loss.

—

"Do you wonder what she will be like, your true mate?" Nick asked the other males as they sat around the dinner table. It was apparent by the looks on their dejected faces that they were once again not happy about being left behind to do nothing. "I mean do any of you have some sort of feeling that maybe one of the four left is yours?"

Kale glanced at the other males attempting to gage the looks on their faces. They were so used to having discord between them that it was hard to reveal something so personal, but he supposed that the only way to truly be united was to begin to trust each other. He knew it was a risk to tell them about the bond, but maybe he could just tell them part of it.

"There was a scent in the room where the lasses stayed that I am drawn to," he admitted. "I didn't ask whose bed it was because I don't want to cause any friction between us. I, just like each of you, long for my mate. It's becoming a fierce hunger that I cannot fill."

They each nodded at him, the low rumble of their agreements filling the room. It was strange, Kale thought, sitting there among other dominants and not attempting to force each other to submit in order to figure out who the Alpha would be. But it was also freeing. To be around other males who were going through the same things, having similar dispositions and therefore able to understand one another, was something he never thought he'd experience.

"I too have felt drawn to this place. When I arrived it seemed like fate," Gustavo spoke up. "I wondered if perhaps it was just wishful thinking on my part."

"How long do you think Perizada will make us wait to introduce us to them?" Ciro asked.

"There is no telling with that fae," Kale answered. "Especially if she thinks the meetings will somehow distract them from finding Volcan. But we might be able to speed up the process if we can convince her that it is wiser for us to find out if one of them is indeed our mate. A mated male is a stronger male."

"Perhaps, some of us do have a valid argument," Drayden agreed giving Kale and the two other males who had spoken up a pointed look. It wasn't envious, or threatening, he was simply acknowledging their claims, and he was okay with it.

"Regardless." Kale met their eyes. "War or no war, she has no real right to keep us from our mates. It only makes sense that because of what they are to us—our lights, our peace—that we meet them sooner rather than later. "

The group descended into silence again, each of them lost in their own thoughts. Kale's mind had begun to grow more and more chaotic, and he was feeling his wolf getting more restless. Like most males as old as he was, his time was growing short. And the more violence that he had to take part in, the more the darkness inside of him grew. The violence, whether justified because of a war or not, only fed the darkness. But it wasn't only for himself that he was becoming desperate to find her. He felt as though she was going to need him. The bond between them seemed to be growing tighter, like a rubber band stretched too far. He didn't know if she was in trouble, or if something had happened in the pixie realm to endanger her life, but his wolf seemed to know that one of those three was indeed theirs, and she needed his protection as much as he needed her light and goodness, and the man agreed.

He couldn't, and wouldn't, wait much longer. If it came to it, he would go against Peri's orders and he would find his mate. If he had to tear through every inch of the forest around the pixie realm to find her, he would. Like any male in search of his true mate, nothing would stand in his way. He wouldn't find peace until she was safe in his arms. He wouldn't be able to focus on the coming battle if he did not know that she was under his protection. Kale had spent centuries looking for her, hoping that he would no longer have to endure his long life alone. Now she was so very close and still he could not have her. *I'll see you very soon, lass,* he thought wishing there was a bond for him to send it through.

"Any of you up for a hunt?" Drayden's voice brought the room back into focus.

"Since we aren't getting to sink our teeth into an evil fae, we might as well go kill something," Antonio, Gustavo's Beta, added.

All of them headed for the forest dropping their human form and phasing into their wolves. Kale knew it was not the hunt any of them wanted to be on. The hunt they craved ended with a warm, light filled female in their arms. Much to his wolf's—and his own—dismay, they would have to settle for a rabbit.

EPILOGUE

"I can see inside of you to the places you'd rather keep hidden. I see your wants, your secret desires, and the things that you would never admit to longing for. I will give you those things and not judge you. I will show you what you are capable of and teach you how to wield your power. You will be mine, and you will be thankful that I didn't leave you to be a servant to the Canis lupis." ~Volcan

Jewel hadn't moved from the spot in the corner that she had retreated to when Volcan had released his grip on her body. The room in which he had left her had obviously been decorated for a lady of distinctive tastes. With its four poster bed, lace curtains, and decorative pillows, it looked like a throwback to the Victorian era.

She sat with her knees pulled up to her chest, her back glued to the wall behind her, and her eyes fixed upon the door. She didn't know when he would be back, but when he did return she wanted to be ready. There was no way she was going to become his, whatever it was he expected, without a fight. She knew a little self-defense from books she had read and would resort to scratching and clawing if she had to. She was not above resorting to crazy girl tactics. Jewel tried not to let her mind wander back to her last minutes with Dalton. The look on his face when Volcan had flashed away with her tore her soul in half. She wished that she could rewind the clock and have him holding her again, marking her, and claiming her for all to know that she was his. Jewel hadn't realized how intimate it would be, and after having that level of closeness with him, being separated was nauseating.

"I do not understand why you think to resist me, Jewel," Volcan's voice skittered over her nerves like tiny ants as he walked in the room. "You and I both know that you have it in you to be a great witch, a witch *queen* even. Like so many before you, you crave the power that dark magic would give you. Save yourself much trouble and just join me. I have plans for us and I do not like to be delayed."

"What sort of plans?" she asked, ignoring his summary of her.

"I've realized that it would be smarter of me to keep you alive, instead of draining you of all your blood for its power. You see, there is another way in which your blood can be used for power. It simply needs to flow in the veins of another magic user."

"So you're going to take my blood and infuse it into witches you create?"

"Wrong again, little healer. I am not going to be the one creating the witches, well maybe in a roundabout way. But really it will be you and whatever male I send to you that will create them."

Alarm signals were blaring in Jewel's mind as she processed what he had just said. *Create witches? And it would take a male?* It hit her like a bolt of lightning and she was on her feet.

"You will have to kill me before I become an incubator for your spawn." He wanted her to procreate with different men in order to become pregnant and bear him witch children? Dude was delusional.

"No, actually I will just have to restrain you. But don't worry, we have a little time for you to warm up to the idea. Jewel, once you begin to feel the power I will give you running through you, you will understand why this is where you belong. This is what you were destined for. You will be the mother of all witches, and my queen, and we will rule this world and all other realms. Never again will you be made to feel helpless or inferior."

Jewel could admit that without all the killing, world domination stuff, knowing that she could have the knowledge of magic, dark and light, was slightly enticing. But she could never hurt innocent people and she could never sleep with a bunch of men she did not love. That part of her was for one male only—one broody, broken, beautiful male— and she intended to keep it that way. She needed a plan, a strategy. She knew that she couldn't defeat him physically and she couldn't wait him out either. She would be better off beating her head against a brick wall because it might actually crack, whereas Volcan was immovable in his resolve to have her.

"We will start your training tomorrow," he told her with an excited gleam in his eye. He reminded her of a cat licking its lips because of the mouse it had just found. Not a good analogy she realized because that would make her the mouse.

"What will my training entail?"

"Secrets to my magic that I have never shared with anyone else." He turned for the door and called out over his shoulder. "I suggest you get some rest. Being wicked is not for the weary."

Jewel climbed up on the bed, though a part of her wanted to defy him just because it would give her some measure of joy, but she was tired—exhausted in fact. Her talk with Dalton had been emotionally taxing, though his blood had given her physical energy, she could now feel it wearing off. She couldn't feel him through their bond though she knew the bond was still there. She had managed to talk to him one last time just as Volcan dropped her in the room. But since then there had been nothing.

As she laid back and closed her eyes she thought about all that had become of her life in just a few months. Her mother had warned her multiple times over the past year that something was coming. She had told her that she would have to make a choice, but she never elaborated on what the options were. Thinking about her mother made her wish she could have seen her one last time. With all Gem's quirky ways, Jewel still loved her very much. She didn't want to die before getting to see her again. But she knew the probability of that happening was pretty great.

"Jewel."

Jewel's eyes popped open at the sound of her mom's voice. She waited to see if it would come again. Perhaps her mind was so desperate for her that it was causing auditory hallucinations. It was a valid conclusion, though her mind felt fully intact, if not just a bit worn out.

"Jewel, you must resist him." "Mom?"

"Yes, I can only hold this for a few moments longer. You must resist. You must hold out for your mate to get to you."

"I won't give into him."

"You are more intelligent than you know and your logic will not always lead you in the right direction. When you make your decision, though it may feel right, remember my words; what begins as a farce more often than not ends as the truth. I love you, daughter. I believe in you."

"Wait, I don't understand." Jewel looked frantically around the room, though she knew her mother wasn't there. She knew that her mother had rules that she followed when it came to revealing the future and so she often talked in riddles, but she wished just this once that she could have just spelled it out for her.

"What begins as a farce more often than not ends as the truth," she repeated her mother's words. So basically she was saying that people begin to believe whatever lie it is they have been telling or living. What did that have to do with her and the situation she was in? What lie would Jewel tell that would become her reality?

She laid back down, her body beyond exhausted and her mind longing for rest. She would think more on her mother's words tomorrow when things would be clearer. Right now her brain was muddled and all she wanted to think about was the man she had left behind. In such a short time he had maneuvered himself into her heart and she missed him fiercely. She missed his voice, the deep rumble that lulled her even when she was unconscious. She missed his warm hands running through her hair and holding her smaller hand. And even though it had been so very brief that he had held her, she missed that as well. To think that she could have had a lifetime in those arms, safe, sheltered, and loved. The tears started then. She had been holding onto them for as long as she could but her strength was gone for the day. She cried herself to sleep; the ache in her chest was even prevalent while she slept. She didn't know how long she had been asleep when the dream began, but she prayed that she would never wake up.

"I've been waiting for you," Dalton told her as he crossed the room to get to her.

"How could you be waiting for me, this is my dream?"

"Is it?" His head tilted ever so slightly as his lips twitched in amusement.

Jewel realized he was trying to tell her that this was no dream; it was real.

"How?" she said as she hurried into the arms he held open to her. She let out a sigh as everything fell into place. Being with Dalton was her destiny. When she was with him, everything made sense.

"I have a powerful high fae as an ally. She has the ability to manipulate dreams. But Volcan will eventually realize what's going on. Magic always leaves a trail." He brushed her hair back from her face and ran a thumb across her lips. "Are you alright? Has he hurt you?"

Jewel felt Dalton's fear and rage as he asked her and she wanted to calm him, to soothe his wolf who was pacing to get out. "No, I'm fine."

"Do you know where you are?"

She shook her head. "I've only been in the room where he left me."

"Has he talked to you?"

"Yes," she said because she didn't want to tell him more but neither did she want to hide anything from him. "He wants to teach me dark magic. He wants my blood, and he wants me to be a breeder female, basically with any male he sends my way." Jewel's body immediately tensed as she felt first his jealousy, and then his protective anger flood her mind.

"I'm sorry you're in this position," Dalton told her as his face softened to the Dalton that was reserved for her alone.

"It's not your fault. It's my own. I need you to know something. You aren't going to like it."

He nodded indicating her to continue.

"I won't be forced. I won't lie there just to survive. And I know that no amount of fighting would get me anywhere. I will leave this life before I let a single male touch me." She waited for his anger but what she got instead was his compassion.

"I don't want you to die. I don't want you to have to take your own life. I'm your mate, it goes against everything I am to condone you hurting yourself. But neither do I want you to suffer abuse at the hands of men who care nothing for you and want to use you. If you leave this world, I will follow. I made sure of that when I completed the Blood Rites."

"So you aren't going to argue with me and tell me to do anything I have to in order to survive?"

His hand wrapped around the back of her neck and tilted her head up to look at him. "There are some things that you can't survive. Just because you live through it, doesn't mean you survived. I will not condemn you for either decision. If you fight, if you endure, then once I have you back in my arms I will do everything I can to take those horrific memories from you and replace them with love, adoration, and faithfulness."

Jewel couldn't believe that this man was intended for her. Who was she to deserve such a blessing? How did she ever think she could live without him?

"I, I'm...," Jewel's tears streaked her cheeks as she tried to tell him how sorry she was. How wrong she had been.

"Shhh, Little Dove. That is not necessary. I love you. I'm coming for you and I won't stop until you are back in my arms where you belong."

She laid her head on his chest and couldn't believe that even in the dream she could smell his masculine scent. His hands rubbed her back pulling her tighter against him until she could feel his heartbeat against her cheek. She wanted to crawl inside of him and never be parted from him again. But like all good things, this too was coming to an end.

"I must go and you need rest," Dalton told her as he leaned down and kissed her on the forehead and then both cheeks.

"Why didn't you kiss my lips?" she asked, not thinking to censor her question.

"Because the first time that I have the privilege of tasting you, it will not be in a dream. I want you, your physical body. As hard as it is not to lean down and kiss your beautiful mouth, I will wait and it will be worth it."

"Did you know a long lasting kiss quickens the pulse and heightens the level of hormones in humans' blood so much that it shortens their lifespan by nearly a whole minute?" Jewel wanted to smack herself in the head. Why that suddenly popped into her head she had no idea other than the fact that she was slightly embarrassed for just blurting out the question and putting him on the spot.

Dalton's eyes began to glow as he studied her. "Well then, our lives are going to be considerably shorter because I plan to take many long, passion filled kisses from you, mate."

That did not help ease her desire to have him kiss her now, but she was glad that he had the self-control to wait until they were together again, if that day ever came.

"Keeping fighting, Little Dove. I love you," he whispered against her ear.

She squeezed him tightly to her as she whispered back. "I love you. I can't wait for that kiss."

"Tell me one more fact, Jewel. I love when you spout off random information. It actually drives me a little crazy with desire for you."

"So you only want me for my brain?" she teased.

He shrugged. "Well the brain's container isn't too shabby so I'll just take it all."

"Okay, so did you know that your lips are a hundred times more sensitive than your fingertips?"

"I did not, but that is definitely good information to be filed away for use at a later date."

Jewel was enjoying this side of Dalton. The playfulness in him was a rare gift, and she had a feeling he was making an effort in order to distract her. She loved him for it.

"I have a fact for you," he told her. She could tell that the dream was ending because he was beginning to appear washed out. "No one has ever made me want to be a better man until you. I want to be worthy of you."

"You are." Jewel reached for him as he faded even more. She didn't want to leave on a sad note because she knew they both needed to be strong for what lay ahead. She didn't want Dalton worried that she was cowering in a corner lost and beaten down. He was a powerful, dominant male in his race and she would be a mate he could be proud of. "Don't keep me waiting too long, Dalton Black.

She felt his breath on her neck as he whispered, "Nothing could keep me from you." And then he was gone and she was alone.

Though she wasn't fully awake after having the dream, she was aware of the pain twisting in her heart as her soul cried out for its other half. Knowing that she no longer would be alone, that she would have Dalton, gave her the desire to want to survive. She was smart. She knew that if she just searched diligently in the many deep wells of information in her mind, she would be able to outsmart her opponent. She knew that would have to be her plan because she couldn't fight him. But she believed she could outthink him.

As she gave into her mind and body's exhaustion just as she was slipping off to sleep, she whispered into the empty room. "Let the games begin."

Please Enjoy this Excerpt of Elfin,
Book 1 in the Elfin Series

1

"Halloween is here and once again I'm struggling to pick a costume. Once again I am trying desperately to ward off Elora's attempts to turn me into some sort of gothic princess or dark fairy. If you happen to see me strutting down the street in a halter top with wings, glitter in my hair, and three inch heels, please shoot me on sight." ~ Diary of Cassie Tate

"I'm not wearing that Elora. You might as well take that pattern and stuff it back into the bag of long lost costumes that should never see the light of day." Cassie climbed into her best friends beat up Dodge Neon. The door creaked ominously as she opened it. Chipping red paint sloughed off, revealing a layer of blue beneath it. Who knew what color lay beneath the blue. Elora's car had been painted several times by her older brother, Oakley, when he had started working at the auto body shop his senior year and the original color was since long forgotten. Few little sisters would have voluntarily allowed their brothers to practice painting on their vehicle, but Elora didn't have much of a say in the matter. At least he had finally covered up the skull and cross-bones he had jokingly, and quite poorly, painted on the hood.

"I'm telling you now, as your friend, if you try and wear a costume like you did last year, I will personally put you out of your own misery, not to mention my own," Elora said in her signature dry voice. She rolled down the window, letting the crisp fall air blow through the car that had, despite the increasingly cool temperature, still grown hot from sitting in the asphalt parking lot that boasted absolutely no shade for the student parking.

"Seriously?" Cassie's jaw dropped open. "That costume was so creative."

Elora rolled her eyes as she started the car. She shifted into drive and pressed the pedal to the metal, coaxing the sputtering little engine to deliver its maximum effort, which resulted in a loud squeal from the tires as the girls pulled out of the school lot. Cassie latched onto the door unconcerned about the loud noise; well acquainted with her friend's maniacal driving skills.

"You were an ant." Elora's face scrunched up in distaste.

"Yeah, but I wasn't just an ant. I was an ant *on a picnic table.*"

"Exactly," Elora responded deadpan. "You were wearing a table. I'm sorry Cass but I draw the line at wearing furniture. We're seniors this year; we have a responsibility to blow the minds of all the underclassmen peons."

Cassie laughed. "What about Charlie's Angels? They are some kick butt females."

Elora raised a single pierced eyebrow at her best friend.

"Do you really see *this*," she motioned to her face and then her body, "as Charlie's Angels material?"

Cassie looked over at her friend. There was no doubt that Elora was beautiful, but not in a typical way. She was heavy into the Goth scene. Her hair was dyed jet black, with the exception of the bright red chunks she put in it. She wore it in long layers with bangs sweeping across her face intentionally creating a mysterious air. She had a stud resting in her left brow; four piercings in her left ear, five in her right, a stud in her right nostril, and, of course, a stud in her tongue. She wore dark eye shadow that gave her purple eyes, made possible by colored contacts, an enigmatic sparkle. She was naturally fair skinned, so she didn't bother with any powder on her face and her skin was flawless anyways. She wore black, black, and more black and she rocked it. Black miniskirts with black fishnet tights drew attention to her insanely long legs on her five foot, seven inch frame, which was completed by black combat boots and an off the shoulder shirt revealing a black halter top. Around her neck dangled various crystals, all of which were, according to her mother, effective to promote healing, positive energy, or some other such nonsense. Various rings, ranging from skeletons to talons, adorned nearly every finger.

Cassie's mouth quirked up. "I see your point."

"Just leave the costumes to me. I'm sure my Lisa can help me come up with something dark and sexy." Elora turned onto Cassie's street and her tires screeched to a halt in her driveway.

Lisa was Elora's mom and that is what Elora had always called her. Elora wasn't into titles that she claimed society put on people to set them apart, when, as she put it "*we are all human beings who picked their noses as children in front of people without shame and then in secret as adults.*"

"Who says I want to look dark and sexy?" Cassie asked.

"I do," Elora answered giving Cassie a *what kind of question was that* glare.

"Just remember that we are not standing on a corner trick or treating for the wrong kind of tricks and treats, okay?"

Elora rolled her eyes but then added, "That was actually a pretty good analogy."

"So glad I meet your approval."

"I'll call you later tonight. No doubt you are going to need my help on our English project." Elora began to back out of the driveway. Cassie motioned for her to roll down her window.

"I have to go up to my dad's work remember?" Cassie yelled to her.

"Why do you have to go again?"

"His assistant is out for the week and he asked me to do some of the filing and whatever other meaningless tasks she does," Cassie said in exasperation.

"Okay. We'll work on the paper tomorrow. It's not due until Friday anyway," Elora waved as she continued out of the driveway and peeled and puttered off down the street.

Cassie looked at her watch and realized that she was already late. She walked over to her less than impressive, not to mention ancient, Honda Civic, digging her keys from her backpack. Once she had them, she tossed her backpack into the back seat, slid into the driver's seat, and started it up. She backed out of the driveway in a much more reasonable fashion than Elora just did, and headed towards her dad's work in downtown Oklahoma City.

—

"Dad, I'm here." Cassie hollered as she walked into the reception area of Woodland Oil Company, Inc. From what little she knew of her dad's work, he handled the company's financial stuff and had the words "President of," in front of his name. She walked past the reception desk and down a long hallway passing office after office on either side. Her father's office was the last one at the end of the hall.

She knocked and opened the door when she heard his voice. William Tate, III sat at his paper-covered desk, tie loosened around his neck, his salt and pepper hair rumpled from continually running his hands through it.

"Come on in, Cass," her father said and she noticed how tired he sounded. He always sounded tired, Cassie thought to herself. He worked way too much. Though he never complained about it, Cassie could tell the long hours were wearing him down. She made a mental note to bug him later about taking her on a vacation. It was for his own good.

"Hey," she said with her brightest smile, hoping to bring a little energy into the stale room. She wanted to wrap him in a hug when he returned her smile and he immediately looked at least ten years younger.

"So what do I need to do?"

William stood and his six foot, three inch form seemed to make the large office shrink a bit. With a flat stomach, large muscular arms and powerful legs, William Tate was an avid athlete. He tried his hardest to make time to do push-ups and sit-ups in his office throughout the day. Aside from his graying hair, he looked much younger than his forty-six years. He laid the papers that were in his hands down as he came around his desk and motioned for her to follow him back down the long hallway to the reception area. His assistant, an older, frumpy woman named Martha, kept her desk in meticulous order. He pulled a box of papers out from under the organized desk.

"These need to be filed alphabetically into these file cabinets." Then he pulled another box from the other side of the large file cabinets.

"These need to be shredded," he motioned to the box. "The shredder is actually in the break room which is out those doors," he pointed to the main office doors. "Down the hall, on the left."

"That seems like an odd place for a shredder," Cassie said absently.

Her dad let out a huff of laughter. "You don't have to tell me. But do you want to be the one who tells Martha where she should put her shredder?" He turned to go back to his office then paused. "You'll be okay out here by yourself?"

Cassie rolled her eyes. "Dad, I'm eighteen. Technically I no longer require supervision."

He let out a groan. "Don't remind me," he said, leaving her to it.

An hour and three paper cuts later, Cassie finally finished the filing. She stood and stretched her legs and then her arms. She looked down at the box full of papers to be shredded and quickly decided that she was not going to be able to carry it down the long hall. She looked around the office for some sort of cart.

"Bingo," she smiled as she pulled a rolling cart from a closet to the right of Martha's desk. She hefted the heavy box onto the cart and then steered it from the office and down the long hall. Cassie had to admit that it was kind of creepy being alone in a large building, knowing there was no one else inside. It reminded her of a movie that she once saw where the lead character woke up from a lengthy coma and staggered from the hospital only to discover that there was no one left alive in the city.

She found the door that her dad had been talking about and poked her head inside to make sure that it was indeed empty. She saw that no one occupied the room and proceeded to pull the cart inside and over to the shredder sitting at the back of the room. She began the monotonous task of pushing paper into the machine and listening to the grinding sound it produced as it cut the paper into tiny pieces that would be impossible to read. Just as she grabbed the last of the papers, she heard raised voices that sounded as if they were coming from just beyond the wall to her right.

Cassie froze. Without thinking, she tried to quiet her breathing, which had inexplicably begun to speed up. Cassie stood and walked over to the wall and pressed her ear to it. The voices were intoxicating, smooth and intriguing, like melted milk chocolate. She found herself wanting to get closer, wanting to find out who could have such a voice. Before she realized it, she found herself walking back out of the break room and to the very next door in the hall. The wall of this office was made of glass instead of painted sheet rock. The blinds that hung in front of the glass were closed, blocking her view to the inside of the room. She walked a few steps down the hall, passing in front of the glass. When she reached the end of the glass, she saw that there was a small, roughly four inch opening where the blinds weren't quite covering the window. She peered in through the opening and her breath caught in her throat.

A long table filled the room and was surrounded by chairs, half of which were filled with men, though they were far from normal looking. These men were beautiful, regal, and masculine all at the same time. Each had long hair, board straight and shiny, with unorthodox coloring. The hair of one of the men was stark white, though he looked as if he were in his early twenties. Another sported hair of pale blue, while another's was light purple. This was bizarre in and of itself, but that was far from their most unusual feature. Cassie's mouth dropped open when she noticed that their ears were pointed at the tips. Not *sort of* pointed, like some people have, which are often described as 'elfin' in appearance. No, these ears were well and truly pointed, strikingly different from anything she had ever seen before. Cassie blinked her eyes and rubbed them fiercely, trying to make sure that she wasn't just seeing things that weren't really there. She looked away from their ears and instead studied their faces. Again she noted that they were inhumanly good looking. Everything about their faces was perfect. High cheekbones, straight, perfectly proportioned noses, pale, smooth, flawless skin that seemed to shimmer under the florescent lights. Then she noticed that their eyes, like their pointy ears, seemed unbelievable. They sparkled, containing unnatural colors that appeared to match the color of their hair.

One of the beautiful men stood from the table and she saw that he was unusually tall. His fitted clothes left no wonder to his body structure. This man's hair shimmered a dark blue, and his eyes were a matching sapphire. He was muscular, but far from bulky. He was built for speed and agility. He wore loose fitting brown pants that looked as if they would allow him to move without hindrance. The material of his white shirt appeared to be the same as his pants and while it also seemed to be fitted for allowing maximum movement, was tight enough to reveal a flat stomach. His chest was broad, but not too thick. His arms, even covered by the sleeves of his shirt, were obviously muscular.

He began to walk around the table and she noted that his movements where so smooth as to be catlike in their grace. He walked confidently, owning the room and commanding the attention of the others. As he drew closer to the back of the room, nearer to where Cassie stood on the other side of the glass, she held her breath, wondering if he could hear her. He stopped only feet away from her on the other side of the glass and his eyes snapped up, meeting hers. His piercing stare seemed to root her in the spot, even though everything inside her was telling her to run as fast and far as she could from the room, and the beautiful men that occupied it. His lips began to move and the motion of another man standing behind him broke her eyes from the intense stare. She saw that the man was moving towards the door. Cassie made a quick decision, albeit the wrong quick decision. Instead of heading in the direction of her dad's office, she turned and ran in the opposite direction, grabbing the first door she came to.

The door opened into an empty office next to the conference room. She rushed inside and pulled the door closed, pushing the lock in place, not bothering to check and see if the room was empty. Once again, not her brightest moment.

Her breath came in rapid pants and her heart was beating so hard it felt like it was going to jump straight out of her chest. She pressed her ear to the door, listening to see if she had been followed. When she didn't hear anything she turned, pressing her back to the door and tilting her head up. Her eyes closed as she let out a long, nervous breath. She stood there for several moments composing herself before she felt someone's eyes on her. Letting out an inward groan before she opened her eyes, she nearly whimpered knowing that she was going to find someone staring at her. Deciding that there was nothing left to do but face the individual, she opened her eyes and slowly scanned the room. They stopped on a figure with his arms crossed, leaning against the wall that separated the room from the conference room where the impossibly beautiful men sat. He looked as if he didn't have a care in the world and didn't appear to be surprised to see her there.

She couldn't move or speak. Like the men she had just seen, he was gorgeous, unbelievably so. For a moment the person seemed to flicker and someone else stood before her, equally gorgeous, and then he returned to his original appearance. She frowned, puzzled by the strange occurrence, but was quickly distracted when he spoke to her.

"Well hello, beautiful." His voice was deep, resonating to her very soul. It was smooth and as flawless as his form.

Cassie still couldn't speak. Her mind was too busy taking in his appearance. His hair, dark as midnight, fell across his forehead and was long enough to tuck behind his ears. Long lashes framed his silver eyes, which shined when they caught the light. He had high cheekbones and a straight, aristocratic nose. His lips were red and full, and appeared to Cassie as if they were made for all things pleasurable. He was tall and, like the other men that she had seen, muscular but not overly so. If his looks were not enough to disarm her, then adding the clothing would take care of it. If she had to describe his clothes in one word it would be 'medieval.' He wore black pants, that appeared to be the same material as the others, fitted to his form, a black shirt that was molded to his arms and over the shirt he wore a black vest that looked like it was designed for protection more than style. He had on black boots that came up over his pants and laced all the way around his claves. Her eyes ran slowly back up his body and when they returned to his face, she saw a smug, knowing smile. She blushed at having been caught obviously ogling him.

"Had your fill?" He asked her and the teasing was evident in the mischief dancing in his unusual silver eyes. He continued to watch her and seemed to be waiting for something but Cassie's mind was lost in a fog of desire and longing.

"I'm wondering if someone as beautiful as you can speak," he said. "And if so, will the intelligence level be so wanting that it ruins the outer package."

That caught her attention and pushed through the fog.

"Are you asking if I'm an idiot?" Cassie asked incredulously after finding her voice.

He smiled a slow, Cheshire Cat smile and the look in his eyes made her shiver.

"She speaks," he uncrossed his arms and one hand came up to cover his heart as he pushed away from the wall and took a step towards her, "and her voice is a caress to my soul. I suppose if you have a voice like that then I could tolerate you not being the brightest bulb in the box."

Cassie's mouth dropped open at the insult. She too pushed away from the door, not considering the fact that she was in a locked room with a guy that she didn't know, who looked dangerous and unpredictable.

"What makes you an authority on intelligence levels?" She snapped.

He took another step towards her, his eyes never leaving hers.

"I'm a genius," he answered with a look that said "duh."

"Oh. Well in that case, you being an ass is totally okay." Cassie let out an exasperated breath as she continued to watch him.

"Perhaps I am being a tad rude." He stepped closer still and was suddenly only a foot away from her. He swept down in a dramatic bow and stood back up, looking at her with smoldering eyes that had her holding her breath.

"My apologies, my lady. Will you let me start our introduction over?"

Cassie could still hear the playfulness in his voice but there was something else as well, something that made her feel like he really wanted to know her. He reached his hand out, waiting for her to place hers in it. She looked at the hand and then back up at him. Something in her screamed, 'don't do it' and yet she slowly lifted her hand and placed it in his. He wrapped his strong fingers around it and his eyes squeezed closed. She felt a jolt of power burst up her arms. She wanted to pull away, yet she also wanted to wrap herself in his arms, to have him touch her, kiss her, love her.

Her eyes, which had closed at some point, popped open. *Love? WTH*, she thought to herself. *Cassie get a clue, he's dangerous, it's written all over his lovely form.* Yes, he is, but I still want him. She frowned at the petulant voice her subconscious had suddenly become. She shook her head, trying to clear it. She felt her feet moving forward and realized that he was pulling her to him. She was standing mere inches from his face. She tilted her head back to look up at him and found his silver eyes staring back at her. His brow was furrowed and she could see the questions on his face.

"You saw me?" He asked her disbelievingly. "My true form, you saw it."

"What do you mean?" She asked, her voice wavering under his intense scrutiny.

"Cassie, beautiful Cassie, what are you? How could you possibly see my true form?" He still held her hand in his and with his other hand he ran a finger down her jaw causing her to shiver again. She wanted to take a step back, needed to take a step back, but she couldn't move.

"How do you know my name?" She asked.

His lips lifted in a crooked smile. "I saw it in your mind." He said it like it was the most normal thing in the world.

Cassie tried to pull her hand away but he tightened his hold.

"You think you can read my mind?" She asked slowly, as if speaking to a child.

"Not think, know," his finger was now trailing slowly, so very slowly across her bottom lip. "I know that you think my lips are made for pleasure."

Cassie felt the blood rush to her face in embarrassment. "Oh," she squeaked out.

She cleared her throat and tried again. "I don't know what you're talking about." It came out more as a question than the firm statement she had been going for.

His finger continued to run gently across her jaw and down her neck to her collarbone.

"I know about the time you fell out of the tree in your front yard and broke your arm because you were trying to rescue the neighbor's cat. I know that you aren't sure you even believe in prayer or the

One you pray to, but it comforts you. I know that you think that your best friend is prettier than you are and I know that you do not see yourself clearly if you think that."

Cassie's breath was coming in short gasps as she listened to this guy she had just met, and didn't even know his name, tell her things that there was no possible way that he could know. She felt like she was suffocating; she couldn't get enough air and her sight started to fade.

"Come on beautiful, breathe for me." His voice sounded far away though she knew he was standing inches from her.

She felt his breath on her face as he spoke. His scent swirled around her and as she breathed in and out, she felt like she might be drunk on the smell. She felt him brushing her hair away from her face and then tilted her chin back to look up at him. She blinked as she looked at his inhumanly handsome face. She saw his features flicker again. For a brief moment, he had long, pitch black hair, pointed ears, and eyes so silver and clear that they shimmered like diamonds. His face shifted slightly. If she thought that he couldn't be even more beautiful, she was wrong. Then, in the blink of an eye, she was again looking at the man with shorter dark hair, regular ears, and eyes that were a more subdued, yet stunning grey.

"Wwwhat was that?" She stumbled over her words. Finally getting her feet to move she pulled back from him staring up at his widened eyes. When he continued to stare at her instead of answering her, she gathered her thoughts. She turned to look back at the door where she had entered. She could hear the other men out in the hall, speaking in low tones.

"They are going to find me soon. I need to go." She looked back and nearly jumped when her face almost ran into his chest. She tilted her head to look up into his face.

"They won't look for you in here," he told her confidently.

"They will eventually. It's pretty obvious since its right next door to the room they were just in and I hid so quickly," she reasoned.

His lips formed a wickedly crooked smile. "They won't find you because I won't let them."

"And who *are* you, exactly?" Cassie raised a single eyebrow in question at him.

He leaned forward until his mouth was mere inches from hers.

"I'm yours," he whispered.

Cassie snorted out a short, abrupt laugh to cover up the gasp his words caused. "Does that work on all the girls?"

Suddenly his head whipped up as the handle of the door began to jiggle. Cassie's body tensed as she turned to look at the door, ready to bolt like a frightened animal.

"Cassie, are you in there?" Cassie let out a relieved breath as she heard the voice of her father.

She took a step towards the door but was stopped abruptly when an arm snaked around her waist. She let out a gasp of air as her back came in contact with a very firm chest. She felt his breath on her ear as his lips grazed her skin.

"I *will* see you again, beautiful."

She closed her eyes briefly as she tried not to enjoy the sensation of being held so confidently. When he released her she headed quickly for the door and as she unlocked it and began to turn the knob, she felt his breath on her neck again and then a whisper.

"Trik, my name is Trik."

She turned to look over her shoulder at him but there was no one there.

From the Author:

Thank you so very much for taking your time and money to read Wolf of Stone. I truly appreciate it. I could not write my books without the support of the amazing readers. God bless you all!

ABOUT THE AUTHOR

Quinn is an award winning author who lives in beautiful Western Arkansas with her husband, two sons, Nora the Doberman and Phoebe the Cat (who thinks she is a ninja in disguise). She is the author of twelve novels including the USA Today best seller, *Fate and Fury*. Quinn is beyond thankful that she has been blessed to be able to write full time and hopes the readers know how much all of their support means to her. Some of her hobbies include reading, exercising, crochet and spending time with her family and friends. She gives all credit to her success to God because He gave her the creative spirit and vivid imagination it takes to write.

Connect with Quinn
www.quinnloftisbooks.com
Twitter: @AuthQuinnLoftis
Facebook: Quinn Loftis Books

38032240R00208

Made in the USA
Charleston, SC
26 January 2015